Second Chance Christmas

Nicki Edwards

To Haylee Nash. For taking a chance on me.

Second Chance Christmas

Australian celebrity chef Jack Carter is determined to convince his estranged wife he's not the smooth-talking workaholic she married six years ago. Olivia has invited him to Canada for Christmas, not for herself but for the sake of their three-year-old daughter Scarlett. Jack willingly agreed, hoping this is the second chance he's been looking for.

Olivia has been hurt too many times by her soon-to-be-ex-husband and she doesn't trust him anymore. But she has to deal with him for Scarlett's sake, because her child deserves to grow up with both parents.

But when Jack joins them in Niagara-on-the-Lake for Christmas and asks Olivia to reconsider the divorce, she is shocked. And more than a little worried that a part of her wants to say yes.

Jack promises he'll give up everything for her and Scarlett, but Olivia is not convinced. Can he really turn his back on his high-flying television career in Australia, and the lifestyle that comes with it?

Will ten days over Christmas be enough time for Jack and Olivia to mend their broken hearts? Or will it take Jack's career or an unexpected accident, to rip them apart again?

Chapter 1

Olivia Carter was trying to keep herself busy in a desperate attempt to stop her mind from racing. The wait was giving her heartburn. After dropping her daughter, Scarlett, at the child care centre, she drove to *Common Grounds*.

She'd usually drop Scarlett, then run ten kilometres along the Niagara Parkway and follow it up with a takeaway coffee from her favourite café before heading home for an hour or so before collecting Scarlett at the end of her program. But today she had too much to do, so she'd ditched her normal routine, including the run.

The skies were a vivid blue and the sun was shining bright, but an icy breeze had picked up, coming straight off Lake Ontario. Olivia huddled deeper into her coat. It hadn't snowed yet, but the air was tinged with the promise of snow, and with temperatures set to plummet over the next twenty-four hours, with any luck they might get a white Christmas after all. Scarlett would be so excited. She was old enough now to understand what Christmas was about, and had been begging Santa to bring her snow ever since the first frost back in November. Olivia was looking forward to her first white Christmas in years too.

Pushing the door open, she entered the toasty warm café and

inhaled the heady aroma of freshly-brewed beans.

Niagara-on-the-Lake had all the usual major coffeehouse chains, but *Common Grounds* prided itself on being different. Independently owned and operated, it offered fair trade coffee and local, organic products. With its array of yummy baked goods, a great location and a friendly atmosphere, it reminded Olivia of the cafés back in Australia. As well as great coffee, she also loved the quirky floor tiles and their ginger cookies.

'Not running this morning?' Connor greeted her with his usual trademark grin.

Like all good baristas he set about making her order—a double shot latte—without being asked.

Slipping off her gloves, Olivia stuffed them in the pockets of her jacket and unwound her scarf. 'No. I have a busy day.' She glanced around the uncharacteristically quiet café. The only other people in the café were a young couple at a table in the corner. 'Unlike you by the look of it.'

'Yeah, it's been like this all morning. I guess everyone's doing last-minute shopping.'

Barely drawing breath, Connor launched into a conversation about the weather that would make a meteorologist proud, as he placed the metal milk jug under the steam jet. Olivia listened with half an ear and watched the clock. She didn't want to appear rude, but she didn't have time to chat with Connor today. She had a long list of items to tick off, and she didn't want to linger.

Oblivious to anyone else, the couple in the corner shared a long, passionate kiss. Remembering what it used to feel to be in love like that, Olivia hastily looked away, turning her attention back to Connor.

She and Connor were around the same age and both had broken marriages behind them, but that was where the similarities ended. At first, she'd found everything about him easy-going, but once or twice over the past month he'd hinted he'd like them to be more than casual acquaintances. Olivia wasn't interested in starting anything with anyone, no matter how casual. So far, she'd managed to deflect his attention, but she had a feeling it was only a matter of time before he asked her out on a date.

'Not working today?' he asked.

'No. I have two weeks off.' She didn't elaborate, though it was obvious he was itching for details.

Connor saw her every day at the café, but he only knew what she wanted him to see—the public aspects of who she was. He knew little about her former life in Australia and even less about her ex-husband, and she was happy to keep it that way.

'Ready for Christmas?'

'Almost. You?'

'Yeah, all good. Wrapped the last present last night.'

She smiled. 'I'll bet you didn't wrap your own presents.'

He laughed. 'You're right. I got my sister to do it.' He eased the plastic lid onto her coffee and handed the cup to her, refusing to let her pay. 'Consider it my Christmas present to you.'

She gave him a quick smile. 'Thanks, Connor. That's too kind of you.'

'My pleasure, eh.' He winked. 'Least I can do to keep my favourite customer coming back every morning.'

'Thanks.' She dipped her head and took a sip of her coffee. As usual, it was very good. No doubt about it, Connor was an excellent barista.

Resting one arm on top of the coffee machine he flicked a tea towel over his shoulder. 'Hey. I was wondering if you have anything planned for New Year's Eve. I thought we could hang out together and go to the Falls Festival.'

And here it was. The dreaded date invitation. Olivia hastily swallowed her mouthful, scalding her mouth and throat in the process. 'Oh, well, um. Actually, I . . . er . . . I have plans already,' she said. 'I have someone coming to stay.'

He cocked his head to one side and grinned. 'You don't have to lie. No need to invent an imaginary friend. You could have just said you're not interested.'

Connor was attractive in a Canadian lumberjack kind of way, but even if she wasn't still technically married, plunging headfirst into the dating pool again was not on her agenda. Not today, or any day soon. She had far too much going on in her life already between work, caring for her grandmother, and raising Scarlett, and did not need the complication of a man in her life.

She re-wrapped her scarf around her neck. 'I'm not lying.'

'But you're not interested in going out with me.'

She shook her head. 'No. Sorry.'

'Shame.' Connor grinned again. 'I thought we were more than friends.'

Definitely not.

An image of herself with Connor flashed through Olivia's mind and she shuddered and pushed the thought right out of her head. There'd only ever been one man in her life, and she was over him. Fresh remorse seeped into her bones, but she ignored the feeling. She was *not* the one to blame for her failed marriage.

Unable to think of a single thing to say, she forced a laugh, brought her cup back to her lips and took another sip.

Connor gave her a wry smile. 'And here I was, thinking my charm and personality had made an impression on you.' He shook his head ruefully. 'Olivia Carter, you've severely dented my ego.'

She smiled back. He had thicker skin than she'd given him credit for. 'I'm sure it will quickly recover.'

'Gotta give a guy points for trying.'

'Indeed.'

Another customer entered, bringing a gust of icy air into the café.

'Don't give it another thought, Olivia,' he said. 'I'll be fine.'

'I'm sure you will,' she said.

'Morning, Molly. How's my favourite customer today?' Connor beamed at the woman who had just entered, as if he'd already forgotten Olivia was still there.

'I'd better get going,' Olivia said, but Connor's attention was elsewhere. He'd probably invite Molly to the Falls festival the minute Olivia was out of earshot.

She had her hand on the doorknob when Connor called out 'See you at dinner, Olivia.'

She spun around, wondering for a second what he was talking about, before remembering. 'Yes. The dinner. Of course. I'll see you then.'

She opened the door and Sally Simpson walked in.

'Olivia!'

Stepping into her arms, Olivia hugged the woman who was like her second mother to her.

'Do you have time to stop for a coffee?' Sally asked.

Olivia held up her takeaway cup. 'I haven't even finished this one, but I'm more than happy to sit for a bit while you have one.' Suddenly her long list of things to do didn't seem as important.

She took a seat near the window and waited for Sally to place her order with Connor and bring her coffee and a cookie back to the table.

'You look like you've left all your Christmas shopping to the last minute,' Olivia said, indicating the bulging bags Sally had deposited at her feet. 'Did you leave anything in the shops for anyone else?'

Sally laughed.

'What have you been buying? More gifts for that grandbaby of yours?'

'The grandbaby who isn't due for another three months.' Sally giggled. 'Les thinks I'm mad buying presents already, but that little bubba is already so loved.'

'How's Aimee doing?' Les and Sally's only daughter was pregnant with their first grandchild.

'Great. It's been a dream pregnancy.'

'When are you heading up to see her?'

'We'll drive up early on Boxing Day and stay for the week.

What about you? Do you have many more gifts to buy?' Sally asked.

Olivia held up a finger and smiled. 'One more. A toboggan. I think Scarlett's old enough this year.'

'I'm sure she is.'

'I hope it snows in time for Christmas.'

'For Scarlett's sake, I hope so too. It's cold enough out there, that's for sure. You're not working today?' Sally asked.

'I've got two weeks off.'

Sally shook her head. 'With two weeks off, I don't know why you're hanging around here. Heck, if I had holidays when I was your age, I would have been on the first plane out of here to some place warm. I hate the winter.'

Olivia smiled at Sally and her constant complaints about the weather. Her friend sang that particular song from October to May. 'No one's stopping you and Les from moving somewhere warmer.'

'You'd miss me. Besides, we're too old to change towns.'

Olivia laughed. 'Since when is sixty too old?'

'Pfft. Spoken like someone still in their thirties.'

'Is everything ready for Sunday night?' Olivia asked, changing the subject.

'Just about.'

Sally and Les owned and operated *Harbourside,* a small restaurant and hotel on the lakefront. Each year on Christmas Eve they closed the restaurant to patrons and served a free meal to the less fortunate in the community. Most of the locals pitched in to help however they could. She'd volunteered every year since she was in her teens. This was her first Christmas back home since moving to Australia to live six years earlier. She couldn't wait to see how much the community dinner had grown and changed in that time.

Olivia had zero confidence when it came to cooking. She *could* cook but only the basics, therefore she preferred to stay clear of the kitchen. In past years, she'd always helped set up the restaurant, serve meals or wash dishes instead.

'Nan said you're expecting almost two hundred people this year.'

'Crazy, isn't it?'

'She's gutted she can't help this year.' Olivia's grandmother was one of the founding organisers of the dinner, but her recent vision loss meant she could no longer get involved the way she had every other year.

Sally's smile faded. 'It's been tough on her, hasn't it?'

Olivia nodded. 'Really tough. For someone so independent, this has been the worst.'

'Joan's lucky to have you back home helping her.'

Olivia put a hand to her heart. 'I'm lucky to have her. And you. Without both of you looking out for me when I was growing up, who knows where I'd be.'

She touched Olivia's cheek tenderly. 'You know you're like another daughter to me.' Sally smiled sadly. 'I wish that beautiful smile of yours would come back.' She shook her head. 'It's a shame about your marriage. What you two had was very special, you know.'

'Yeah, I guess so.'

But he blew it.

Olivia glanced at her watch. 'Sorry, Sally, I have to keep moving. I still need to get that present for Scarlett and I promised Nan I'd be home to help her do some baking.'

Olivia had promised nothing of the sort, but she needed an excuse to escape before Sally launched into another lecture. She loved Sally dearly but, like Nan, Sally seemed to believe everyone deserved a second chance.

She stood and gave Sally another hug. 'I'd better keep moving but I'll see you at dinner on Sunday night. Call me before then if you need a hand with anything.'

'Will do. Now give your little princess a kiss from her Aunty Sally.'

'Of course.'

With a wave, Olivia left the café, pushing thoughts of her almost-ex out of her mind and going through the list of all the things she still had to do. Head down against the wind, she strode purposefully up the main street.

After buying a toboggan she needed to get home and get the spare room ready. She checked her watch and her chest tightened. Nine-thirty already. Jack's flight would land in Toronto in less than two hours and he'd be here in less than four. Her stomach twisted as emotions warred within her. Had she made a stupid mistake asking her estranged husband to come for Christmas?

Chapter 2

As the plane touched down on the tarmac with a shudder and lurch, Jack tipped his head back, closed his eyes and let out his breath. The window-seat passenger nudged him with an elbow. Jack removed his headphones and glanced over at him.

'Not a fan of flying?' the guy asked with a grin.

'Just glad to be here,' Jack replied.

The flight had been delayed leaving Vancouver and he was now two hours behind schedule. Olivia hated his ability to be perpetually late. Not that he had any control over time, but if he did, he'd turn back the clock eighteen months. And he'd never be late again.

'Where are you from?'

'Australia.'

The man's eyes bulged. 'That's a long way, eh?'

'Sure is,' Jack agreed.

He'd taken off from Brisbane twenty-eight hours earlier, excited but nervous. Twelve months was too long. He wasn't worried about whether Scarlett would remember him, but he was anxious about seeing Olivia. Last year was a disaster and he didn't want a repeat of that.

'Hope you like the cold.'

Jack glanced past him through the tiny oval window at blue, cloudless skies. 'Looks okay out there. I expected snow to be honest.'

'Still two days. Plenty of time for it to snow before Christmas.'

'That's good.'

A white Christmas would be nice, but that wasn't why he'd flown halfway around the world. He'd come all this way to see his wife and daughter, and they were his priority. His stomach re-knotted itself, as it had done since Olivia's invitation. A lack of snow was the least of his worries.

The guy was still making small talk, going on about the weather. Jack tuned back in.

'It's summer in Australia, isn't it?'

'Yeah.'

The guy shook his head. 'Dunno why you'd come all this way in the middle of winter. Must be mad, eh? Where're you headed?'

'Niagara-on-the-Lake.'

'Nice one,' he drawled. 'Got friends there? Family?'

The knot tightened. 'Family.' *My wife. My daughter.*

Missing Scarlett was a constant hum in the background, no matter how busy or chaotic his life was. And no amount of Facetime would ever compensate for holding her in his arms.

'Nothing better than spending Christmas with family,' the guy said, putting a hand to his heart and tapping his chest with a closed fist. A wedding ring shone. 'Home. The best place on earth.'

'Yeah, nothing better.' Jack tried to smile but his face felt stiff and heavy.

When the flight attendant announced they could disembark, Jack quickly stood and retrieved his carry-on case from the overhead locker to avoid further conversation.

'Merry Christmas.'

'Yeah, Merry Christmas to you, too, mate.'

Having already passed through customs in Vancouver, all Jack needed to do was pick up his suitcase and find the car hire company and get on the road.

While walking to the carousel, he inserted the Canadian SIM card into his phone and switched it back on. Within seconds, it pinged with dozens of messages and missed calls. His mouth went dry as he quickly scrolled through them, terrified there'd be a message from Olivia saying she'd changed her mind. But there was nothing from her. All the messages were from Maddie, his business manager. He debated ignoring them—ignoring her—but it wasn't worth the grief. She was persistent and would keep trying until she got hold of him. He wished he could see her face when she found out he was in Canada.

Trying not to smirk, he rang her number, even though Australia was sixteen hours ahead and he knew his call would wake her. Maddie never put her phone on silent.

It took her longer than he expected to answer, her voice raspy with sleep. 'Jack? What's wrong? What time is it?'

'I dunno. Around midday I think.'

'*Midday*?' Her voice came out as a screech and he held the phone away from his ear. 'Where the hell are you?'

'Canada.' He glanced up at the large "Welcome" sign at the top of the escalator. 'Pearson International Airport in Toronto to be precise.'

There was a long pause. 'You're going to see Olivia.'

'Yes.'

A shorter pause. He pictured her swinging her legs out of bed, switching on the light. 'Does she have any idea how busy you are right now?'

'I'm sure she does but—'

Maddie didn't let him finish. 'Of course not. Olivia has no clue how busy you are. Your *ex*-wife, has never shown any interest in your career.' She swore. 'I cannot believe she'd ask you to go there now of all times. It's totally unacceptable. The timing is terrible, what with the—'

This time he cut her off. 'It's Christmas, Mads. I'm going to see my daughter.'

He heard a click, a quick inhale, then an exhale of puffed cigarette smoke.

'How long are you away for?'

'I fly out on New Year's Day. I land back in Melbourne on the second.'

There was a pause while Maddie calculated how long he'd be gone. 'Ten days?' She swore again and her voice rose. 'Are you joking? We're supposed to open on the fifteenth and with the way things are going, that doesn't seem likely. That's why I've left you all those messages.'

'Sorry.' *Not sorry.* 'I was in the air.'

'Surely you had a stopover and could have checked your phone then.'

When he'd landed in Vancouver, he hadn't bothered to put his SIM card into his phone nor connect to the airport Wi-Fi. Instead, he'd used the six-hour break between flights to take a quick shower and nap in the Premium Lounge before his connecting cross-country flight to Toronto.

The carousel was already moving, and a few bags had appeared. He kept his eye trained for his case.

'What's up, Maddie?'

'Where do I start? Apart from the delays with the fit-out, I haven't seen your menu yet.'

'What delays?'

He heard her blow out another puff of smoke. 'It's Christmas. You know what tradies are like this time of year. Notoriously lazy. No one wants to do a bloody thing until the end of January.' She carried on, bemoaning the fact the builders were useless.

He'd heard enough. 'What else is wrong?'

'You haven't given me your menu. I should have started our marketing campaigns weeks ago, but you've been dragging your feet.'

'I've been busy,' he reminded her.

'Listen, Jack. Just because *Atlas* was a huge success, doesn't mean *Globe* will be the same. It's a cold hard fact that, sixty percent of restaurants will fail in their first year of operation.'

'*Atlas* hasn't. No reason why this one will be any different. We're trading on my name, now, Maddie.

'Argh,' she growled. 'You can be so pigheaded and full of yourself at times, Jack.'

He ignored the dig.

'You are so frustrating,' Maddie went on. 'You think because anyone in Australia who watches television knows who you are, it means they're going to rush through the doors the moment we open. It might not happen. Melbourne is a different market from Noosa. There's no magic formula, you know.'

'You worry too much.'

'And you don't worry enough.'

There was an element of truth in what Maddie said, but Jack had always been a glass-half-full kind of guy. It was Maddie's job to worry—and she was very good at them both: her job *and* worrying—and it was his to build hype around any new venture. Sure, there were always teething issues with anything new, but he had full confidence that the new venture in Melbourne would lead to even bigger things.

Another sigh of exasperation came down the line. 'What's our selling point, Jack? And don't tell me it's you. People want to know what's on the menu. Your customers need one good reason why they should come to your new restaurant and pay over three hundred a head instead of going to *Dinner by Heston, Vue de Monde* or *Attica*.'

The thing was, it *was* him and Maddie knew that. That's why people come in droves. They felt like they already knew him because they'd seen him on television. When they came to his restaurant and watched him cook, and then had the opportunity to chat with him afterwards, it formed an emotional connection.

'You know it's me, Maddie. After they leave, they don't remember the amazing food or the great wine or the exceptional service, they remember how I made them feel. *That's* our selling point.'

'And how am I supposed to market that?'

'I don't know. That's what I pay you to do.'

His bag came into view and he excused himself as he pushed between two people to pluck it off the moving carousel.

'Jack?'

He ran a hand through his hair. 'Maddie, I need to do this. I've been working twenty-hour days for the last month to get *Atlas* ready and I'm exhausted. I need a break.'

'You can take a break once we're open.'

'No, I can't. Once we're open, I'll need to be there overseeing things. This is the perfect time.'

'I think you're taking a big risk.' He pictured her grounding out her cigarette butt the way she did when she was annoyed and trying to hold it in.

He *was* taking a risk—a huge risk—but not the way Maddie thought.

'I have to go, okay?'

'Promise you'll check your emails.'

'Promise. Have a great Christmas, Maddie.'

'Yeah, right. I'll be working at covering your backside.'

'Talk to you later, Mads.' He ended the call and slipped it into his pocket.

Ten minutes later Jack sat in the hire car, heater blasting, while he programmed the GPS. He'd told Olivia to expect him around one-thirty, but with the flight delays it would be nearly three before he made it to Niagara-on-the-Lake. He knew she'd be ticked, and blame him for being late, but this time the situation was out of his control.

He typed out a quick text message to her.

Hi Olivia. Sorry, flight was delayed. On my way now. Looking forward to seeing you guys. Jack

The reply pinged back immediately. She must have been waiting for him to call or text.

See you whenever you get here.

The sledgehammer came down on his heart, but he recovered quickly. He didn't need to be a psychologist to read between the lines of her typed words. Determined to fight the fear welling within him, he reminded himself that *she'd* invited *him*. It wasn't as if he was coming unannounced.

Chapter 3

An hour and a half later, Jack slowed as he came to the outskirts of Niagara-on-the-Lake. He hadn't been here since their summer wedding six years earlier, but he remembered it like it was only yesterday. This time though, instead of colourful baskets of flowers hanging from leafy trees, Christmas decorations and lights adorned the bare branches.

Niagara-on-the-Lake was a picture-book kind of town that tourists loved. The parks and gardens were full of large, shady trees. The buildings were clean and freshly painted in muted tones of green and yellow, and burnt red and blue. It was no wonder the town had featured in over thirty television shows and movies.

It was famed for its gorgeous architecture and award-winning wineries. In the summer, the Shaw Festival, showcased a series of theatre productions. But even when it hummed with tourists— which was pretty much year-round—it felt like the type of place where time stood still. This town was the total opposite of the hustle and bustle of the life they'd led in Australia, where he jetted between Melbourne, Sydney, Brisbane and Noosa on a regular basis.

A life Olivia told him she couldn't stand. A life she'd walked away from eighteen months earlier without offering him a valid reason why. Olivia had taken Scarlett and returned to Canada and Niagara-on-the-Lake.

She'd grown up in this town and gone to school here and the only time she'd left was to visit Australia on her dream "bucket list holiday" where she'd met him.

Growing up in Melbourne, he and his family had spent every summer in Aireys Inlet on Victoria's southern coast. Some of his happiest memories were of the long weeks spent there, surfing and hanging out with his mates, but the best memory was the year he turned twenty-nine. The year he met Olivia. Memories bloomed and he couldn't help but smile. It had been love at first sight.

Olivia Donahue. Eleven years ago.

Felt like a lifetime.

Without needing the GPS now, he turned right off Mississauga onto Queen Street. Heart pounding, he was only minutes away from seeing Olivia and Scarlett for the first time in a year. He drove along the main street, past the clock tower war memorial in the centre of the road, until he got to the corner where the Prince of Wales Hotel stood.

He turned left down King Street, then right onto Ricardo. If he'd kept driving straight, he would have ended up at Queen's Royal Park and the cute little gazebo where they'd gotten married. He pulled up in front of Olivia's grandmother's house and turned off the engine. The modest two-storey home in Old Town Niagara-on-the-Lake was one of the smaller homes on the street, but it was as gorgeous as its neighbours. Set close to the street with its red weatherboards, sage green front door, cream-coloured trim and grey shutters, it looked like something from a postcard. Lights adorned the trees in the front yard and they'd already been switched on, even though it wasn't yet fully dark.

He climbed out of the car and stretched, rolling his neck back and forwards and easing out the kinks. Buying time. It was hard to stay calm when the thunder in his chest was rumbling so loudly. He inhaled deeply. The air was cold and wet and infused with the smell of smoke from wood fires.

Leaving his bags in the boot, he pushed open the front gate. Three steps later he stood at the door, hand poised, ready to knock when it was swung open from inside. His breath caught and he tried to swallow the lump in his throat and ignore the tightening band around his chest.

'Hi, Liv,' he finally managed to say.

Olivia looked fantastic. Since last Christmas she'd grown her hair long and it fell well below her shoulders, hanging in a thick, dark, glossy wave. Her dark denim jeans clung to her slim legs and the pale blue jumper she wore matched her eyes, covering the curves he remembered. Flashes of fire ran through him until he tingled all over. The memories of how her silky skin felt under his fingertips circled around him, tempting him. It took everything in him not to reach up and cup her cheek the way he used to. But he'd lost the right to touch her eighteen months ago.

He had no idea what he was supposed to do. He would feel foolish shaking her hand like she was an acquaintance. What about a friendly kiss on the cheek? Or at least a hug. No. The likelihood of her wanting his arms around her was less than zero percent. There was no rule book that told him how to handle this situation, but judging by her folded arms and her scowl, it wouldn't be smart to overstep any boundaries right off the bat.

Mental note: go slow.

'Hi, Jack.' Her half-smile didn't come anywhere near her eyes.

He knew he was supposed to say something intelligent, but he was having trouble thinking. 'Hi,' he repeated. 'Good to see you.'

'Are you coming in?' There was a hint of irritation in her voice. 'It's cold out.'

'Yeah, yes, of course. Thanks.'

He slipped past her into the warm house. Closing the door behind him he caught a hint of coconut and lime, her signature hand cream.

After toeing off his boots, he followed her through the main living area on the right side of the house. He looked around curiously. The room was deceptively large and furnished with two comfortable looking couches and a leather recliner positioned in front of a large open fire. Heavy drapes hung at the windows and colourful rugs covered the dark timber floorboards. Artwork adorned the walls. A massive Christmas tree filled one corner of the room, covered in baubles, tinsel and lights. A basket of toys sat in another corner of the room, and there was a timber dolls' house under the window and a stack of children's books on the coffee table. It was a lovely room but nothing like the type of home they'd had back in Australia. Even though it was her grandmother's house, he had the sense that Olivia had put her stamp on this room.

He followed her through into the kitchen. It was an equally large room and looked to be recently renovated. It had black appliances, dark grey shaker-style cabinetry, white subway tiles and pale grey marble benchtops. Again he saw evidence of Scarlett everywhere from the fridge covered with pre-school paintings to a stack of colourful plastic plates and cups on the open shelving, but there was no sign of his daughter.

'You look tired,' Olivia said.

The cross-country flight from Vancouver to Toronto on the back of the long-haul flight from Brisbane would make anyone look tired but he wasn't about to point that out. 'I'm okay. I slept a bit on the plane.'

'No doubt first class.'

'Business.'

'The jetlag will hit tomorrow.'

'I'll be alright.' Too much small talk. 'Where's Scarlett?' he asked.

Olivia flinched at his question then wiped a bit of nothing off the spotless countertop with a Christmas-themed tea towel. 'She's not home from day care yet. Nan and our neighbour, Paul have gone to pick her up.'

He smiled. 'I can't wait to see her.'

'She doesn't know you're coming.'

He rocked back on his feet as if she'd physically slapped him. His smile vanished. 'You didn't tell her?

She stopped the wiping and finally looked up. 'Neither does Nan.'

He frowned at her. 'Why not?'

She shrugged and didn't answer but he already guessed her reason. She hadn't believed he'd show up. The tightness around his chest doubled in intensity. He honestly had no idea what he'd done to deserve Olivia's lack of trust in him. He'd been a good dad and had never let Scarlett down. Not once. If he had a chance, he'd find a way to gently remind Olivia he wasn't the one who'd taken their daughter to the other side of the world.

'Will Joan mind me staying here?' he asked.

'Nan still loves you.' Her lips settled into a thin, flat line.

'Right.'

He'd anticipated a frosty greeting, but this was icy to the point of South-Pole-cold. From the moment he'd stepped through the front door her brusque behaviour was like an impenetrable wall.

'How are your folks?' she asked.

'Good,' he replied carefully.

Olivia had never hit it off with his parents and to be fair, he could understand why. Whilst he loved them, he didn't always like them or the way they chose to live or do things. Over the years he'd come to realise his parents were business partners first and husband and wife second. He wasn't even sure if they loved each other and often wondered why they stayed married. The counsellor said it was little wonder he'd struggled to be a good husband when he didn't have good role models.

'They send their regards,' he lied.

Her eyebrows rose. She'd always seen through his lies. 'Sure.'

His parents had tried to talk him out of the trip, and Jack was still seething over the argument he'd had with his father the night before he flew out. Not that he should have been surprised. One of the hardest things he had to deal with was proving to his father that he knew what he was doing. No matter what Jack did, it was never done the right way, according to Tony.

Over the years Jack had accepted things for what they were and did his best to keep the peace. He and his father generally got along relatively well if they didn't spend too much time together, but that didn't stop Tony from voicing his opinion often, and loudly. Jack often wondered whether his relationship would have been different with his parents had he chosen a different career, instead of following his father's footsteps into the restaurant and hospitality business.

Her hand hovered over the kettle on the stove. 'Are you hungry? Thirsty? I can make you a coffee.'

'That'd be great. Thanks.' He didn't need a coffee, but anything to fill the void in the conversation.

While she kept herself busy making him a coffee, he glanced around the small, well-equipped kitchen. Nothing was out of place and he suspected Olivia had spent all morning cleaning and tidying in preparation for his visit.

A few moments later they were facing each other across the vast expanse of island bench. Olivia's face was pale and set like stone.

'Can we sit down?' he asked.

She silently led the way back to the lounge.

He perched on the edge of an armchair while she stood behind the leather recliner, as if using it as a barricade. He let a couple of beats of silence pass. Olivia kept her eyes fixed on the fire crackling in the hearth behind the heavy fire screen.

For the past three months, ever since she invited him for Christmas, he'd thought about what he was going to say. He'd thought about it so often, rehearsing it over and over in his head, but now he was here, feeling the full force of her anger, he had no idea how to say it. Olivia was hurting, and he wasn't sure why.

He took a breath. 'Thank you for asking me to come. I'm sure that wasn't easy for you.'

'I did it for Scarlett.' She looked down at her hands.

He nodded. 'Thank you. I appreciate that.'

The silence was so thick.

He stared down at his socked feet for a moment before looking up. His eyes met hers. They were as grey and stormy as the clouds that had swept across the lake in the last half an hour of his drive. He drew in a deep breath and let it out with a rush. 'Olivia, I don't know how to say what I want to say without it sounding like it's scripted, so I've done what we used to do before we were married…'

The V between her eyebrows deepened.

He reached into the back pocket of his jeans and pulled out a crumpled piece of paper. Unfolding it, he smoothed it flat against his thigh. 'I've written you a letter, and I'd like to read it to you.'

She started to speak, but he held up a hand.

'Listen, Liv. Please.' He heard the desperation in his voice and wondered if she could hear it too. He only had one chance to get this right. Stuffing up wasn't an option.

She clamped her lips shut and her eyes darkened.

'I know a letter won't fix what's broken between us. I know you'll probably think these are just words, but I wanted to write down everything, so I didn't miss saying what I want to say.' He lifted the letter and began to read. 'This is a sincere apology for my part in our marriage breakdown.'

He glanced up at her but couldn't gauge the look on her face. He kept going, forcing himself not to rush.

'I realise I've made a lot of mistakes during the last six years and I want to take full responsibility for those right now. I should have been more attentive, more grateful for everything you did for me. I should have communicated with you by listening instead of always talking.'

He dragged in another breath and realised his hands were shaking.

'I know the wall around your heart was built because I have hurt you so much by pushing you out of my life, and I'm sorry for that. I want to fix what I broke. If you'll allow it, I'll spend the rest of my life taking down each brick and rebuilding our relationship into something better than what we once had.'

He folded the letter and finally looked up at her. She hadn't uttered a word but her eyes glistened. A rush of sadness went through him. He was the reason for her tears.

'I still love you, Olivia and I always will. I'm not going to beat around the bush. You know me. I don't normally look backwards, but in the last year I've done a lot of thinking and a lot of soul searching. I've looked at the past to see what I've done wrong. And I've come to a conclusion…'

She stared at him, face like granite, eyes wide, mouth slightly parted.

He tried to smile, but his face felt frozen. Best to man up and say what he had to say.

'I'd like you to give us a second chance.'

Chapter 4

Olivia hadn't expected this. She folded her arms across her chest, stared at him, searching for words. Was it a trick?

Jack ran a hand through his hair but didn't say another word and didn't take his eyes off her face. He looked as if he was struggling to keep a lid on his emotions.

Her blood made a whooshing sound in her ears. 'No! No way. I'm not falling for your words again, Jack.'

No way was she falling for Jack's crazy ideas. Or Jack. Ever again.

Been there, done that.

No matter how sincere or convincing he sounded, or how attractive he still was, Olivia knew better. She wasn't going to let him hurt her again, not after leaving a long string of broken promises, shattered hopes and unfulfilled dreams in his wake. She forced herself to breathe slowly but there was nothing she could do to slow down her racing heart. He was kidding if he thought he could come here and "fix" their marriage.

She risked another look. He didn't appear to be joking. He sat in the chair, hands clasping the letter he'd penned. His face was pale, his eyes imploring her to give him another chance.

Her stomach clenched. Less than ten minutes and he'd turned her world upside down.

She dragged in a ragged breath, closed her eyes and tried to ignore the way her heart thumped and the fact her legs felt like jelly. She was totally unprepared for the out-of-control emotions tumbling through her, or the way her body was reacting to being in the same room as him. She scrubbed her face with her hands and tucked her hair back behind her ears. Jeepers. How was she supposed to convince herself she was over him?

'No, Jack. I can't do it.'

Jack sat, straight-backed, watching her, smiling but not speaking. The house seemed quieter than it was before.

'I've changed,' he said.

Yeah, right.

He rubbed his jaw. When she heard the scrape of skin against stubble a little piece of her heart went out to him and she felt fleetingly sorry for him. The least she should do was offer him a shower and a bed.

Jack looked exhausted. Dark smudges underlined his eyes and he needed a shave, but despite his unkempt appearance, he looked gorgeous. It was no wonder the cameras and half the Australian population loved him. And no wonder every woman who met him swooned.

She looked closer. There *was* something different about him not caused by international travel. The lines around his eyes had settled deeper and his sun-bleached blonde hair was interspersed with some greys. His tan had faded, as if he hadn't had a chance to get out on his beloved surfboard in a while. And his clothes hung from his already slim frame. Funny how the cameras lied.

She never would have admitted to Jack that she sometimes watched his show, but Scarlett loved seeing her daddy on the screen. When Jack emailed YouTube links of every episode after they'd been shown in Australia, Olivia would let Scarlett watch them. Olivia hovered in the background so she could watch too.

'I've been seeing a counsellor.'

Her eyes widened. That was the last thing she'd expected him to do.

'She told me I haven't put you first.'

Olivia blinked.

'And I've cut back my hours at the restaurant and put on a manager. I have a day off every week now. I've even re-negotiated my contract with the network so that we shoot over a longer block of time.'

She couldn't believe what she was hearing. When he was filming, she didn't see him for six weeks at a time.

'All I'm asking is for you to give me a chance.'

Part of her ached to believe him, but she couldn't let her heart go there. No. Nope. Nada. No way! Jack may have swept her off her feet once, declaring he'd do anything to make her happy and convincing her to leave Canada and marry him, but that was when she was younger and didn't know better, and believed every word that came out of his mouth.

Her mind flicked back to the day she met him. She was out in the water trying to put her new surfing skills into practice on a cool summer's morning. She couldn't remember if there had been anyone else in the water that day, because the moment she met Jack, it had been love at first sight.

Without any waves to catch, the two of them had sat on their boards and chatted for what felt like hours. After that, they'd had coffee which morphed into lunch, then dinner. She hadn't gone back to her accommodation that night and they were inseparable from that moment. She cut short the rest of her trip around Australia, returned to Canada to pack her bags and six weeks later moved in with him into his flat in East Melbourne.

There was a term for what happened when she met Jack. *Lovesick.* And she had no intention of catching it again. Especially not from her soon-to-be-ex-husband.

One of her friends once asked if she wished she'd never gone to Australia. But if she hadn't met Jack, she wouldn't have Scarlett and her daughter meant the world to her.

'Why would I want to give you another chance?' she asked, finally finding her voice.

His smile didn't falter but something flashed across his face. Doubt. Hurt. Regret. His lips thinned a little and the grooves around them deepened. Anger? No, despite all his other failings, Jack wasn't the type of guy who got angry. It was weird how she'd lost the knack for recognising his moods when she'd once been able to read him like a book.

There was a long pause as they faced each other across the room. The space between them was filled with a coffee table and painful memories. In the heavy stillness Olivia heard the central heating click and kick in again and on the mantlepiece the old grandfather clock ticked and tocked in the silence.

'Why?' she repeated. 'Why should I trust you again?' Obviously he had no idea how badly he'd hurt her. 'This is another one of your crazy ideas, I know it is.' He'd always been the type of guy to dream the impossible. The type of guy who thought he could fix everyone's problems.

'I've changed, Olivia,' he repeated. 'Give me a chance to show you how much. Please.'

Olivia tightened her grip on the back of the leather recliner. When she'd asked Jack to come to Canada for Christmas, she hadn't expected him to say yes. She also hadn't thought he'd actually show up. And she certainly hadn't predicted the way his presence would make her feel. Seeing him standing in the middle of Nan's lounge room was doing all kinds of strange things to her head and heart. Things she didn't like.

She should have gone with her gut. The moment she'd hung up the phone after he'd agreed to come, she'd wanted to call him back and un-invite him. Tell him to forget it, stay in Australia and have Christmas with his family and friends. Or work late on Christmas Eve like he usually did, then go back to work again on

Christmas Day and Boxing Day the way he had every other year of their married life.

Her mind ricocheted back to their summer wedding six years earlier. To the last time he'd been in her home town. When everything between them was filled with love and promises. Back when she was suffering from lovesickness. She tightened her grip. Nothing in the world could have prepared her for his suggestion.

And nothing would change her mind.

'We can't,' she said.

'We can,' he replied softly, eyes glowing.

She clenched her teeth. As always there was nothing that could damage the man's self-confidence. That was one of his problems, not only did he not know how to say "no", he didn't know how to take "no" for an answer.

His sea-green eyes bore into hers and Olivia was the first to look away. *Damn it.* It was his eyes that had caught her the first time and she wasn't going to let it happen again.

'I really want you to give me another chance. To give *us* another chance.'

He took a step towards her and she let go of the back of the chair, taking two steps back until she was pressed against the bookcase.

'I can't.'

'Can't or won't?'

'Both.'

'What about for Scarlett?'

The fight left her and it took all her strength to stay standing. Jack may have broken his marriage vows and betrayed her trust, but he'd always been a wonderful father. What sort of person was she if she denied Scarlett the chance to spend time with her Dad?

Her conscience warred between her own needs and Scarlett's. She wasn't sure she could risk Scarlett's happiness by letting Jack back on the scene. Sure, he was a great father, when he was around. But it wasn't like he was around very much. Scarlett was an amazing little girl and deserved more than the few minutes she got from Jack when he bounced in and out of her life between his work commitments.

Olivia thought back to last Christmas. Not that Scarlett was old enough to recall any of the details, but Olivia remembered vividly.

Six months after they'd returned to Canada, not long after Olivia finally found her feet back home, Jack called and begged her to bring Scarlett back to Australia for Christmas. Despite her misgivings, she didn't want to deny Jack the chance to see his daughter or give him an opportunity to sling mud at her if their divorce settlement ended up in a courtroom. When she left him she'd made a decision to keep things amicable.

They'd flown halfway around the world, landing at Coolangatta airport on Australia's Gold Coast the day before Christmas, cranky and sleep-deprived. Jack picked them up and took them to the five-star resort his parents owned and operated in Surfers Paradise, and it was a disaster from the moment they hit the tropical-rain-soaked tarmac.

Scarlett had no idea who her grandparents, Tony and Maxine were—which was hardly surprising given the last time she'd seen them she was two—and she refused to let Olivia out of her sight, crying whenever they tried to talk to her.

On Christmas morning, severely jetlagged and overdosed on sugar, Scarlett was plied with so many gifts from Jack, Olivia had to buy a second suitcase and pay for an extra bag to fly them home. Then they'd eaten a meal that cost more than Olivia's weekly grocery budget in a restaurant operated by a mate of Jack's.

Unfortunately, a week earlier the mate had lost the tip of finger after it was bitten off by a lobster, so Jack had offered to step in and help him out. Jack ended up spending more time in the kitchen on Christmas Day than he had sitting at their table. To make matters worse, Scarlett barely touched a thing on her plate and Olivia spent the whole meal ignoring Maxine's barbed comments about Scarlett's dismal eating habits.

Afterwards, Olivia wondered why Tony hadn't offered to help in the kitchen instead of Jack, so that Jack could spend time with his daughter, but by then it wasn't worth asking.

Jack's parents had never liked her and that year they made it more than obvious, clearly furious she'd walked out on their golden boy. They also showed no interest in Scarlett. Instead, all they wanted to talk about was how Jack's restaurant was doing, what the ratings were like for his show, how much money he was making and when he was planning to buy another house.

She'd felt ill, and it strengthened her resolve that she'd made the right decision to leave him. There was every chance Jack would turn out like Tony. He'd say all the right things and she'd agree to give him a second chance but then he'd choose his career over her. She couldn't commit to spending the rest of her life with someone like that for fear that *she'd* turn out like Maxine—living in a loveless marriage because appearances were worth everything.

It had been hard to get over the disappointment of Christmas Day, but to his credit Jack was incredible with Scarlett for the rest of their time in Australia. Olivia spent much of each day alone by the pool at the resort while Jack spent every waking moment with his daughter. He took her to *Dreamworld, Sea World, Movie World* and the Currumbin Wildlife Sanctuary. They fossicked in rock pools, went to *Wet 'N Wild* and had fish and chips on the beach.

Not long after her birthday in September, Scarlett started begging to see her daddy again at Christmas. It took Olivia a while to get her head around asking him but she had, and now he was here. Here in Nan's house. Right here, causing her heart to race at twice its normal speed.

From the moment he'd walked in the front door he'd filled the house with his presence, making it feel smaller than it was, making her feel like she needed to open all the doors and windows to make room for him in it. He had that way about him.

Jack was patiently waiting for her to say something, but she didn't know what to say. Or do.

She crossed the lounge room and went to the large bay window. From her vantage point she could make out Lake Ontario, dull and murky, reflecting the grey, overcast winter sky. The blue cloudless skies of the morning had vanished, replaced by thick clouds. Soon it would be too dark to see anything other than her reflection in the window. She stared out at the water as if it could magically gift her with words, but none came.

It was a long time with nothing but the ticking clock between them before Jack finally broke the silence. 'I wanted to be honest and tell you upfront, Liv. After you left last Christmas, I realised how much I'd stuffed it. I've been thinking about this ever since.'

And yet you hadn't thought to mention it to me until now?

He could have called first, or at least emailed and warned her he had something he wanted to talk to her about.

She turned to face him and risked a glance. He was saying all the right things, but until she saw evidence of change, it was hard to believe him. He sounded sincere, but then again, he was well-practised at saying the right things. It was like he followed some internal script, the same way he followed the scripts his producers gave him.

She met his steady gaze A small part of her hoped he had woken up to himself and made changes—for Scarlett's sake of course, not hers—but she couldn't and wouldn't go there. There was no way she could consider giving Jack a second chance. Not even for Scarlett. No matter how convincing he sounded.

'I want to work on our marriage while I'm here.'

She folded her arms again and shook her head sadly. 'We don't have a marriage anymore, Jack. We have an impending divorce.'

'Not if I can help it.' His words were so soft she almost wondered if she'd heard him correctly.

She released a shaky sigh. When she'd been younger and daydreaming of how she wanted her life to look, she'd never pictured being a single mother forced to justify why she'd left one of Australia's most recognisable and lovable men.

'Liv...'

The way he said her name, the way his voice washed over her, warm and sweet, and full of memories was almost her undoing.

He looked at her with a bleakness that tugged at her heart and raised a million questions.

Then he smiled and it reached his eyes and her heart did an unwelcome flip that felt like love and longing. She nearly wavered and fell at his feet and agreed to give him a chance because, damn, those *eyes* and that smile. And because once she had loved him with all her heart.

Unbidden, a smile tried to come to her lips and she had to consciously stop it from forming. She looked away. Jack's smiles always came easily. Too easily. When he turned on that golden boy thousand-watt smile, the cameras and everyone watching him on television lapped him up. He'd used that smile to win his way into the hearts of Australian audiences and no doubt into the beds of Australian women. Well, to be fair, only two women she was aware of, but she'd bet Nan's house there were others. There had to be others. It went with the territory.

She straightened up, hating the way he still made her heart flutter when he looked at her like that. She couldn't afford for her heart to get involved. She needed to use her head and remember she was older now. Wiser. More immune to Jack Carter's charms. There was no way she could trust him again, let alone agree to a reconciliation.

As for spending Christmas and the next ten days together, they'd somehow make that work. For Scarlett.

'Even if I believed in second chances, Jack, which, for the record, I don't. I can't leave Nan, not now her sight is gone.'

Chapter 5

Jack sank back into one of the armchairs and stared at Olivia, standing stiff as a board in front of the large picture window, arms folded over her chest, glowering at him.

'Joan's gone blind?'

Why hadn't Olivia told him? Fair enough, whenever they spoke on the phone it was usually about Scarlett, but surely Olivia should have mentioned something as devastating as her grandmother going blind.

What a dreadful blow. He'd liked Joan the moment they'd met. After losing her only child to breast cancer, she and Robert were left to raise eight-year-old Olivia on their own. Olivia had told him more than once that Joan was her mother in every aspect except name. It was no surprise Olivia was as strong as she was. She'd had an excellent role model.

Before he'd proposed, he'd called Joan and Robert to ask their permission. Joan had agreed on one condition: the wedding be held in Canada. It had been a no-brainer and Jack happily agreed because from the moment he met Olivia she'd talked continually about her love for her grandparents. And, after meeting them, he could see why.

Olivia's shoulders sagged and she wrapped her arms around her body and rubbed her arms. He had a sudden urge to wrap his arms around her and hold her tight, but he stayed where he was.

'She's almost completely blind. Macular degeneration.'

'When did that happen?'

'It's been gradual. Over the last couple of years it's been getting progressively worse, but then about six months ago she experienced almost total loss in both eyes in a matter of days. Something to do with the blood vessels deep in the eye growing.'

He shivered as a cold sensation swept over him. Poor Olivia. Poor Joan. 'I didn't know.'

Something sparked in Olivia's blue eyes. 'Of course not. You haven't been back here since we got married so how would you know?'

There was something in her voice he didn't recognise. Bitterness. Resentment. Sadness?

'Is that why you came back here? To look after her?' He hadn't considered there'd been another reason why she'd walked out on him.

'She doesn't have anyone else. Not since Granddad died.' Colour flared in her cheeks. 'You remember *that* don't you?' she asked, voice rising.

'Yes, Olivia,' he replied carefully. 'I remember your grandfather passing away.' Robert was a softly spoken teddy bear of a man whom Jack had held in high regard too. He'd passed away in April of that year.

Chin raised defiantly, she glared at him, her eyes piercing right through him. 'Not that you bothered to come to his funeral.'

He hated that he might be the reason there was so much venom in her tone and rage in her stance, so he bit back his retort. The counsellor said if he wanted to win her back, he had to do more than *tell* her he'd changed, he had to show her. And he had to do it slowly, giving her space to heal and not lashing out with his words the way he was apparently prone to doing.

Since last year's disastrous Christmas, he'd spent almost twelve months in therapy, working out what he needed to do to change. It was a painful, eye-opening experience because he hadn't realised how selfish he was until his psychologist turned the mirror towards him. So he'd tried to change. He just had to prove that to Olivia, but now he was here, he had no idea where to start. He hadn't realised the depth of her animosity *towards* him, which only proved how self-centred he'd been and confirmed that every word the counsellor had said was true.

He hadn't gone to Robert's funeral because he'd been in the UK, at *River Cottage*, filming a segment for his show. He'd done everything he could to get time off to fly to Canada for the funeral, but he was contractually obligated to finish filming in a certain time frame. If he'd walked off set, it would have affected so many other people who all had their own timelines and jobs to do. It hadn't been feasible. He'd tried to explain that to Olivia, but she'd refused to listen.

He'd rung and spoken with Joan and she'd told him she totally understood so he'd sent flowers and a substantial cheque to cover funeral costs instead. He bet Olivia didn't know *that*.

'Olivia, please sit.' He patted the seat beside him. Her resistance was deeper than he'd anticipated, and he had his work cut out for him if he was going to convince her how much he wanted their marriage to work.

She moved away from the window and took the chair furthest away from him. Not that he'd expected her to sit on the couch next to him, but it would have been nice. At least the anger that had flared briefly in her eyes was gone.

A thick silence blanketed the room.

She couldn't bring herself to look at him, but he took the opportunity to look at her. Even without makeup Olivia was a stunning woman—a natural beauty. That was the first thing he'd noticed about her when they met.

It had been his first summer back in Aireys Inlet in years.

Since finishing high school he'd taken a gap year which had extended into three. Instead of going to university he'd gone to America and attended the prestigious Auguste Escoffier School of Culinary Arts in Boulder, Colorado, like his father had done. When he'd returned to Australia, he'd moved around a bit ,trying to decide what would be the next best move for his career. When his parents bought a resort in Surfers Paradise, they asked him to join them and his sister up there, but he had far bigger dreams. Dreams which soon become a reality.

In January of the year he turned thirty, he started a job in Melbourne at The Press Club and although he didn't know it at the time, his career was launched from that moment, and the pathway for his future was set.

He'd dated a few lovely women over the years, and even been engaged once, but none of them came close to Olivia, not even his former fiancé. It was impossible to forget Olivia and the way she'd made him feel from that first meeting, and ever since.

It had been an overcast late December morning and they were in the inky water off the beach at Fairhaven, the only two wet-suited souls in the surf waiting for a wave. He'd noticed her immediately because she clearly had no idea what she was doing. He'd padded over to her and introduced himself and she'd explained she'd taken a surfing lesson the day before and was keen to give it another go.

Unlike he and Olivia, everyone else had clearly checked the surf report and seen it wasn't worth getting out of bed that day. So, without any waves to catch, they'd lain on their boards and started chatting. Everything about their conversation was easy. Olivia was Canadian, five years younger than him, taking a break from her job as a nurse and taking a bucket-list holiday, backpacking around Australia for three months over the summer.

They'd fallen hard, fast and deep. At the time they were both seeing other people, but when they met, the attraction and connection was so instant, they knew it was meant to be. Within six weeks of their first meeting, Olivia changed her life. She flew home to Canada, quit her job, broke things off with her boyfriend, packed up her belongings and moved back to Melbourne to be with him.

He split amicably with his fiancé, Chelsea, and he and Olivia married within months back in Canada. The next couple of years passed in a hazy whirlwind of happiness. At least that's what he'd thought until she walked out on him. In hindsight he realised he'd missed all the warning signs. In the early years after Scarlett was born, Olivia had tried to fight for the marriage, but he'd never listened to her. Then she'd stopped going on about needing to get help and he dumbly assumed things had worked themselves out. Little did he realise until it was too late that he'd shoved things under the carpet while Olivia had shut down and given up.

Olivia shifted in her seat and her jumper pulled tight across her chest. Given the tension in the room, now was the totally wrong time to notice the way her clothes hugged her figure, but he couldn't help it. They might be officially separated, almost divorced, and smack in the middle of an argument he wasn't winning, but that didn't mean he didn't still find her incredibly attractive. Seeing her again today was making him feel more alive than he had in a long time. And more desperate to make their marriage work.

'Is there anyone else who can care for Joan?' he asked eventually. His question shattered the silence in the room like a rock breaking through the ice on a frozen lake and he realized how insensitive he sounded. His question made it sound like Joan's blindness was the cause of the breakdown of their marriage. 'What about another relative?'

'There is no-one else. Mom was an only child and so was Nan.'

Olivia was an only child too and the way things were looking, Scarlett was unlikely to ever have a sibling either.

'What about your father?'

Olivia scowled and he immediately wanted to bite back his words. Joan's ex-son-in-law Michael Donahue was a chronic gambling womaniser who hadn't stayed around long enough to see Olivia finish primary school. After Olivia's mother, Christy, died, Michael walked out and from that moment had nothing to do with Olivia, or Christy's family. Perhaps that partly explained Olivia's anger towards him. She thought he was no better than her father. A flash of fury ripped through him. He was *nothing* like her deadbeat father. Even after she'd taken Scarlett and gone back to Canada, he'd done everything he could to keep the connection going between him and his daughter.

Jack met Olivia's father for the first time at their wedding. He'd barely walked her down the path to the gazebo and into Jack's waiting arms before he'd made his way through the tab at the bar paid for by Jack's parents. At the end of the night after their reception dinner, there was an embarrassing fracas when Michael vomited in the flowerbeds outside the hotel before punching a guy who stopped to offer assistance. That was the last time Jack saw or heard of the man. Michael hadn't even been in touch with Olivia when Scarlett was born.

'Where's Michael living these days?' he asked.

Olivia shrugged. 'Who would know? He's onto wife number four and last I heard they were on a Pacific cruise.'

'Wow. How'd he afford to do that?'

'I didn't ask.'

'When did you last speak to him?'

'I haven't. He emailed. I didn't reply.'

'Right.'

'Jack, why didn't you ever come back to Canada with me to visit Nan?'

Her question came as a surprise. Surely she knew the answer but she seemed to be waiting for him to reply. It was impossible to explain again in a way that didn't sound like he was making more excuses. Olivia never seemed to understand how busy he'd been in those early years establishing his career. He'd been more than happy to let her come back to Canada as often as she wanted to visit, but he hadn't had time to join her.

He swallowed and chose his words carefully. 'I couldn't come back. I was under immense pressure to get *Atlas* up and running, plus I had the commitments to Channel Nine for *The Chopping Block*.'

His first restaurant had been an overnight sensation which had led to his own television show and even an appearance on *Ellen*. Portia had tried one of his recipes, loved it and suggested Ellen interview him. To get where he was today had taken a lot of his time and energy and focus.

'I had investors and staff relying on me to succeed.' He leaned forward. 'But more importantly, I was working my butt off to provide for you and Scarlett. I didn't want you to have to put her in child care and go to work.'

Her eyes flashed. 'I *wanted* to work.'

He frowned and sat back. 'You did?' He'd presumed she hadn't wanted to work because it was too much of a hassle to have her nursing registration transferred from Canada to Australia.

'You never heard me, Jack. You were so focused on you and your career you forgot I had plans for my future too. I told you again and again how much I wanted to work.'

'I'm sorry, Olivia, I really am.' Was she right? *Had* he been so self-absorbed he didn't realise their goals had shifted. Another thought occurred. Maybe their goals had never been the same.

'Yeah, well it's too late now.'

He wasn't sure whether she was talking about her career or their marriage or both and wasn't game to ask.

'I saw more of you on the television than I did in person.' Bitterness tinged her voice.

Battling the temptation to return fire with fire, he tried to keep the edge from his voice. 'I didn't have a choice.'

'You can tell yourself that if it makes you feel better, but we all have choices. I needed you. Scarlett needed you. But you made your priorities clear. Work came before us. Even when Scarlett was born you didn't take time off work.'

'You were three weeks early! We were in the middle of filming. You know I couldn't take time off.'

His pulse accelerated and he clenched his fists, forcing himself not to react. The Olivia he'd met and married never got annoyed, but now the anger was coming off her in waves. Then it hit him. Maybe Olivia *had* been angry, but she'd never let it show. Or worse, she'd been angry, and he hadn't noticed because he hadn't been there. In which case, her accusations were true.

That would explain so much. He'd genuinely had no clue she was unhappy, so when he received the divorce papers, he believed what Maddie told him. Olivia had gone home to Canada, back to Mark, the guy she'd left to marry him. He'd believed Maddie, not once stopping to consider why she would know anything about Olivia and Mark. He was an idiot. He should have ignored Maddie and gotten straight on the next plane to Toronto to find out what was going on, but the timing had sucked, and he was unable to get away. By then, he figured it was too late to chase her.

'Being successful and famous isn't all there is to life, you know.'

He flinched at Olivia's words. 'Is that what you think? All I wanted was success and fame?' He shook his head. 'Then you really don't know me.' He let out a long breath.

Olivia lifted her head and for the first time since he'd arrived, met his gaze head on. Her blue eyes flashed.

'You're right, Jack. I don't know you. And you don't know me.'

Chapter 6

Jack's face lost colour and for a second Olivia's heart twisted a tiny fraction, but she straightened her spine. She'd lost count of how many promises Jack had broken. How many nights and weekends and birthday celebrations and special occasions she had sat up waiting for him to come home. All ending with her tossing the cold food in the garbage bin and downing the rest of the bottle of wine on her own. It had happened more often than she wanted to admit.

Since she'd left him, she had no doubt in her mind Jack had found a willing woman to keep Olivia's side of their bed warm. And she knew he'd been in touch with his former fiancé, Chelsea.

But now he was here, looking more gorgeous than ever, sounding contrite and making crazy suggestions about getting together again. She clenched her hands, feeling the pain of her nails digging into her palms. Despite her best efforts to keep the hard shell of protection around her heart, something inside her was softening like butter in the sun. And she didn't like how it was making her feel. She'd gotten over losing him, the way the ache from a broken bone finally stops. And now he was here, stirring up all her emotions.

Jack still hadn't said a word. He sat, unmoving, staring at the fire, shoulders hunched over, elbows resting on his knees.

She'd lied when she said she didn't really know him. She did. Probably better than anyone else, but that didn't change the facts. He'd hurt her and Scarlett, and Olivia wasn't going to let him do it again. If she'd known how tough marriage to him would be, she probably wouldn't have signed up for the ride. Sure, every marriage took work, but with Jack constantly in the spotlight, it added an additional strain to their relationship. The limelight on centre stage wasn't her favourite seat in the house. She preferred the back row.

In truth, she wasn't proud of what she'd done—walking out on Jack with barely any explanation—but once Nan called and asked for help, she felt she had no option. Jack didn't seem to need her, but Nan did. After Scarlett was born, she'd fought hard for her marriage, but Jack always brushed her off and seemed to think everything was fine. He'd say one thing and do another. It always felt like there was something invisible inside their marriage, pushing them apart. Since leaving, she'd realised what it was: Jack's hunger for more and his desire to please. Problem was, he seemed to want to please everyone but her.

Nan losing her sight wasn't the final straw, it was the perfect excuse to leave and escape the pain and shame of a failing marriage.

When she'd lovingly spoken her wedding vows, she'd truly believed the "until death do us part" bit. Giving up on her marriage felt like a betrayal of her vows and herself and everything she stood for. It was a failure on a scale she could never have imagined. Deep down she knew she was taking the easy escape route, but at the time she didn't think she had any other choice.

She'd been unhappy and frustrated with lots of things about her marriage, despite her best efforts to make it work. Exhausted and heartsore, she'd concluded that leaving Jack would make life better. But she was no happier now.

Jack finally looked up. 'Are you sure?'

She sighed. 'You need to accept it's over, Jack. I appreciate that you're here and thank you. Honestly. I'm grateful for you taking time out of your busy schedule to come and see Scarlett, but that's the thing. This visit is for Scarlett, not me. As far as I'm concerned, we're Scarlett's parents, and that's as far as it goes. We have to focus on making this a special time for her and somehow get through the next week or so.'

'Ten days,' he said.

'Right. Yes. Ten days.'

Ten days to hang out and spend time getting to know your daughter again.

She pulled the cover around her hurting heart even tighter. All she had to do was get through the next ten days, one hour at a time, the same way she'd made it through the last few years.

'Ten days to change your mind,' he murmured, so softly she barely heard him.

She heard the lilt in his voice and sure enough when she looked up, he was smiling at her. A little smile, but it was enough to rouse her anger and send her back over the edge.

Typical Jack. He never took anything she said seriously. He always believed a smile and his trademark charm could get him out of anything. Why could he never take "no" for an answer?

She clenched her fists. 'I'm not going to change my mind, Jack. I can't go back to the life we had in Australia.'

He seemed to consider her answer for a moment.

'What was so bad about it?'

She shook her head. Once again, he was demonstrating he'd never listened to her. They'd talked about this. He knew how much she missed Canada.

'What was so bad about our life, Liv? I did my best to provide for you and Scarlett ,and I don't understand what I did wrong. Were you unhappy?'

'Was I unhappy?' Her laugh sounded forced. 'That doesn't

even begin to describe it.'

He sat back in the chair and stared at her. 'Unhappy with what? We had an amazing house, an amazing life. I gave you everything.'

Except the one thing she craved: him. His time, his attention, feeling like she had some place in his list of priorities. But she wasn't going to admit any of that to him. She was done begging. 'You gave me things, objects. That's simply not enough to sustain a relationship.'

Sure, Jack had provided for her—materially speaking— thinking that was the way to show his love, but he never seemed to grasp that she needed him to provide for her emotionally too.

Something glinted in his eyes—something she didn't recognise. Defeat?

'I didn't realise the life I provided for you made you so unhappy.'

'Because you never listened,' she retorted.

'How could I? I came back from that trip to New York and you and Scarlett were gone. Nothing except a note saying you'd come back here to look after Joan. Whenever I tried to call, you wouldn't answer. The next thing I know your wedding rings arrived in the mail and a month later I had an email from your solicitor saying you wanted a divorce.'

She exhaled heavily. 'At the time I was so upset I didn't know what else to do. I had Nan calling me from Canada, needing me, and I had you, always away, always busy. I was so distraught I felt the only way to move forward was to make a clean break. If I hadn't, I think you would have talked me around again like you always did and convinced me to keep going, and we'd be in the same place we always ended up. You at work, me at home, desperately unhappy and lonely.'

He ran his hands through his hair. 'I tried to call you, but you'd changed your number. I figured you'd gone back to Mark.'

'Yeah right. At least *I* honoured our marriage vows.'

'So did I.'

'Until you didn't,' she retorted.

He frowned. 'What's that supposed to mean?'

They were moving into forbidden and dangerous territory. She wanted this visit to be good for Scarlett and that wouldn't happen if she was so angry with Jack she couldn't even look at him without snapping. And that's exactly what would happen if he denied his affair with Chelsea.

It was bad enough hearing it come from Maddie but listening to Jack lie about it would be a million times worse. When Maddie told her what had happened between Jack and Chelsea, it had been too much, especially when it came the day after she found out about Nan's blindness. Confused, angry and feeling betrayed, she hadn't confronted Jack because she was too devastated. And she wouldn't do it now because she had a daughter to protect—the same way Nan and Granddad had protected her after Mom died and her father walked out.

So regardless of how much he might want to deny what had happened, she didn't want to or need to hear Jack's side of the story. At least not now. Scarlett and Nan would be walking in the door any minute and the last thing she wanted them walking into was a fight.

'I don't want to argue with you, Liv.'

At least they agreed on something.

'But we need to talk about what happened. Whatever it was, pretending it didn't happen isn't healthy. You were obviously unhappy in our marriage and I'm sorry I didn't realise how deep that went. I want to talk about it. Work out how I can fix things. Change things. Be a family again.'

Every word was like an arrow straight to her heart. Hearing him say the words she'd wanted to hear for so long was confusing her. Part of her felt a sense of optimism, but another part of her knew it was too little too late. The optimism fizzled quickly, replaced by frustration.

'There's nothing left to fix. That's one of your problems Jack. You think you can click your fingers, and everything will be the way you want. Our marriage, me, our family isn't something you throw on a plate. No one is going to ooh and aah over how good it looks and tastes. Our marriage is not an episode of *Masterchef*.'

He blinked and opened his mouth to say something, but she cut him off.

'Perhaps if you'd put as much energy into our marriage as you did into your work, we wouldn't be having this conversation. Honestly Jack, I think the time to talk about fixing our marriage is long gone. I tried, but you didn't try with me. You were always too busy planning your next television appearance.'

The light in his eyes dimmed a little and his shoulders slumped again. A tiny spot in her heart ached to say sorry for snapping at him and she almost went to him. But she held herself back. If she weakened now, they'd be right back where they were at the beginning when he'd convinced her that life with him was all she'd ever dreamed. Instead it had been a nightmare, trapped in a high-rise penthouse apartment with no back yard for Scarlett and a long way from Olivia's home. Sure, she had the beach at her doorstep, but the squeaky sand of Noosa wasn't the same as the gritty sand on the shore of Lake Ontario.

Long forgotten memories stirred unwillingly, flooding back to the surface. After returning to Canada as a twenty-four-year-old to pack up her life before heading back to Jack in Australia, they'd emailed each other every day. When she'd admitted she was scared about leaving Canada and moving to Australia, he'd promised she could trust him. It hadn't taken long before she'd realised that trust was misplaced.

She didn't want to twist the knife in further, but she needed to be honest. Jack needed to know where she stood. There was no going back to that life. Not now. Not ever.

'I can't trust anything you say anymore, Jack.'

'Can't or won't?'

She hesitated for a fraction of a second. 'Both.'

'I'm sorry, Olivia. For everything.'

She sighed heavily. She was sorry too, but not enough to accept his apology. 'For Scarlett's sake, I'll make an effort.'

Jack gave her a tiny smile. 'Thank you, Liv. That's all I can ask for now.'

Their painful conversation was interrupted by the sound of the front door opening. Perfect timing. She heard Nan's voice urging Scarlett to take her boots off ,over Scarlett's high-pitched nonstop chatter, and Paul's deeper tones.

Olivia's heart rate accelerated and suddenly she had second thoughts about whether she'd done the right thing by not warning them she'd invited Jack for Christmas. But no, she quickly reminded herself. He'd let Scarlett down so many times in the past, promising to visit and always having a reason why he couldn't. She'd kept the potential visit a secret because she didn't want to risk Scarlett getting upset again.

'Hi sweetheart, we're back,' Nan called out before shuffling into the lounge room, using the furniture to guide her to her recliner.

'G'day, Joan.'

Nan stopped dead in her tracks and her smile widened to a beaming grin. 'Jack? Is that really you? What a lovely surprise. How wonderful.'

Jack stood and went to her, towering above her and dwarfing her as he wrapped his arms around her tiny frame.

Before Olivia had a chance to explain what her ex-husband was doing there, Scarlett exploded into the lounge room and launched herself at Jack like a rocket grenade.

'DADDY!' Her voice was loud enough to be heard on the other side of the lake.

Jack scooped her up and Scarlett wrapped her little arms tightly around his neck. For a moment Olivia had to look away as her heart ached with something she couldn't describe.

After hugging her tightly and spinning her in circles, Jack finally put Scarlett back on the ground. Ruffling her hair, he placed his hand on Scarlett's head to measure her against his thighs. 'Look how much you've grown.'

Bursting with pride, Scarlett seemed to grow another ten centimetres before Olivia's eyes. 'I'm nearly four.'

She'd been saying that the week after her third birthday.

Jack ducked down to Scarlett's eye level. 'Yes, you are. You'll be ready for high school soon.'

Scarlett shook her head, face serious. 'Mummy said not yet. I have to go to kidner-garden then school first.'

Olivia stifled a smile as Scarlett struggled over the pronunciation.

Paul entered, weighed down by bags of groceries. He'd been so helpful since Nan had lost her vision and was no longer able to drive, and over the past eighteen months he'd been a constant source of stability in their lives. He was a short, rotund man with a shiny bald head, rosy cheeks, a big smile and few words. Olivia had come to rely on him heavily, and she enjoyed his company as much as Nan did.

Joan turned to him. 'Paul, this is Olivia's Jack.'

'Not my Jack,' Olivia muttered, but no one heard her.

Paul put the bags on the ground to pump Jack's hand. 'Pleased to meet you. I love your show. Watch it on Netflix from time to time.'

'Thank you.'

Olivia waited. This was the moment Jack usually zoned out of whatever was going on around him and went into celebrity mode, turning on the charm to make a fan feel important and heard. It was such an automatic response she wasn't even sure Jack knew he did it which made it so much harder to explain how hurtful it was when he turned his back on her to focus on someone else. It made her sound petty. By the time the conversation wound up, Jack would have a new fan and best friend.

When Jack didn't pursue Paul for more compliments, she frowned. That wasn't like the Jack she knew.

'I'll pop the kettle on shall I?' Paul asked as he picked up the shopping bags.

Joan smiled at him. 'That'd be lovely, thanks, dear.'

Paul headed to the kitchen and Olivia made a mental note to thank him later for not showing an over-interest in Jack.

Joan put a hand on Jack's arm. 'How long are you staying, darling?'

Jack grinned down at Joan and Olivia scowled at him, even though he wasn't looking in her direction.

Typical. There he goes again, charming everyone.

'Until New Year's Day, if that's alright with you.'

'You know it is. I wish I'd known you were coming though. I would have been able to boast to all my friends in the book club. Though I use audio books now that I can't see.'

Scarlett suddenly looked up at Jack, eyes wider than the first time she'd met Santa. 'You're here for Christmas?' Awe and wonder filled her voice.

For a fleeting moment an image of the three of them tangled up on a couch together, laughing and watching television, flashed into Olivia's head. A family. The way she'd always dreamed.

Again, Jack bobbed down to look Scarlett in the eye.

'I sure am, sweetheart. Is that okay with you?'

Scarlett nodded so vigorously her blond curls bounced like springs. 'Are you going to sleep in my room or Mummy's room?'

Jack hesitated. Looked up at Olivia. She gave a tiny shake of her head. Hoped Scarlett didn't catch the unspoken message.

Thankfully Joan caught it and stepped in. 'Daddy's going to sleep in the spare room right next door to you, and over the hall from Mommy. You can come and help me get it ready if you'd like.'

Olivia released a deep breath. For a second she worried Nan would suggest Jack sleep in the main bedroom with Olivia. After losing her sight, Nan had moved to one of the bedrooms downstairs and given up the master bedroom and ensuite to Olivia.

'It's all good, Nan. I've already made the room up for Jack. I did that earlier today while you were out.'

'Tea or coffee, Jack?' Paul called out from the kitchen, thankfully interrupting any further talk about room allocations and sleeping arrangements.

Jack straightened and turned to Olivia. 'What are you having?'

'Tea.' Because she didn't drink coffee after three in the afternoon or she'd be awake all night. She tried to ignore the prickle of hurt when he didn't remember.

He raised his eyebrows. Joan frowned and flicked her head in Scarlett's general direction.

Olivia took her point. *Behave yourself, Olivia. No need to be snitchy.*

'I'll have a cup of tea please.'

'Are you hungry Jack? I baked some brownies,' Joan said.

Scarlett clapped her hands. 'I wuv brownies.'

'Only one,' Olivia said. 'I don't want you to fill yourself up before supper.'

Scarlett looked at Jack and theatrically rolled her eyes. Seriously? *Little Princess.* No doubt she'd learned that at day care because surely Olivia didn't roll her eyes like that.

'Mommy *never* lets me eat what I want.'

'I do, but I don't want you to spoil your appetite.'

'You poor deprived baby girl,' Jack said with a laugh, ruffling her curls again. He looked at Olivia. 'What do you have planned for dinner tonight? Is there anything I can help with?'

Olivia checked the time and groaned. After five already. She hadn't even taken any meat out of the freezer to defrost.

'Don't panic, sweetheart. We brought a rotisserie chicken when we were out,' Joan said. 'We can have that. And maybe while you and Jack toss a salad, Scarlett can help Paul and me hang some more decorations on the tree. What do you think?'

That was an easy question to answer. The tree did *not* need any more decorations. She did *not* want to be alone in the kitchen with Jack. And she did *not* want Nan thinking that Jack's presence in her house meant they were getting back together.

Yeah right. Good luck with that.

From the moment she and Scarlett had arrived back in Niagara-on-the-Lake eighteen months earlier, Nan had refused to accept Olivia's marriage was over. Like Sally, Joan seemed to think there was life left in it. And now Jack was on the same bandwagon. Sheesh.

'I'll go and help Paul get supper started. You two can stay here and catch up. I'm sure Scarlett's not going to want her father out of her sight.' Olivia stomped off to the kitchen. At least she could trust Paul to keep his opinions to himself.

'You okay, love?' Paul asked her gently as she yanked open cupboards, pulled out mugs and banged the doors closed.

'Mmm hmm.'

'She means well,' he said. 'She wants to see you happy.'

'I am happy.'

Paul's raised eyebrows begged to differ.

'Jack and I are no longer on the same page. About anything.'

'You must have been once.'

'Maybe once. It feels like a lifetime ago.'

Olivia would never blame Scarlett on the unfolding of the marriage, but that was when things started to go downhill. They were both so excited about becoming parents but from the moment Scarlett arrived, Jack seemed hellbent on working even harder to provide for them. At times it felt like he deliberately worked longer hours, took on more responsibilities, and said yes to more opportunities which left Olivia stuck at home. Scarlett was a good baby, but the first six months had been so much harder than she'd anticipated.

'You ever see a counsellor together?'

She shook her head. By the time the situation was critical,

Jack wasn't home long enough to get into a conversation about their marriage. And she had always figured a counsellor was out of the question. If anyone found out Jack Carter's marriage was on the rocks, it would have been splashed across the front page of every magazine and newspaper. The media would have savaged his reputation and permanently damaged his image. It would have killed the career he'd worked so hard to build, which was why she was staggered when he said he'd been in therapy for the past twelve months.

'He seems like an okay guy. I know I've only just met him—'

Olivia interrupted. 'He *is* a good person, Paul, but not the person for me.'

'What's he like with Scarlett? He seems to dote on her.'

Olivia poured boiling water into the mugs. She didn't even have to think about that. Jack was an excellent father. She set the kettle back on the stove.

The problem was, Scarlett deserved more than a father who visited on special occasions. She deserved quality time. And by taking Scarlett and fleeing Australia, she was denying Jack the chance to be involved in his child's life. She was hardly being fair.

When Scarlett was little, Jack had tried, but so often he'd make promises he couldn't keep. Promises that Daddy would be home for dinner, home for bath time, home to tuck Scarlett in and read her bedtime stories. He always had valid reasons but over time Olivia saw them as excuses.

And he'd broken his promises to Olivia too, exactly like her own father had.

'He's always been good with Scarlett,' she said.

'What about when he leaves again and goes back to Australia? How will Scarlett cope with that? It's pretty hard for a kid to watch their parent walk out.'

Pain twisted her gut. She knew exactly how hard it was. As far as she could remember, her dad had been a good father before Mom got sick. Olivia had been a couple of years older than

Scarlett was now when her mother was first diagnosed. Old enough to remember how her father slowly drifted away from home during the months of chemo and radiation. Olivia vividly remembered her mum's tears on more than one occasion when it was Granddad who drove her to and from her appointments at the hospital. A week after the funeral, her father had walked out without a backwards glance, leaving nothing but a note saying he needed a break.

There was no telling how Scarlett would cope after spending ten days together with Jack, then watch him leave again. And it wasn't right that it might be another month, six months, or even a year before she saw him again. It wasn't right and it wasn't fair.

She leaned back against the counter, exhausted from overthinking everything. 'Paul, have I made a stupid mistake asking Jack to come to Canada for Christmas? Have I invited more heartache into our lives?'

'Time will tell, love,' Paul said, giving her shoulder a light squeeze.

The ache in her gut intensified. Olivia was too angry and wary of Jack to believe him simply because he said he'd changed. Sure, the attraction was still there—and she hadn't expected to feel that—but a five-minute conversation with him wasn't enough for her to be tempted to change her mind. What kind of changes was he talking about anyway? She doubted they'd be real and permanent. And certainly not enough that she'd risk her heart for—or, more importantly, Scarlett's?

Having him here for Scarlett was the right thing to do, but nothing altered the facts: She wanted a divorce, he wanted a second chance. *Give him a go,* a small voice whispered in one ear. *What do you have to lose?*

She knew exactly what she had to lose. Everything. That's why she'd travelled halfway around the world to start again. Finally she was in a place where Nan was okay, Scarlett was settled and she was finding some emotional resilience.

You're mad. Another voice whispered. *He's only interested in his career.*

Her thoughts raged like a winter snowstorm. If she only had herself to worry about, she might have taken another risk and given him a second chance, but she had to protect Scarlett from getting hurt. Olivia couldn't afford to expose her little girl to the kind of heartache she'd experienced herself at that age.

Even if she gave in and offered Jack another chance, she had no idea what she'd do if she fell for him again, then discovered he hadn't changed. Her heart would be broken all over again. Sure, she'd eventually learn to get over him, but she wasn't sure whether Scarlett would.

Firming her resolve, she picked up a cup of tea in each hand.

What did she have to lose if she said yes to Jack? Everything!

No. She was never coming second again.

Ten days. That's all she had to endure. Ten long days and he'd go back to Australia and out of her life again. Nothing he could do or say would make her change her mind.

Chapter 7

While Olivia was in the kitchen with Paul, Jack sat on the floor in front of the fire with Scarlett. As he helped his daughter dress her dolls, he chatted to Joan and filled her in on what was going on in his life.

'It's so lovely to have you here,' Joan said. 'It must be difficult to leave the restaurant, especially at this time of the year.'

'It is,' he agreed. 'And I'm opening a second restaurant in January, so there's lots going on.'

'That will keep you busy.'

'Yeah. Plus, we start filming for season three of *The Chopping Block* when I get back. My business manager wasn't happy with me taking the time off right now.' That was an understatement, but he didn't care what Maddie or his father thought. Yes, it wasn't great timing, but it was worth it to fight for his family and show Olivia he was serious about their marriage

Paul entered the lounge and handed Joan her cup of tea before taking a seat beside her on the couch.

'Scarlett will love having you here.' Joan smiled. 'As will I.'

Gratitude flooded through him. Even though Olivia said Joan loved him, he'd been worried she'd be on "Team Olivia" and not want him to stay under her roof.

'Thank you, that means more than you know.'

As he watched Scarlett playing with her dolls, his heart filled with fresh regret. He'd missed out on so much of her young life and hated to think how much more he was going to miss if he left again. He closed his eyes and exhaled slowly. He couldn't go back to Australia.. Not unless Olivia and Scarlett came with him.

'I've missed my little girl,' he said softly. 'When I couldn't get here for her birthday this year, I knew I couldn't miss Christmas too. I've missed too much of her life already.'

Olivia returned to the lounge bearing two cups of steaming tea. She handed him one and kept the other for herself.

'You know what, Jack?' she asked, voice cracking. 'You *did* miss out on a lot but don't blame me for that.'

'It wasn't always my fault.'

The moment he saw the agony in her eyes he knew he'd done it again—gone to his usual default position of defending himself. He dragged in a deep breath. This was what the counsellor had talked about. He had to listen to Olivia and validate her feelings.

'I'm sorry, Olivia. You're right. I could have arranged time off.'

Her eyes narrowed as though she didn't believe him.

'I'm sorry,' he repeated. 'I should have been there for you and Scarlett.' He hoped it sounded like he meant it, because he did. He'd never intentionally meant to make her unhappy, he simply hadn't realised how much his blinkered pursuit of his career had hurt her.

Surprisingly, his apology appeared to have worked. Olivia blinked twice before sinking back into the cushions and taking a sip of her tea. Her anger seemed to dissipate like slowly melting snow.

He set his cup down and smiled to ease the tension. 'Why don't I bring my bags inside?' He'd left everything in the car in case Olivia changed her mind about him staying. 'I have presents.'

Scarlett looked up from her dollhouse. 'Presents?'

Jack grinned at his daughter. 'If Mum says yes, you can open one now, but we'll put the rest under the tree for Christmas morning.'

'Want a hand?' Paul asked.

'That'd be great, thanks.'

'I can help too,' Scarlett said, running to the front door.

Jack went to her and crouched down. 'No. You need to stay here inside,' he said. 'It's too cold outside and by the time you get all your warm clothes and boots on, I'll be back with the presents.'

Jack had expected an argument but, although Scarlett pouted, she didn't argue back. Jack made a mental note to thank Olivia for the amazing job she was doing raising Scarlett into a darling little girl. It couldn't be easy doing it alone.

Olivia shot him a grateful look and he caught it. It was a long way from a smile, but it least it wasn't a grimace.

Outside, the icy wind tore through his puffer jacket and he glanced up at the thick clouds, expecting to see snow any second. He rubbed his hands together. First thing tomorrow he'd head out and buy some thick gloves and a beanie. He'd packed for cold weather, but not this cold. It was impossible to buy ski gear in Australia in the middle of summer and he'd figured he'd use what he had and buy whatever else he needed once he was there. He'd had months to plan for the trip, but he'd been so busy with work, the date had crept up on him.

Seeing him shiver, Paul said, 'I can loan you a warmer coat if you'd like.'

'I'll be fine. Thanks anyway.'

'They've forecast snow tomorrow. Maybe even tonight if we're lucky.'

'Amazing. I was hoping I'd get to experience a white Christmas. Olivia used to talk about them so fondly.'

It didn't take long for him to lug his suitcase and bags of presents out of the car and back to the house. But by the time he ducked back inside and closed the front door, he was shivering.

He followed Olivia up the stairs to the spare bedroom, passing Scarlett's room on the left. On the right, he caught a glimpse of a larger room behind a partially closed door. Olivia's bedroom. He quickly averted his eyes from the large red and white quilt-covered bed, forcing his mind elsewhere. One day he hoped he could share her bed again but right now that seemed far from likely.

She showed him to his room which was opposite hers, across a wide expanse of hallway. The small room with a narrow window overlooked the street and contained a single bed, a chest of drawers and a lone lamp.

'Do you need anything else?' Olivia asked. She stood on the threshold, shifting her weight from one foot to the other, as though afraid to enter. 'The bed's already made up and I've left you plenty of towels. Do you think you'll be cold? I can get another quilt.'

He glanced at the bed and knew his feet would probably hang over the end by about twenty centimetres. 'I'll be fine,' he lied, dumping his carry-on bag on the bed and blowing on his cold fingers.

'They've forecast snow.'

'Paul said.'

He went to the window, stared out over the frozen front garden. Olivia had once described this time of year before it snowed as the "butt-ugly end of Fall" and he could see why. The brown grass and bare boned trees weren't very pretty. He hoped it would snow so he could experience the white Christmas Olivia used to talk about when they were first married. Her eyes would take on a dreamy look and her voice would waver. She'd always said winter was her favourite season and Christmas was her favourite time of year.

'Olivia?'

She paused, hand on the doorknob.

He went to his carry-on bag and unzipped it. 'I have something for you.'

She froze and he watched her swallow as though her throat was full of razor blades. 'I don't need a present.'

'It's just something little.'

'I said I don't need your presents.'

He winced. She'd loved the little gifts he'd showered her with when they were first married. But she didn't consider them married now, so the rules had clearly changed. Still, it might work as a peace offering. He pulled out the brown paper bag and she stared at it, eyes wide, as if it contained live spiders. He pulled out the jar of Vegemite and held it in the air.

Her shoulders relaxed.

'You're the only non-Aussie I know who likes the stuff,' he said.

The first time she'd tasted it, she'd been hooked and, as far as he knew, it had been her breakfast staple ever since. Maybe it still was. Maybe it wasn't.

'Thank you.' She took a step towards him, accepted the jar and stepped back. 'I brought some home with me last Christmas.'

His smiled faded. He hadn't thought of that.

'But we've run out,' she quickly added. 'Thank you. Scarlett will be thrilled.'

'Do you still like it too?'

She nodded and gave him a tiny smile which ignited an optimistic spark within his heart, warming him. A truce, even if it was only momentary. He knew they'd need more than a spark to kindle their broken relationship, but he'd take a small smile as a victory.

'Is there anything you'd like for Christmas?' he asked.

She shook her head and the smile disappeared in a flash making him wonder if it had ever been there in the first place. He massaged his temples. What just happened? One second something warm and wonderful passed between them and she'd seemed pleased with his thoughtful gift, now her expression had hardened again.

'I told you, I don't want your gifts. You can't buy me back or bribe me. That didn't work on me when we were married, and it won't work now.' Her words were harsh, her tone harsher.

'I wish I knew what you *did* want from me,' he muttered.

She stayed silent. Maybe he should have accepted she didn't want to be married to him and let her have what she wanted. But he couldn't. Scarlett needed a dad, and Jack needed his wife and daughter back. He would do whatever it took for them to be a family again.

Receiving those divorce papers eighteen months ago had been a massive eye-opening kick in the rear end. And he'd paid attention, gone to counselling and started making the changes he needed to win Olivia back. Firstly, he cut back his hours at *Atlas* and even took a day off each week. Then he employed a manager to run the restaurant and actually let the guy do his job. The counsellor said he had control issues. He hadn't thought he did, but apparently there was a fine line between being a perfectionist and a control freak.

The only sticking point to all the changes he'd been making in his work life had been around the timing of the opening of *Globe* in Melbourne. The issues it was experiencing were out of his control and he'd had to invest a lot more of his time and focus there than he'd hoped. But the good thing was, he was now aware he was a workaholic and he was trying to change that, and that was the main thing.

And he was here now, ready to do whatever he could, so that should count for a lot too. He should never have left the problems between them fester for so long. In doing so they had become worse than sour milk. Rather than deal with them, he'd buried himself in work until she walked out.

Jack inhaled slowly and counted to five before speaking, choosing his words carefully. 'I can see I've screwed up badly, but I'm not sure how. I thought I was doing the right thing, making a life for us, providing for our family. Clearly it wasn't what you expected or wanted.'

'What I *wanted*, Jack, was time with you, not expensive presents. I wanted to know what it felt like to sit with a glass of wine after dinner, after Scarlett was in bed, and chat. I wanted to know what it was like to go for a walk down the street and not have everyone stop and stare and talk to you like they knew you. What I wanted was something you couldn't offer me.'

He frowned. 'But when we met, I was already a chef. You knew about the crazy hours I worked.' It was like she'd bought a chocolate cake, and now she was complaining she was allergic to cocoa.

'I was okay with that because when we first got married you used to do split shifts at least. You'd come home and we'd carve out time to be together. But once you opened the restaurant in Noosa and then the show started, it stole the little bit of time we actually had together.' She lifted her hands then let them fall to her sides. 'And after Scarlett was born, I saw even less of you.'

He stared at her. Her brow was creased in a way that made him want to reach over and smooth it out, but he kept his hands by his sides. She wasn't finished.

'I wanted home cooked meals and time with you. Instead I got fancy dinners in restaurants with music so loud it was impossible to talk, filled with people who wanted to have their photo taken with you. It was impossible to have any privacy. Impossible to be us.'

He squeezed his eyes closed for a second as he drew in a long, deep breath. 'Why didn't you tell me? I know you didn't enjoy it in the beginning, but I thought you'd get used to it. Maybe even start to like it. When you stopped coming out with me, I thought it was because you didn't like leaving Scarlett with the nanny.'

Olivia exhaled slowly. 'You're right, I should have said something.'

Her honest admission was a good start. He licked his lips. 'I'm sorry, Olivia, I really am, and I want to make it up to you.'

'Well you can start by not thinking the way to win me back is by giving me gifts.' The gifts were lovely, but they always made her feel as though he was buying her off. Buying her silence. Well, she wasn't going to be silent anymore.

'Okay.'

'I'll leave you to it then,' she said, taking another step back. 'Feel free to freshen up and come down when you're ready. I'll go and get supper started.'

'I'm happy to help you.'

'No. It's fine. I've got it.'

She turned on her heel and he chose not to argue. A bit of time and space would do them both good. As he'd discovered, there was a massive chasm of misunderstanding and broken dreams between them and he had a lot of work to do to rebuild his side of their fractured marriage.

It didn't take him long to unpack. He hadn't brought a lot of clothes with him, mostly filling his case with presents for Scarlett. Other than the jar of Vegemite, and a tube of her favourite hand cream, he hadn't bought anything special for Olivia yet, which was probably just as well. But his fingers touched on one tiny gift box he'd hidden away, tucked into an inside pocket of his carry-on luggage.

His heart sank. Even if things went according to his ten-day plan, he was no longer sure she'd accept it.

Chapter 8

Olivia escaped downstairs back to the kitchen, totally off balance and in unfamiliar territory. The man upstairs in the spare bedroom was not the Jack she'd left in Australia. It was a new version, or more correctly, it was a version of the old Jack. The one she'd fallen for. His apologies seemed genuine, he'd talked about cutting back on his hours and he seemed willing to talk in a way he never had before. He was also taking responsibility for his actions, which put him in an entirely different light. She didn't know what to make of it.

She looked at the jar of Vegemite in her hands. Such a simple present; a thoughtful and practical one. Not like the expensive, useless, countless gifts he'd showered her with when they were married. She used to wonder whether Jack walked into a shop and asked whoever was behind the counter what *they'd* like as a present. Or worse, had asked Maddie to buy them for her. Even when he brought her flowers, they were generally huge long-stemmed scentless roses. Lovely, but she would have preferred a pot plant or something that lasted longer than a week. She'd tried to be grateful, but his gestures of generosity left her heart untouched and widened the gulf of hurt.

Regret tightened her stomach. Once they'd had something incredible. Something special. So how had they let things slide so far from where they'd started?

She wanted to believe him but how could she, when experience showed that his words were like vapour?

And yet, if he was being honest with her, he was taking action and that spoke far louder than his words.

Sadness flooded her. Their marriage was over and as much as she lay the majority of the blame at Jack's feet, she to admit she'd had a part to play in the breakdown. She hadn't clearly expressed how sad and lonely she'd felt. If he'd known how unhappy she was, he might have changed while he still had a chance.

Scarlett was still playing with her dollhouse and Olivia left her there with Nan. There was no sign of Paul; he'd obviously headed back to his house next door. She trudged into the kitchen, heart heavy and a niggling headache forming behind her eyes.

He offered to cook. The thought lobbed into her head and she batted it away. *He was just being polite.* Jack hadn't offered to cook for her after the first six months of their marriage when he was still trying to impress her and ask her opinion on the different dishes he was preparing. Once the restaurant opened, everything slowly changed until those meals got further and further apart until he no longer cooked at home.

She remembered the one and only time she'd asked Jack if he could cook dinner for her. She'd spent the entire day with a clingy Scarlett who had a cold and wouldn't leave her side. Jack's snarky response had floored her.

'I cook all day for a living, Olivia. The last thing I want to do is come home and cook a meal for an unappreciative audience.'

As soon as he'd spoken, he'd apologised profusely explaining that he'd had a terrible day at work. But rather than accept his apology and forgive him, she'd held her tongue and called for a pizza.

Pushing the memories away, she picked up a knife, chopped

some potatoes and sweet potato and placed them on a baking tray, drizzled them with olive oil and salt and pepper and popped them into the oven. After pulling apart the store-bought rotisserie chicken and covering it in foil to place in the oven to warm later, she popped some beans into the steamer then put together a simple Caesar salad.

She was stirring the gravy when she heard movement behind her. She tensed, knowing it was Jack.

'Can I give you a hand?'

She kept stirring, still feeling totally off-kilter. 'I'm almost done. Why don't you set the table? Plates are in that drawer.' She pointed.

She listened to him in the other room setting the table, teasing Scarlett who was going nuts begging Jack to let her open her presents. Olivia's protectiveness towards Scarlett filled her chest until she could hardly breathe. Argh. She wanted Scarlett to spend time with her dad, but she wished he wasn't here. Unfortunately, she couldn't have it both ways. She rolled her neck to try to relieve the tension in her shoulders.

Moments later Scarlett skidded into the room with Jack trailing behind. 'Daddy brought lots of presents. Can I open them now? Daddy said I could.'

Jack shot her an apologetic look before putting a hand on Scarlett's shoulder. 'No, sweetie. I said you had to ask Mum first.'

'I don't think so Scarlett. If you open your presents now, what will you open on Christmas day?'

'Daddy bought lots of presents.'

Of course he did.

'Sorry, Liv. She saw me putting them under the tree,' Jack said. 'I should have asked you first what you'd prefer.'

Once again, she was surprised by how remorseful he sounded and how willing he was to check with her to see what she wanted. Another first. 'That's okay. I usually wrap her presents and put them under the tree on Christmas Eve. A bit earlier won't make any difference.'

'Can I, can I, can I,' Scarlett begged, hopping like a one-legged kangaroo.

'Just one,' she said. No point denying Scarlett that.

'YES!'

'After dinner.'

'Ohhhh.'

'That's only fair.' Jack gave her backside a quick tap. 'Now go and let your nan know dinner is ready and I'll help Mum serve up.'

Olivia picked up an oven mitt, opened the oven and pulled out the vegetables. 'I'm fine.'

'I'd like to help, Liv.'

'Whatever,' she said under her breath.

He heard her, but ignored her.

They worked side by side, serving food onto plates. 'Sorry about the present thing. I didn't think. Scarlett asked if she could open one now and I said yes.'

'It's not a problem.'

'I hope she likes what I bought her.'

'Whatever it is, I'm sure she'll love it.'

Unlike Olivia, Scarlett loved every gift Jack had ever sent.

A nasty thought occurred. Maybe he sent Maddie out to buy them on his behalf.

Dinner was weird with everyone pretending it was perfectly normal sitting around the table eating together as a family. But she got through it. Nan was in fine form, keeping everyone entertained with stories of Christmases past and thankfully Olivia barely had to say a word.

'I love this time of year,' Nan said after setting down her knife and fork on her empty plate. 'You can never have too much food, too many sugar cookies, too many Christmas decorations or too many presents. I might not be able to see, but I had a feel under the tree a little earlier and I can't imagine what's in all those packages.'

'They're mostly from Jack,' Olivia said, 'for Scarlett.'

'She's a lucky girl,' Joan said.

'I don't want to spoil her,' Olivia replied

Nan made a tsking sound, tongue against the roof of her mouth. She glared at Olivia, her cloudy eyes wide. 'Oh, don't be a grinch, Olivia. The girl is young enough to be indulged without it going to her head. She deserves it. And if Jack can afford it, why shouldn't he spoil his child?'

Rather than argue, Olivia stood and began clearing the plates. When she returned to the loungeroom, Nan was sitting alone, in front of the fire.

'Where's Jack?'

'I told him Scarlett always has her bath after dinner. He's gone upstairs to get her ready for bed. I said she could come back down and open a present.'

Olivia planted her hands on her hips. 'Jack doesn't have to do that.'

'Olivia,' Joan warned, drawing out her name. She patted the seat beside her, and Olivia plopped obediently into it. 'He wants to help, sweetheart. Let him be a dad to Scarlett.'

'You mean let Jack hurt Scarlett again by leaving.'

'He told me he's asked you to reconsider the divorce.'

Olivia's head snapped around. Jack had no right telling Nan that. It would only get her hopes higher. He shouldn't have dragged Nan into their mess—that wasn't fair.

'He can ask until he's blue in the face. It's not going to happen. Our marriage is over.'

She would hold onto the "marriage is over" line in public, but already she was starting to wonder if she'd been too hasty. Not that she'd admit that out loud in case she decided against it.

'You're not divorced yet.'

'He just hasn't signed the paperwork yet.' She'd given up asking him to do it. Now she knew why he hadn't.

'You wouldn't even consider staying together? Not even for Scarlett?'

Olivia stared at Nan, open-mouthed. 'You actually think it's worth reconciling a broken marriage for the sake of a child?'

'Sweetheart, stop.' Joan put a hand on Olivia's knee and patted it gently. 'You invited Jack here, so the least you can do is be kind to him. From the moment I walked in the front door this afternoon and found Jack in my house, all I've heard come from your mouth is hurt. I know how hard this must be for you, but you invited him here so you need to be a bit kinder. I can hear you're trying to hold back that anger and hide it, but that's not healthy. You need to find a way to deal with all these emotions that Jack is bringing out in you. If you don't, Scarlett is going to know something is wrong.'

The gentle rebuke hurt, but Nan was right. She couldn't afford to have Scarlett upset with her dad too.

'Out of the overflow of the heart, the mouth speaks, darling.'

Olivia sighed heavily. Nan had a series of special quotes and sayings and this was one of her favourites.

'I know, but I'm not ready to trust him. He's all words. He promises the world, delivers nothing.'

Nan looked at her, head cocked. 'Is that right? He hasn't changed?'

Olivia sighed. 'He said he's made changes to his work situation, but I don't know if I believe him.'

'Give him a chance.'

'I've already given him so many chances.'

'What if he's changed?'

'And what if he hasn't?'

'Then you're in exactly the same place you are now.'

Olivia was quiet for a moment. Were she and Jack ever as happy as everyone said they were?

'Do you think I was happy when I was with Jack?'

'Happier. In fact, when it came to Jack, it was as if you were lit from the inside. From the moment you two met, you only had eyes for each other. You were so happy in the beginning. Even from the other side of the world I could feel the joy in you. Every time we spoke on the phone or you emailed me, I just knew you were perfect for each other. I don't know how or what snuffed out that light, but you must believe it was there, Olivia. What you and Jack have is rare. One of those relationships that others only dream of having.'

Olivia closed her eyes, wishing she could believe what Nan said was true. She was about to say something when she heard Scarlett thumping down the stairs. She was in her pyjamas and dressing gown, face flushed, hair still damp. Olivia couldn't remember a time when Jack had bathed Scarlett. Olivia imagined she'd find the bathroom floor covered in soap suds and wet towels and none of the toys put away. But it was nice that he'd done the bath routine and somehow she'd find a way to thank him.

'Look, Mama.' Scarlett wiggled her foot. 'Daddy gave me new gugg boots.'

'Ugg boots,' Jack corrected. He glanced at Olivia. 'Not really a present. I just figured she probably didn't have any. Every Aussie kid needs a pair of Uggs.'

There was nothing wrong with Scarlett's thick cottage socks, but Nan's warning words filled her ears and the pink boots *were* cute.

'That's very thoughtful of you, thank you. And thank you for running her through the bath. Scarlett, I hope you said thank you to Daddy.'

Scarlett wasn't listening. Her eyes were wide as she surveyed the presents under the tree.

Jack smiled. 'She gave me a hug. I presume that means she likes them?'

'It does.'

Watching the two of them together, Olivia's stomach twisted. Despite not having seen Jack since last Christmas, Scarlett wasn't holding any grudges. Rather than taking time to warm up to her father like Olivia expected she might, Scarlett hadn't left his side. Olivia acknowledged the twinge of jealousy that Scarlett had basically ignored her from the moment she'd laid eyes on Jack. But the bigger part of her was thrilled they had a bond. A bond she'd done nothing to foster, if she was honest.

Jack leaned down and whispered something in Scarlett's ear and she giggled. Despite herself, Olivia smiled. It was so good seeing them together. And they looked so much alike. Her smile slipped. She had to stop thinking of the past and the way things used to be. This was just ten days. Ten days out of another year when Jack could act like he was father of the century. Truth was, he had never been home more than a few nights at a time when they lived together. The reason he'd rarely done the bath and bed routine was he was always at the restaurant or the studio.

This was a big mistake. When Jack left on New Year's Day Scarlett would be devastated and Olivia would be left to pick up the pieces. She needed to protect her daughter the way she'd protected herself—by not allowing herself to get close.

'Mama? Mama? Are you listening to me?'

Olivia tuned back in and put on a smile.

'Can I open this one?' Scarlett asked, plucking the largest of the presents from the cache under the tree.

Jack laughed. 'Why am I not surprised?'

Olivia smiled too despite her misgivings. The present was almost the same size as Scarlett. The amount of wrapping paper suggested Jack had used at least three rolls.

Jack settled onto the floor near the tree with his back against the couch and crossed his ankles. He looked tired, but relaxed.

'That present must have taken up half your suitcase,' she said.

He flashed her a smile. 'It did.'

'Come on Scarlett, open it up,' Nan urged, 'and tell me what it is.'

Scarlett tore into the wrapping paper and squealed as she

pulled out a large grey soft toy koala before throwing herself into Jack's lap and hugging him. 'Thanks, Daddy. This is the bestest present ever.'

Olivia frowned. Scarlett already had dozens of soft toys so Olivia had no idea why this one was a winner except that Jack had given it to her.

Scarlett brought it over to her for her to admire and she tried to show an interest. 'Look, Mama, it's a koala bear!'

'Yes, it is,' she said, running her hands over the soft grey fur.

'A koala,' Jack corrected. 'They're not bears.'

'We have bears,' Scarlett said, all-of-a-sudden-serious. 'Up at Papa Paul's cottage.'

'Really?' Jack leaned in, lowered his voice, equally serious. 'Have you ever seen one?'

Scarlett nodded. 'Last summer we saw a mommy bear and a baby bear. Black ones.'

'They're the dangerous kind, aren't they?'

Scarlett nodded again. 'Papa Paul said we had to be real careful about where we put the garbage.'

'Is that right?'

'Yep.'

Scarlett hugged the koala to her chest.

'What are you going to name him?' Joan asked.

'He's not a *boy*, Nan,' Scarlett said, with an eye roll. 'He's a girl.'

'Oh, I see,' Joan said with a chuckle. 'Can I feel her?'

Scarlett took the toy over to her great-grandmother and let her stroke the koala's soft fur.

Olivia glanced across at Jack who wore a huge grin.

'What are you going to call her?' Jack asked.

Scarlett didn't hesitate. 'Milo.'

'That's a perfect name,' Jack agreed.

Scarlett plonked back into Jack's lap and a hard knot formed in Olivia's chest. She'd hoped the outcome of Jack's visit would be exactly what Scarlett wanted, and so far it seemed that it was. But Olivia hadn't anticipated how much it would hurt watching the two of them together.

'I miss chocolate Milo.' Scarlett twisted around to look at Olivia. 'Why don't we have Milo in Canada, Mummy?'

'I don't know.' She stood. 'Maybe because we have Tim Hortons instead.' She clapped her hands together. 'Anyway, it's late. Come on. Time for bed.'

'Can Milo sleep with me?'

'I'm not sure she'll fit. Maybe she can sit at the end of your bed and watch over you.'

'Okay. Daddy are you going to read to me?'

Olivia stiffened. That was her routine, her favourite time with Scarlett.

As if he read her mind, Jack said, 'Not tonight, sweetheart. I'm here for ten whole nights. I can read to you another time if that's okay with Mum.'

Scarlett gazed up at him. 'I wish you lived here with us all the time.'

Olivia saw him swallow and watched his Adam's apple bounce. He glanced at her briefly and looked like he was trying to choose his words carefully.

'I want to be with you all the time too, sweetheart. But I have to work, and my work is in Australia.' He helped Scarlett to her feet. 'But I'm here for the next ten days and after that I'll talk to Mummy and work out how I can see you as often as I can next year.'

Satisfied with this, Scarlett hugged him tight, before hugging Joan then running up the stairs with Milo firmly in her grip. Olivia dragged her feet up the stairs after her daughter, heart heavy.

Nothing was going as she'd planned.

Chapter 9

When Olivia woke the next morning, she yawned and rubbed her eyes. She'd forgotten to close the curtains the night before and sunlight bathed her bed. Scarlett's voice filtered through the closed bedroom door and Olivia sat bolt upright. What time was it? She reached for her phone and gasped. Nearly nine o'clock. Scarlett usually woke her which meant she'd clearly woken Jack instead and he'd kindly let Olivia have a sleep in. Another first.

A barrage of thoughts hit her like snowballs.

She never slept in. She had a million things to do today. And Jack was here.

Darn, darn, darn.

The memories of yesterday rushed back in and with it, the question that had weighed on her mind since Jack walked in the door yesterday. Could she give him a second chance?

It was no wonder she'd had trouble falling asleep and it had taken her hours to drift off. Her mind had refused to co-operate and shut down, instead her thoughts circled around and around. Could she, would she, should she, give him another chance? Having Jack here with her and Scarlett, having him behave as he did when she first fell in love with him, made it so hard to stand her ground. Yes, she ached to feel loved again and to be part of a family, but the cost was so high.

Olivia swung her legs over the side of the bed and pushed the questions from her mind. If she kept busy, she wouldn't have to think of an answer.

She tied her robe around her and stopped at Scarlett's bedroom door. As usual, Scarlett was chatting without drawing breath. Jack was trying to convince her that she needed to get out of her pyjamas if she wanted to go outside and build a snowman. Olivia hadn't checked out the window but evidently it had snowed overnight.

Neither of them noticed her for a moment and she stood watching. Jack looked as sexy as anything in his boxer shorts and T-shirt. His boxers had ridden up his leg and she couldn't help but admire his quad muscles and note the contrast between tanned skin and pale upper thigh. He was more quiet than usual, and she'd noticed him stifle a yawn more than once. Poor guy. The Jack she remembered was usually the chirpy one in the mornings, while she took at least two coffees to get her engine started. She wondered what time Scarlett had woken him up.

'Jetlag?' she asked.

Jack spun around and his eyes grazed up her body. She wished she was wearing something other than her thick flannel pyjamas and old robe.

'Ah, no.'

'What time did she get up?'

'Around seven.'

'Sorry she woke you.'

'She didn't. I've been awake for hours.'

She frowned. 'Why?'

'There's a few problems back home I had to deal with.'

This would be interesting. He never talked about work with her. 'What kind of problems?'

He shrugged. 'Just stuff with the restaurant in Melbourne.

Council won't give us a permit. I haven't done the menu. The wrong tiles got delivered. That's only the tip of the iceberg.'

'When were you supposed to open?' She wasn't testing him, but she was interested to see if he'd open up and confide in her. If he did, maybe that was a sign that he was changing.

'We're already weeks behind. Originally we were meant to open mid-January but looks like I'm going to have to push that out to the end of Feb.'

'Sorry.'

Another shrug. 'It's not your problem.'

And there it was. Olivia tried to hide her disappointment that he'd shut her out again. Jack always presumed she didn't want to be involved, wasn't interested or didn't care. That his work problems weren't *their* problems.

Perhaps if he'd talked about his job over the years, she might have been more understanding of the late nights. Instead, she'd convinced herself that all the late nights and missed birthdays and weekends, followed by the expensive gifts added up to guilt offerings. When he didn't come home, it hadn't been a stretch to think he was spending his nights in the company of another woman.

He'd assured her he had never been unfaithful, and she'd believed him until Maddie told her otherwise. But now, seeing how tired he looked, she was having second thoughts about what Maddie had insinuated. Perhaps all those longs hours he put in really were spent working on his businesses, the way he'd always assured her.

'If you'd like to talk, I'm happy to listen.'

'It's all good. I don't want to dump my problems on you.'

She wanted to tell him it would be nice if he used her as a sounding board, but she couldn't dredge up the energy.

'I'll have a quick shower, then I'll take Scarlett with me down the street while you have a sleep if you like,' she said.

'What are you doing down the street?'

'I need to buy a few last-minute presents.'

Assuming Jack wouldn't come for Christmas, she hadn't bothered to get him a gift. She'd bought presents for him on behalf of Scarlett—a grey wool sweater and some aftershave—and Nan had bought him a cookbook. But Olivia hadn't bought him a thing.

'I'll come. I can nap this afternoon.'

*

'Will you be okay while we go out,' Olivia asked Nan after eating some Vegemite on toast and swallowing a cup of tea. 'We should be back around lunchtime. Can I bring you something home?'

Joan rolled her eyes. 'Will you stop worrying about me? I may have lost my sight, but I haven't lost my other faculties. I'm more than capable of reheating leftovers.'

'I know, but—'

'But nothing. Paul is coming over to help me wrap some presents so don't come home too early or you'll spoil the surprise.'

Laughing, Olivia kissed Nan's cheek and gave her a hug. 'I love you.'

'Love you too. Now take your time and enjoy yourselves. I can feel from that sunshine coming through the window that it's a glorious snowy day out there.'

Nan was right. It was a perfect winter morning. The fresh snow glistened in the sunshine and blue skies stretched above them from east to west. The snow plough hadn't been down their street yet, so the overnight fall of snow lay crisp and fresh and unmarked by salt or slush or tyre tracks.

She loved these types of mornings. Most people were still inside in the warmth of their homes and it felt like they were the only people in the world as they walked down the deserted street. Olivia had a car, but she enjoyed walking whenever she could. The fresh air, even when it was freezing like today, was good for her soul. In this part of town, there was no traffic so they were able to walk down the middle of the street, their feet making fresh tracks in the snow.

'It's beautiful out here,' Jack said as they headed down the street towards the lake. 'And so quiet.'

They continued along Front Street with the lake on their right. On the waterfront was the little white gazebo where they'd married six years earlier. She didn't say a word, but she caught Jack glancing towards it.

They passed some of her favourite homes and as Jack commented on how pretty each one was, she saw them through his eyes. He was right. They were beautiful. And the freshly glistening snow added another dimension to the prettiness of the quaint streetscape. It made her realise again how much she loved living here.

'It is beautiful,' she agreed. 'Like a Christmas card.' She already felt in a better mood than yesterday. Perhaps a sleep in was exactly what she'd needed. 'I'm glad you're going to get a white Christmas.'

'If it hadn't snowed, I would have had words with the man upstairs,' he said with a chuckle.

They walked about a hundred metres in silence, with nothing but the crunch of snow underfoot. A minute later, a snowball in the centre of her back stopped her in her tracks. She turned to see Scarlett, grinning, holding another balled-up wad of snow in her hand. She pulled her arm back to throw it and she ducked, and the snowball hit Jack square on the jaw, splattering in a shower of powder.

Grinning and laughing at Scarlett, Jack pretended the snow she'd thrown at him had packed a powerful punch, when it was obvious it hadn't. He bent and scooped up handfuls of fresh snow and began forming them into balls. But he was too slow, not used to how the game was played. By the time he'd thrown one perfectly formed ball which missed its mark, Olivia and Scarlett had pummelled him with dozens of sloppy snowballs between them.

The three of them chased one another down the middle of the empty street, giggling and breathless. When they arrived at the lake, they collapsed against the large grey rocks that lined the shore, laughing.

'You win.' Jack said, shaking snow off his puffer jacket. 'You girls are experts. Do they teach you that in school?'

'Yep. And how to make snow angels,' Olivia said.

'Snow angels?'

'Scarlett, show Daddy how to make a snow angel.'

Without hesitation, Scarlett threw herself on her back and slowly flapped her arms up and down and moved her legs in and out. When she was done, Olivia reached down and helped her up. They stared down at a perfectly formed snow angel.

'That's awesome,' Jack said, beaming.

'Your turn, Mummy. Do yours next to mine.'

Olivia lay down and made her snow angel. As she was about to get up, Jack reached down and offered his hand. She nearly didn't accept it, but Scarlett was watching. She took his hand and let him help her to her feet before quickly letting go of his fingers so she could brush the snow off her jeans and pretend she hadn't noticed the fizz that went through her when they touched.

'Daddy, do yours now.' Scarlett pointed to the other side of her angel. 'Do yours here so I can be in the middle of you and Mommy.'

Jack didn't hesitate. He threw himself to the ground and enthusiastically squirmed in the snow. 'Am I doing it right?'

Scarlett giggled. 'We can't tell until you get up.'

Olivia tried not to smirk. The way he was moving, Jack's snow angel would be nothing but a mashed-up mess.

'Can you help me up, sweetheart?' Jack put out his hands and Olivia made a note to buy him a pair of gloves. His hands must be freezing.

Scarlett heaved and grunted, but Jack didn't move. 'You're too heavy, Daddy. Mommy will have to help.'

'I think Dad is more than capable of getting up on his own.'

'I think I'm stuck.'

He smiled up at her and something inside her shifted.

'Come on, Liv, give an old man a hand.'

'You're not that old.' Olivia rolled her eyes at him and held out a hand.

As she tugged, he tugged harder. She slipped in the snow and lost her balance, falling onto him so hard the air escaped from her lungs in a whoomph. She tried to roll off him, but he rolled with her, pinning her to the ground, arms above their heads. Their noses touched and she felt his breath, warm and minty against her lips.

Her heart hammered and her eyes widened with each passing moment in time. What did he think he was doing?

Scarlett squealed with laughter and clapped as though this was a new game her parents had invented.

Jack grinned. 'This is payback for all those snowballs you threw at me.'

'Is that right?' She slowly pulled one hand free from his grip, grabbing a fistful of snow as she did. As he released his grip on her other hand, she flung the snow in his face.

Laughing, he rolled off her and called a cease-fire. 'Truce. You win.'

He jumped to his feet and looked at the chaos in the snow. 'I think we'd better make new ones. That was fun.'

'I think we'd better get into town before the shops close.' She brushed crusted snow off her jacket and tried to gather her swirling thoughts. She had the oddest feeling that if Scarlett hadn't been watching, Jack would have tried to kiss her.

And she had an even stranger feeling that she would have let him.

Jack bent down and carefully brushed snow from Scarlett's hair and face. His eyes were full of love for his daughter and watching them together caused a dull ache in the centre of Olivia's chest. It wasn't fair. Once he left, Scarlett would miss him so much.

Her good mood faded, and she clapped her hands together. 'Come on, let's go.'

They headed for the main street, Scarlett between them.

'Joan tells me you've been working a lot,' Jack said conversationally.

She glanced sideways at him. 'What else did she tell you?'

'That you're saving up for a place of your own.'

She shrugged. 'Not likely to happen any time soon on my part-time salary. At least not around here. House prices are insane.'

'Do you enjoy it?'

'My job?'

'Yeah.'

'I love it.'

'You're in ICU?'

'That's right. I'm working there as a registered nurse but next year I'm planning to do further study, then I'll be a Clinical Nurse Specialist.'

She was proud of her achievements considering her initial training had been conducted years ago. She'd had a long break when she lived in Australia and had Scarlett. Returning to Canada had been the best thing for her career because nurses were in high demand. She'd worked hard, but had also been lucky enough to be in the right place at the right time. When the role came up in ICU, she'd jumped at it and was excited about furthering her training and education.

'Who looks after Scarlett while you're at work?'

'Nan, day care, my friends, Lexie and Beck. I have an awesome network of people who help me.'

Jack didn't ask any more questions until they arrived on the main street.

No wonder the side streets were deserted. Everyone seemed to be in town doing last-minute shopping. The store windows were all lit up and decorated, and she caught a whiff of coffee, roasted nuts and hot apple cider.

'Okay if I take Scarlett with me? I want her to help me pick out a present for Joan.'

She frowned. 'I thought you said you'd done all your shopping.'

'I have. I want to get something extra. And I'd like to get a small gift for Paul too.'

'Okay.' She checked her watch. 'Let's meet back here in an hour.'

'I have a better plan. That café over there looks like it sells good coffee.' He pointed to *Common Grounds*. 'We'll meet you there instead, okay?'

She smiled. 'Can't take the Melbourne coffee snob out of the boy, can you?'

'Definitely not.'

They parted ways, with Olivia warning him not to be late.

She strolled down the main street, smiling at people she knew and wishing them a merry Christmas, but inside panic was building. She had no idea on God's earth what to buy Jack, the man who had everything and needed nothing.

It took nearly an hour but, in the end, she settled on buying him a piece of Canadian art. It was way over her budget, but the moment she spotted it, she knew he'd like it. The artist was a local, and she was willing to remove the canvas from the frame so it could be rolled up and transported easily back to Australia.

After making her purchase, she continued shopping, picking up little souvenir type gifts she thought Jack might like. Her purchases included a bottle of real maple syrup, a pair of fleece-lined deerskin gloves and a *Roots*-branded beanie.

It took longer than she'd hoped, and she was running late to meet Jack and Scarlett at the appointed time, so she had to jog to get to the café. She arrived, out of breath, to find Jack and Scarlett seated at a large communal table, surrounded by a group of people. No sign of Connor which brought a sigh of relief.

Jack saw her when she walked in and beckoned her over with a grin. 'This family is visiting from Australia.'

Olivia gave a little wave and tried to smile. Trust Jack to find fans. Even on the other side of the world he couldn't go unrecognised.

'It's their first white Christmas too.'

'Where are you staying?' Olivia asked politely.

'Niagara Falls,' the older man said.

'It's an amazing part of the world,' the woman said. 'Have you been here before?'

'I actually live here,' Olivia said.

'Oh.' The woman glanced from Jack to Olivia and back again. 'I thought I detected an accent. I didn't realise you and Jack had a place here in Canada too.' She grinned. 'Must be nice being famous and having houses all around the world.'

'Liv's Canadian,' Jack said hurriedly, realising her discomfort. 'Her grandmother lives here, and Olivia and Scarlett wanted to spend Christmas with her.'

He somehow made the lie sound like the truth.

'Would you like to join us for a coffee?' the man asked, pulling out a chair and shoving coffee cups aside to make room for her at the table.

Jack smiled as he stood. 'Thanks for the offer, but we should get going. I'd like to spend time with my family if that's okay.'

He glanced at the shopping bag in the crook of her elbow, the large cardboard tube sticking out. 'Looks like Olivia has finished her shopping.' He smiled at her. 'Do you want a takeaway coffee, or would you prefer to sit for a bit before we go home?'

She didn't recognise this man. Jack usually loved being the centre of attention. 'Thanks, Jack. A take-home cup would be great, thanks.'

Jack strode over to the counter to place her order while Olivia politely answered questions about her hometown. A couple of minutes later Jack joined her and handed her the cardboard cup. When he casually draped an arm over her shoulder she stiffened. She wasn't used to him showing any affection in public.

'Nice to meet you all.'

'Enjoy your holiday,' Olivia said, as she gathered Scarlett close and ushered her out the door.

Jack followed and she strode ahead of him down the street, not sure why she was so angry. Was she annoyed because he'd acted like they were a couple or cross because she wished they still were?

They crossed at the lights and Scarlett tugged the hem of her coat. 'Can I run home through the park?'

Olivia nodded. She needed some space to work out what was going on in her head and heart.

'Are you sure that's safe?' Jack asked.

'Perfectly,' she replied. The streets were empty of cars and Scarlett didn't have to cross any roads to get home. The front door would be unlocked, and Nan wouldn't be concerned if Scarlett arrived without them as Olivia often let her run the last hundred metres home. It was one of the things she loved about living in a small town—it was safe.

Scarlett scampered off and Olivia headed for the lake, not surprised when Jack followed her to the gazebo. She stood at the timber railing and stared out across the grey water towards Fort Niagara on the other side of the river that fed into Lake Ontario. The gazebo—erected for a movie set in the early 1980s and donated to the town afterwards—was one of her favourite places to come to think, year-round. It was also where they had been married.

She remembered their wedding day. It was a Saturday afternoon in the middle of summer and the water had sparkled under brilliant warm sunshine. The air was so clear and the cloudless sky so blue it had been easy to see the skyline of Toronto on the other side of the lake. Despite what Jack's parents had wanted and expected for their son's wedding, Olivia and Jack opted for a small, private ceremony without any fuss or fanfare, even choosing not to have a bridal party. The ceremony itself almost didn't go ahead on time though when Jack's parents and his sister missed their connecting flight from Los Angeles and arrived in Niagara-on-the-Lake jet-lagged and grumpy less than an hour before the wedding was due to start. Then there was her father's poor behaviour. Already halfway towards drunk when he'd arrived to pick her up from Nan's house, he'd somehow managed to hold her arm and walk her down the street and across the grass towards the gazebo without tripping.

Olivia had never felt so nervous in her life as she took the steps onto the gazebo, but the second the celebrant joined her hands together with Jack's and quietly told them to take a deep breath, her nervousness disappeared, and for the rest of the service she forgot about feeling embarrassed about her father or worrying about Jack's parents falling asleep at dinner.

Despite everything, the ceremony was perfect—casual and relaxed, yet elegant at the same time. Even the little white gazebo shone, freshly painted and decorated by Nan and Sally with hundreds of hand-picked flowers. Olivia closed her eyes and remembered reading their vows, exchanging rings, and their first kiss as husband and wife. She also remembered the letter Nan had given her on the morning of her wedding day. It was a complete surprise and one of the best gifts Olivia had ever received. Written not long before her mother had passed away, the letter was full of loving words and the kind of advice only a mother could give.

Though Mom hadn't been there physically, Olivia had felt like she was standing there beside her throughout the day. After the ceremony they took a horse-drawn carriage ride to the reception venue, stopping along the way to take photos in a nearby winery. She'd smiled so much that day her face had hurt.

'Olivia?' Jack's voice, filled with concern, eventually

permeated through the fog in her head. 'Are you okay? What happened? What did I do wrong?'

She pinned her bottom lip with her teeth and tried to hold everything back, hoping he wouldn't notice how much she was trembling. She couldn't find the right words to explain how she felt.

Another beat of silence passed.

She wanted to tell him that everything *wasn't* alright. That she was a mess. That she didn't know whether she belonged with him or not, but she couldn't form the words. Yesterday she was in control of her world. Today she was not. An hour or so ago they were wrestling in the snow and she'd thought he was going to kiss her and now she could barely look at him.

Jack cleared his throat. 'What is it, Olivia?' His voice was low. 'Tell me.'

She sank down onto the seat beside him and faced him. His green eyes were darker than the ocean on a cloudy day and they were filled with an earnestness she hadn't seen in years. He held her gaze with his and she felt intoxicated by him.

She had to give Jack credit. He'd said he'd changed, and so far she'd seen enough evidence to believe he was telling the truth. Despite her anger towards him from the moment he'd arrived, he'd leaned in towards her instead of running in the opposite direction. He was a decent man trying his best and she wasn't doing anything to help him out.

She looked over at him and realised it had only been twenty-four hours but already her impression of him had changed. He wasn't the consummate charmer she'd left. He was much more than that. Perhaps time had changed him. Perhaps the best thing she'd done was walk out because it had forced him to his senses. But despite the changes, she wasn't sure she could be as vulnerable and honest with him as he was being with her.

She hesitated while grappling with the right words to explain how she felt. 'I didn't like the way you pretended we're still together,' she said softly.

He exhaled slowly. 'I'm sorry, it felt natural to put my arm around you. I didn't think.'

He was right. It did feel natural, and that's why she was freaked out. A part of her ached for him to hold her again and another part ached to be the one to reach out and touch him.

He scooted a fraction closer, and their shoulders almost touched. She breathed in the scent of his aftershave, and she could feel the warmth of his body where their legs touched. The back of his hand brushed hers causing a rush of blood to course through her, the way it had the first time they'd entwined fingers all those years ago. Once upon a time she would have reached for his hand and squeezed it three times—her way of saying "I love you".

His eyes locked with hers, holding her gaze and making something in her chest flutter wildly. Somehow his eyes managed to convey even more than his words ever did. She blinked first, breaking the stare but in that moment, before she blinked, she knew with certainty that what he said was truth. He *did* still love her, and he honestly believed he deserved a second chance. Her insides pinched and she inched away from him. She wasn't ready for this.

'I know it's going to take time for you to trust me again,' he said, voice low.

She tucked a stray strand of hair behind her ear and pulled her hat down lower.

'It's all going to work out,' he added. 'I promise.'

She stared out at the water. 'How?'

She felt him shrug. 'I'm honestly not sure, but I know what I want, and I'm prepared to do whatever it takes to have you and Scarlett back in my life. Forever,' he said softly.

She wanted to ask if he could live in Canada but dreaded his answer. Instead, she stayed silent.

Minutes circled slowly around the clock and they sat in silence until the sky turned from a bruised grey to a dark slate.

He put one arm around her waist, drawing her close and with his other hand he reached for hers. This time she didn't stiffen. Instead, a shiver of desire lurched through her core, swirling deeper and lower, prickling her skin and tightening her gut and reminding her of all the good times they'd shared.

Jack looked at her the way he had on their wedding day and when he moved his face closer to hers, Olivia's pulse pounded so fast and furious she was surprised he couldn't feel it. She closed her eyes as he brought his lips to hers it was impossible not to surrender. Something shifted in her chest and the space that was left was filled with a warm glow. He reached for the nape of her neck with one hand, claiming her as his and it sent a warm flutter through her body. She found herself wrapping her arms around his neck and kissing him back. He tasted so good.

He deepened the kiss but when his tongue flicked past her lips, she pulled back breathlessly. Putting her hand on his chest she pushed herself away from him, heart hammering furiously. Tears pricked her eyes. Oh God, what had she done?

'Liv.'

She raised a hand, indicating she needed a moment to compose herself as the reality of kissing him sank in.

'I can't.' She stood and buried her hands deep in her pockets. 'I don't want to lead you on, Jack. Give you the wrong idea.' Tears blurred her vision. 'I'm sorry, Jack. I can't do this.' The kiss had brought all the past rushing up to the reality of where she was today. Jack may have changed, but she hadn't. She was still deeply hurt by him.

He'd tasted exactly as she'd remembered and that was dangerous ground. Even though she was enjoying his company for the first time in years, things were going too quickly, and she needed to slow them down before they got further out of control.

Wrapping her scarf tighter around her neck she tried to stem the tears that ached to fall, like a swollen river about to burst its banks. It would be so easy to allow herself to fall into her dream here. The dream where they were a perfect family. But she'd given up dreaming a long time ago.

Jack didn't say a word. He stared out across the lake as if lost in his own thoughts, hands between his thighs to keep warm.

Finally, as if he couldn't stand the silence any longer, he stood and let out a long sigh. 'I'll go home and check on Scarlett.'

Turning on his heel he walked off without a word, leaving her alone in a bubble of silence. Everything within her wanted to call him back, tell him that she was sorry, that she would try to forgive him, that she was willing to give him another chance, but she couldn't. There was still too much they hadn't figured out and one heat of the moment kiss wasn't going to resolve anything.

Instead, she burst into tears and sobbed until there was nothing left.

Chapter 10

Jack left Olivia alone by the lake and trudged back to the house with his hands clenched into fists and jammed into his pockets. She clearly needed to think, and he needed space too.

Stupid, stupid, *stupid*. Why the hell had he kissed her? It seemed like they'd moved forward today, laughing and playing in the snow with Scarlett. Then he'd ruined it because he didn't know how to keep his hands off his wife. Now they'd gone backwards at least three steps, maybe more.

By the time he arrived home, dark clouds had gathered along with his dark thoughts, snow was falling more heavily. And he was freezing.

He pushed open the door and heard giggling coming from the kitchen. By the time he'd hung up his coat and toed off his boots and walked into the kitchen, Joan, Paul and Scarlett wore innocent expressions. Empty rolls of wrapping paper, sticky tape and ribbons covered the kitchen table and wrapped presents were stacked on the floor.

He dropped a kiss on the top of his daughter's head. 'Looks like you've been busy.' He smiled for Joan and Paul's benefit. 'Thanks for looking after her.'

'Our pleasure,' Paul said.

'We were worried when she came home without you, but Paul said he'd seen you two head down to the lake.' Concern filled Joan's cloudy eyes. 'Everything okay?'

Probably not. 'Yeah. Olivia needs to clear her head.' If she didn't walk in the door in the next five minutes, he was going back outside to get her.

'Are you hungry? I've got fresh baked cookies.'

'No. Thanks anyway.' He put a hand to his abdomen. 'I have to stop eating so much.'

'Pft. It's Christmas. Calories don't count.'

He heard the front door open. Knowing it would be Olivia and she would need more space, he said to Joan, 'Is it okay if I go and sit for a while in the lounge?'

'Do whatever you need to do.'

He stretched out on the couch in the lounge and stared into the crackling fire until he could no longer keep his eyes open. Moments later he sensed Scarlett climbing up beside him. He lifted his arm and Scarlett tucked herself against him. Dropping his arm around his daughter, he spooned her to his chest and within minutes, they were both sound asleep.

When Jack woke, Scarlett was gone. He sat up, yawned and stretched. Checking the old grandfather clock on the mantlepiece, he was surprised it was almost four o'clock and already dark outside. He'd slept for hours. The smell of food wafted from the kitchen and he realised he was hungry again.

He shuffled into the kitchen and found Joan at the stove, stirring something. The kitchen was warm and smelt of gravy and cinnamon and vanilla. He inhaled deeply.

'Good sleep?' Joan asked, without turning around.

'It was.' He stretched again, cracking his back.

'You must have needed it.'

'I did. Where are Olivia and Scarlett?'

'Upstairs getting ready for supper.'

'How was Olivia when she came home?'

'Quiet.'

He rubbed his temples. If only he had someone to talk to. He'd totally stuffed things up by kissing her, and had no clue how to navigate his way out of the mess he'd created. He hadn't planned to kiss her, but sitting by the lake it had felt like they were on some kind of trajectory that he couldn't stop even if he'd wanted to. It was all so confusing and complicated. She was his wife and he wanted to be with her so badly it was a physical ache, but in her mind they were no longer together.

It was bad enough that he wanted her but what was worse was he'd seen the look in her eyes. She wanted him too. The problem was, she didn't trust him yet. He'd seen that as clearly as if it was written in the sky.

Joan stopped stirring. 'Want to talk about it?'

He exhaled loudly. 'I think I rushed her.'

'Keep doing what you're doing.'

He exhaled slowly. 'That's my problem. What I'm doing isn't working.'

'Time, Jack. Time. That's all. It heals everything.'

'Time is something I don't have. I only have another week to show her how much I still love her.'

Joan pulled out a chair at the table and sat opposite him. She reached across the table, searching for his hands. 'You have the rest of your life to show her.'

'What if she won't let me?' It seemed as though she wasn't prepared to give him another chance.

'I know my granddaughter and she will.' Joan pulled her hands away and reached behind her, taking an envelope out of the drawer in the side dresser. She handed it to him.

He frowned. 'What's this?'

'An early Christmas present from me. I wanted to give it to you without anyone else around, especially Olivia.'

Puzzled, Jack put his finger under the flap of the envelope and opened it. He pulled out a legal document and a typed letter.

'It's the deeds to this house.'

His head snapped up. 'Why are you giving this to me?'

'Read the letter. It's not just for you. I'm giving it to both of you. You and Olivia.'

'I don't understand.'

'I'm getting old, Jack, and the problems with my vision has knocked the wind out of me. Not that I'd admit that to Olivia, but I'm struggling. This house is too big for me and I can't live here on my own any longer.'

'But Olivia is here with you.'

'Exactly. Which is not where she's supposed to be. She's supposed to be with you.'

He put the papers down on the table. 'She won't be happy about this.'

'That's her issue. I've made my choice and I've seen the lawyer. It's all signed, sealed and delivered, as they say. I don't mind whether you live here, rent it out for holiday accommodation or keep it for whenever you want to visit. The house is yours.'

He scratched his jaw. 'But where are you going to live?'

She flashed him a smile so wide it revealed all her dentures. 'Next door. With Paul.

Jack grinned. 'Wow. Good for you.'

Colour tinged her cheeks. 'Olivia's probably not going to like it and I'd rather you didn't say anything to her yet. I'm waiting for the right time to tell her. She was very close to Robert, but he's been gone a long time now and I'm getting lonely.'

'Paul is a good man.'

'He is. He and Robert were good friends you know. When Paul's wife Janet was alive, the four of us were close. But after Janet died last year, Paul and I discovered we had feelings for each other.'

'Are you going to get married?'

Joan's blush deepened. 'I'm probably too old for a wedding.'

'I don't think so.'

'Well, we'll see about that.' She pushed back from the table and went back to stirring the soup on the stove.

'I'm happy for you, Joan. For both of you.'

'Thank you, sweetheart.'

Now if only *his* story could have a happy ending.

Chapter 11

That afternoon Olivia stood at the island bench in the kitchen re-reading her mother's recipe for the third time. She stared at the cookies on the baking tray and had no idea what she was doing wrong. The first batch were like hockey pucks. The second batch were crunchy around the edges and looked alright, but sank like soft sand in the middle and tasted dreadful. These ones had spread like pancakes. She wanted to cry, but pride and stubbornness wouldn't allow it.

One of her favourite childhood memories was decorating sugar cookies with Mom before she passed away. This year, because it was Scarlett's first Canadian Christmas, she'd decided to pass down some of her own fond memories to her daughter.

She'd rifled through Nan's cupboards and found the old recipe book, but despite her best intentions, the kitchen was a mess, the third batch of cookies were doomed for the rubbish bin and she was close to admitting defeat.

The front door opened and closed. Jack was back from his run earlier than she'd expected.

She brushed hair away from her face with the back of her hand and let out a sigh. Brilliant. Now she would feel further embarrassed by her lack of baking abilities.

Before meeting Jack, she couldn't boil eggs. It wasn't her fault; Nan had loved cooking and always shooed her out of the kitchen. After marrying Jack, he'd helped her gain confidence in the kitchen and she'd learned to cook the basics by necessity because he was rarely home. It turned out that it wasn't too hard to follow a recipe, but cooking didn't come naturally, and it certainly wasn't something she enjoyed doing.

She could cook and made plenty of nutritious—if bland— meals for herself and Scarlett, but she also kept the local pizza place on speed dial. Judging by today's efforts, she still hadn't mastered baking.

'I'm in the kitchen,' she called out.

She picked up a measuring cup and checked the recipe again. One and three-quarter cups of flour. Was that enough?

Jack appeared seconds later, stopping in the doorway and staring, mouth open, at the scene in front of him. 'What's going on?'

What does it look like, dude?

'I'm cooking,' she huffed, blowing away at the loose strand of hair that kept getting in her eyes.

'Oka . . . aay.'

He pulled up a barstool at the island bench and she found herself looking at his broad chest. Beneath the black top he'd worn for his run she saw the outline of his pectoral muscles and her stomach contracted remembering how she used to run her hands over his smooth skin. Swallowing hard, she pushed the flicker of desire away. She had no right to be thinking about his body like that.

She forced her gaze up to his face, flushed from the freezing air. 'How far did you go?'

'Fifteen k.' He pulled off his peaked cap and ran his hands through his hair.

'You must be freezing.'

He spun the cap in his hands. 'I'm glad I took your advice on how many layers to wear but I should have worn gloves and a beanie. Everyone I bumped into reckons it's going to snow again soon.'

'Yeah, I think it will.'

'Where's Scarlett?'

'Paul and Nan took her to Niagara Falls to see the lights.'

Not long after Jack went for a run, Paul had arrived and suggested he and Nan take Scarlett with them to the Falls to see the lights and give Olivia some time to herself.

To keep busy and take her mind off Jack, she'd foolishly decided to attempt the cookies as a surprise for Scarlett. She thought it might be fun for them to decorate them together when she got home. But the problem was, with everyone out of the house, it was so quiet it gave her too much time to think. She should have concentrated on the recipe instead of Jack and that kiss.

Jack hadn't said a word. She glanced at him, saw disappointment in his eyes and a shot of guilt hit her. She'd gotten too used to not including Jack in her decision-making when it came to Scarlett.

'I'm sorry, Jack. It was a spur of the moment decision. You'd already gone on your run and I didn't think to call you and tell you. I promise she won't mind going again with you after Christmas, if you'd like.'

'I would like that.' He turned away from her, grabbed one foot and began to stretch out his quad muscles but not before she saw a shadow cross his face. He must think she was being deliberately mean-spirited.

She averted her gaze from his lycra-clad legs and focused on his mouth. 'I'm really sorry, Jack. I should have called you.'

'It's okay.'

He shrugged, but she knew his body language well enough to know he was upset.

She chewed on her bottom lip. What else could she say other than sorry?

He swapped legs and stretched the other one. 'I've loved hanging out with her today. She's an awesome kid.'

Olivia smiled at him.

Jack had been incredibly patient with Scarlett all morning, building Lego, dressing her dolls, reading books to her, colouring in, watching movies. Olivia had mostly sat back and watched them interact, genuinely surprised by how good he was with Scarlett. She couldn't remember them ever spending so long together without Jack being distracted by work. He'd always been an amazing dad, albeit an absent one. But it clearly hadn't affected Scarlett. She'd let Jack back into her life like he'd never been gone.

'She is a great kid,' Olivia agreed.

Jack finally met her gaze. 'You've done an amazing job raising her, Liv.'

The unexpected compliment warmed her. She dipped her head. 'Thank you.'

'What are you cooking?'

She ignored the way he was inspecting the batch of rocks to her left without appearing to be looking at them.

'I'm trying to bake sugar cookies.' She picked up one of the blackened puck-like rocks. 'Although given what these things look like, I clearly wouldn't last one round on *The Chopping Block*.'

He chuckled. 'I didn't realise you were planning to audition.'

'I'm not.' The last thing she'd ever want was to be part of his show. Her hands shook as she picked up the baking tray and dumped the whole batch into the bin.

'I didn't think you liked baking.'

'I don't.'

'Then why are you doing it?'

'Because I like sugar cookies.'

And because it's the best memory I have of Mom at Christmas.

He leaned over and slid the tattered recipe book towards him. His eyes widened. 'Where did you get an *Australian Women's Weekly* cookbook? This is vintage.'

'I have no idea. Mom used it as long as I could remember. I think that's why I always wanted to visit Australia.'

They shared a quick smile.

'What type of flour are you using?' he asked.

'It says self-raising flour, but I don't know what that is. I'm using all-purpose flour.'

He ran his finger down the list of ingredients. 'Are you using caster sugar?'

'No. I only had brown sugar. I didn't have time to go to the store.' She chewed the inside of her lip. 'Is that wrong? Is that why they're not working?'

He closed the recipe book and pushed it to one side. 'Would you like my help?'

'Can you do that without taking over?' The sugar cookies were her link to her mother, and it was important she pass that link to Scarlett on her own terms. It wouldn't be right if Jack made the cookies and created the memory with Scarlett that she was planning to create, would it?

'When have I ever taken over your kitchen?'

'You never took over. You never helped either.'

There was silence for a moment.

'I'm offering now.'

She hesitated, then put the measuring cup down. She saw the earnestness in his eyes and could hear it in his voice. He was trying to make a connection with her. And part of Olivia wanted that too.

Setting her ego aside she gave him a nod. 'Thanks, Jack.'

He joined her on the other side of the island bench. He was so close she could hear his breathing. He took the tray from her hands and placed it in the sink. 'Can I ask you a question?'

She bit her lip and waited.

'What's so important about the sugar cookies? It's obvious

there is more to it than a sudden urge to bake.'

Tears pricked and she ducked her head. Her throat tightened and it was a moment before she could speak. 'Mom and I used to bake cookies together every Christmas. It was our thing. I wanted to make them for Scarlett so she and I could create our own Christmas memories.'

He touched her gently on the shoulder and his fingers burned through her sweatshirt. 'I'm sorry. I never knew that. I can see why it's so important for you.'

She sniffed and tried to blink back the impending tears.

He squeezed gently then let go. 'Give me a few minutes to shower and I'll be right back down to help.'

While Jack was gone, she dried her eyes and blew her nose, then cleaned up her mess. She washed all the dishes she'd used, wiped down the countertops and put things away. One thing she remembered was Jack liked a tidy workspace.

When he re-appeared ten minutes later, her breath caught. His hair was damp and tousled, and his face flushed from the heat of the shower. He'd swapped his running clothes for a pair of grey trackpants, a white T-shirt and thick socks, yet somehow, he managed to make the outfit look sexy. When he came close, she caught a hint of lemon myrtle, eucalyptus and mint and it invoked a million memories of the past. He'd used the same body wash for years.

Raw sex appeal hummed around him, tugging her closer and she struggled to concentrate. The breadth of his shoulders was so familiar, and all it would take was one step and she'd be back in his arms.

Wordlessly, he joined her at the bench. When he reached for the recipe book, his bare arm touched hers and she jumped as if zapped. She pulled her hand back quickly, spooked by the shooting tingles across her skin and by the stirrings deep in her belly, like someone waking from a coma. He caught her gaze and her breath hitched again. His eyes were full of a longing that tugged at her reserve. Her heart began to hammer, and she had a sudden desire to reach for him. To stand on tiptoes and press her lips to his and taste him again. But she couldn't. Wouldn't.

He turned away and reached purposefully for the flour, breaking the moment. 'Let's get started.'

Something in his manner changed in that brief encounter. It was as if the enormity of what he was asking of her had suddenly occurred to him.

Or perhaps it was something else. There was a tug of attraction, hovering below the surface and maybe he'd felt it too.

She found a smile. 'What would you like me to do?'

'Why don't you sit down and watch?'

'Too easy.' She pulled up a bar stool and sat.

Jack worked quickly and efficiently, using her mother's recipe. Watching Jack in this kitchen reminded her of all the years her Mom had stood at this same bench, always laughing and smiling, and telling stories while she baked. Even the Christmas before she passed away when she knew she was sick and dying, Mom had worn a confident and calm smile. Olivia learned later she had been dosed on morphine so she could stand up long enough to make cookies.

Memories flooded in and Olivia fought back tears. She missed her mother dreadfully, but always more at Christmas.

After Jack whipped up enough mixture for two batches of cookies and slid them into the oven, he began pulling ingredients together to make something else. Everything he did looked effortless. It was like he'd been born with a wooden spoon in one hand, a silver one in the other.

'What are you making now?' she asked.

'Raspberry and white chocolate muffins. I'll add in a touch of cinnamon too.' He passed her a roll of baking paper and a pair of scissors. 'Can you cut some squares to line the muffin tins please?'

'I think I can manage that,' she replied when he started to demonstrate what size paper he wanted. She took the scissors from him and he went back to adding all the ingredients together into a large stainless-steel bowl.

When she was done cutting the paper, he expertly spooned the batter into the tins and wiped the bowl clean with the rubber spatula. He hadn't left a single drop of batter or mess anywhere.

After removing the cookies from the oven, he slid the muffin tins in, set the timer then washed his hands. Leaning back against the bench he looked at her. The smell of cinnamon and vanilla filled the toasty kitchen and her stomach rumbled. She took a cookie and blew on it to cool it down before taking a bite.

'Mmmm.' Perfect.

She closed her eyes and went straight back to her childhood when she used to sit on the kitchen bench and try to snatch cookies when Mom wasn't watching.

A stray tear slid down her cheek.

Before she had a chance to wipe it away, Jack took a step towards her and used his thumb to tenderly brush her cheek. Their eyes locked and she became acutely aware of his attention, of the heat coming off him as well as the warmth of the oven behind her. Her heart raced and her fingers itched to touch him. They were merely inches apart and all she had to do was stand on her tiptoes to meet his lips.

Her thoughts crashed into her. Damn him for coming back into her life just as she was starting to find routine. She needed to stay strong. He was not going to get under her skin again.

But there was no denying the giddy heartbeat or the tug in her gut—the stirrings of something she thought she'd forgotten. Her skin prickled with a memory of the first time they'd made love. Was she doing the wrong thing letting Jack go?

'Jack—'

Her phone rang, and they sprang apart as if they'd been caught doing something wrong.

She turned away quickly so he couldn't see the confusion on her face and glanced down at her phone, frowning.

It was Sally.

'Hi, Sally. Is everything okay?'

'Olivia.' She sounded out of breath. 'Glad I caught you.'

'What's wrong?'

'It's Aimee. They're taking her to hospital now. There's something wrong with the baby and she wants us there.'

Aimee lived on the other side of Lake Ontario in Peterborough—at least three hours' drive depending on the weather. Much longer if the forecast snow hit.

'What's wrong?'

'I don't really know. Something about a slow heartbeat.'

Olivia heard the panic in Sally's voice.

'They're going to do more scans tonight and we'll know more then. Les is already packing the car.'

'Is there anything I can do?'

'I don't think so.'

'Did they say whether they'd induce her?'

'Maybe. Aimee wasn't sure.'

'How many weeks is she?' Olivia couldn't remember.

'Twenty-six.'

'If they induce her, they'll have to take her to Toronto,' Olivia said. There were only three hospitals in Ontario that had a Level Three Neonatal Intensive Care Unit.

'I know.'

'If you need anything, or even if you have questions, please call me.'

'I will.'

'What are you doing about the dinner tomorrow night? Do you have a contingency in place?'

'I'm sorry, Olivia, we're going to have to cancel it.'

'Oh no. What a shame.'

Olivia was gutted on Sally's behalf. She and Les always put so much time and effort into the dinner, and it had become an institution over the years. The whole town would take a hit if they cancelled the community meal. It was the highlight of the year and something the locals looked forward to. Cancelling it would take as much work as running it, but she couldn't do it on her own. Les and Sally were the backbone of the whole thing. Without them, it would never work.

'I hate to dump our problem in your lap, but could you do the cancelling for us? We have to focus on Aimee and the baby.'

'Of course you do.' After all Sally and Les had done for her over the years, she'd do anything to help.

'Thank you, Olivia. It would be such a relief knowing you'll take care of everything.'

'What do you want me to do with the food?'

'Do whatever you need to do. We trust you.'

'Give Les my love and tell Aimee we're praying for her and the baby and sending our best wishes.'

'Thanks, Olivia. Will do.' Sally ended the call.

'Who was that?' Jack asked

'Sally.' She yanked the apron over her head, balled it up and dumped it on the bench. 'I have to go.'

Jack frowned. 'Go where?'

She ignored him.

Jack put a hand on her arm. 'Hang on. Stop. What's going on? Where are you going?'

She didn't have time to explain. There was too much to do. 'I need to get down to the restaurant and…' She froze.

And what? She had no idea where to start. She blew out a long breath, sank onto a kitchen chair and put her head in her hands.

Jack squatted before her. 'Restaurant?'

'I'm one of the volunteers for the community meal tomorrow night.' Olivia ran her hands through her hair. 'Sally feels like they have to cancel, but I can't let her do that. People will be so disappointed.'

Jack still wore a confused expression.

'Who is Sally?'

'She's a chef. She and her husband Les own one of the restaurants in town and they host a community meal every year. I've known Sally my whole life. She was like a second mother to me after mine passed.'

The oven timer chimed. He got up, removed the muffins from the oven and placed them on a cooling rack. 'What sort of community meal does she run?'

'It was something Nan's local church started years ago. A free meal provided for those who didn't have family or someone to spend Christmas with. Since then it's morphed into a dinner for around two hundred locals.'

Jack's eyes widened. 'Two hundred? At once? A sit-down meal? How do you feed that many people? What size is the kitchen? Is it a traditional Christmas dinner?'

Jack was lobbing questions at her, but Olivia couldn't arrange her thoughts in a straight line in order to answer him.

She stood up and snatched a pen from the jar on top of the fridge then rifled through the junk drawer and found a notebook. She would start by making a list of people she'd need to call.

'Do you have to cancel it?' Jack asked.

That was an excellent question. Maybe she could run it. She shut that idea off straight away. She was the least qualified person to co-ordinate a meal for two hundred people.

But Jack wasn't.

An idea formed but she pushed it away. It was an insane idea. There was no reason why Jack would want to help cook food for a community meal. It was hardly fine dining and there wouldn't be any cameras or accolades.

'When's the dinner?' he asked.

'Tomorrow night.'

'And Sally would have bought all the food? Everything?'

Olivia nodded. She wasn't entirely sure, but she knew Sally, and Sally was always organised.

'I can do it.'

She stared at him. 'Really?'

He shrugged. 'Sure.'

'Why would you want to?'

'Because I can see how much it means to you.'

She didn't know what to say.

He grinned at her. 'Who knew you were going to need the help of one of Australia's best chefs?'

Who knew indeed?

Chapter 12

Later that night, after supper, and after reading Scarlett three books, before her eyes finally began to close, Jack came downstairs to find Olivia at the front door, pulling on her boots.

'Where are you going?' he asked.

'To the restaurant.'

He frowned. 'Why?'

'I have to see what needs doing.'

'Can't it wait until the morning? It's pretty late and you said there's going to be snow tonight.'

'I won't be able to sleep until I know what Sally's already done.'

Fair enough. He understood what that was like. 'Let me come with you.'

He saw her hesitate.

'Someone needs to stay with Scarlett.'

Joan came out of the kitchen. 'I've already called Paul. He'll be over in a few minutes. We'll sit up until you get home. Take Jack with you, Olivia.'

She winked at him, and Jack bit back a smile. At least someone was still on his side, but he had a feeling he'd need more than that.

That afternoon Olivia had seemed happy to accept his help, but now it felt like she'd changed her mind and he didn't know why. He wasn't sure if he'd done something to upset her again or if it was the stress of the dinner. She'd taken on the responsibility of it without the first clue how to go about getting it done.

'I'm leaving now, okay?'

'That's fine.' He reached past her into the hall cupboard and grabbed his black puffer jacket from the hanger.

'Did you bring something warmer?' Olivia asked as he slipped it on. 'And better boots? Yours will be useless if it snows. You'll slip everywhere.'

He shook his head. It wasn't like he had options. He only had one pair of boots with him, thinking his leather soled *RM*'s would have been fine. 'I don't have anything else.'

'Give him Grandad's old boots,' Joan said.

'No.' Olivia's reply was sharp and quick. 'He can't use those.'

'Oh, Olivia,' Joan tutted. 'Your grandfather has been gone a long time. I keep Robert's things for anyone who needs them and right now your husband needs them.'

'He's not my husband.' Olivia mumbled.

The words shot straight through his heart. He *was* her husband.

'And you know my opinion on *that*,' Joan said with a shake of her silver curls. 'Now stop being so petty and stubborn. Jack can use one of Robert's old coats too. And from memory there's a box of hats and gloves on the top shelf.'

Jack could see how upset Olivia was. She must be worried sick about her friend's pregnant daughter, so he let her snippiness over her grandad's boots slide, because that wasn't the real issue. Olivia obviously didn't want to let her friend, or the townspeople, down and he respected her for that. Rather than make more waves and upset her further, Jack took the decision from her hands.

'I'm fine, honestly. Thank you, Joan. My boots are fine, and this jacket is plenty warm enough. It might look light, but it's from Japan and they have plenty of snow in Japan.' Using the stair banister to get his balance, he put one foot into his leather-soled boot and pulled it on over his thick socks. 'And Olivia's partly right, Joan. I might still be her husband legally, but I lost the right to be called that.' He pulled his other boot on, avoiding looking at Olivia. He wasn't sure he was ready to see the expression on her face.

'It's not your fault,' Joan said, patting him on the back. 'It's probably mine. If this damned eyesight hadn't gone, Olivia wouldn't have felt obligated to come back here to look after me.'

'That's not true,' Olivia said quickly.

Olivia and Joan were very close, but Jack wondered if Joan knew the real reason why Olivia had left him. If she did, maybe she'd let him in on it.

Joan wasn't to blame. If he'd been a better husband, he and Olivia wouldn't be in this situation. Which was why he was doing everything in his power to fix things between them.

'You're a good man, Jack Carter,' Joan said.

He wasn't sure Olivia would agree.

She was waiting for him at the front gate. She'd wrapped a thick blue and white tartan scarf around her neck and mouth, and he could barely make out her eyes under the navy-blue beanie pulled low over her ears.

'We're walking?' he asked, pulling the hood of his jacket over his head. The air was so icy his lungs were turning into blocks of ice.

'It's only three blocks and it's easier to walk than drive.'

She took off and he had to jog to catch up, his feet slipping on the icy footpath. Two houses down, Jack slowed his pace. He couldn't keep up with Olivia in his leather-soled shoes. He should have ignored her protestations and taken Robert's boots.

He also slowed because it had started to snow.

He looked up in wonder as tiny flurries landed and melted on his cheeks. He resisted the desire to squeal and shout like a child. He was nearly forty-years-old and he'd never seen snow falling. No wonder he was excited.

He stood, palms raised, as the flakes fell soundlessly from the black sky like tiny white parachutes from an unseen plane, taking their time to land. At first, they fell tentatively, almost awkwardly, but soon they were coming so fast everything was quickly blanketed in a fresh white coat. And it was so strangely quiet.

Olivia walked back to join him. Her beanie looked like it was covered in white confetti.

'It's beautiful,' he whispered as he gazed at the untouched snow all around him. The swirling flakes stained the shrubs and trees white and the ground looked as smooth as icing on a wedding cake. He'd never seen anything so pretty. It was like something out of a Hallmark Christmas movie.

'Now it's beginning to look a lot like Christmas,' she said with a chuckle. 'But if you stand there much longer, you'll turn into a snowman. Come on!'

As the snow came down heavier, the temperature dropped considerably. He shivered as he shoved his hands deeper into the pockets of his jacket, but it did little good. He should have borrowed a pair of gloves and a beanie.

As they walked up the middle of the deserted road, their breath puffed steam into the frigid air. A gust of wind fresh off the lake sent flurries of snow flying, pricking his skin like ice needles. He huddled into his coat and hoped the restaurant wasn't far away.

At the next intersection Olivia turned right and stopped in front of an historic-looking brick building. 'This is *Harbourside*. The hotel is small, only fifteen suites. The restaurant is this way.' She led the way down the snow-covered path to the front door.

He frowned at the darkened interior. 'Why isn't it open tonight?'

'Sally would have cancelled bookings tonight because of Aimee.'

'But surely there's someone else who could have opened for them.' The idea of closing a restaurant three days out from Christmas was unbelievable and unheard of. The loss of revenue alone was massive, let alone turning away customers—that was a sure-fire way to ruin the restaurant's reputation and lose repeat business. 'A sous chef at least?'

'Sally's the head chef. They have a sous chef, but he broke his leg playing hockey and he's out for another six weeks with plaster up to his groin. I think there might be some cooks who come in and help with food prep but I'm not sure. As you'll see, it's not a large restaurant and mostly caters to the guests here at the hotel, or to us locals. Everyone knows it's closed Christmas Eve for the community dinner.'

'What about Christmas Day?'

'Closed. They open the day after Boxing Day for lunch.'

'But surely those are be their biggest trading days.'

'No. They're the biggest *family* days. People spend Christmas and Boxing Days with their families.'

He felt her barb sink through his jacket into his skin, but he kept quiet.

Putting a key into the lock, she turned it before pushing the door open and leading him into the darkened restaurant. He saw cloth-covered tables and chairs and estimated seating for about sixty to seventy people at a stretch.

'Can I ask you something?'

She paused, her hand hovering over the light switch. 'What?'

'You were okay earlier today when we were in the kitchen at home, but now you're clearly angry again. Did I do something wrong?'

She huffed out a breath as she flicked on a switch. He blinked and she dimmed the lights before moving across to the fireplace. She turned on the gas log fire and it burst into life and warmth. Yanking off her gloves, she stood in front of it, her back to him, rubbing her outstretched hands together. He joined her. He'd never been so cold in his life.

'I'm not angry with you,' she said finally. 'I'm angry with myself.'

'Why?'

'Because I'm in over my head. Sally wanted me to cancel the dinner and you've talked me into doing it.'

'I only offered to help. You can go ahead and cancel it if you want to, but I don't think you do.'

She sighed heavily. 'I don't want to cancel it but I'm in way over my head.'

Which is why he'd offered to help.

'There's too much pressure.'

He frowned. 'Pressure from who?'

'Everyone. Once they find out you're a famous chef they'll expect this dinner to be better than it's ever been. And you'll do what you do, and you'll take over and you'll be amazing, and everyone will fall in love with you and rave about how incredible you are and how amazing the food is and once again the focus will be on you.'

He blinked. Did she really think that about him?

She pulled her beanie off, raked her fingers through her hair and tied it back into a high ponytail. Her cheeks were flushed pink from the warmth of the heater.

'I know that makes me sound jealous and petty, but the thing is, Jack, your celebrity status will overshadow the purpose of the dinner. For many people this meal is the only time they feel special and valued and I'm worried all the attention will be on you, not them.'

That was the last thing he wanted.

'What if I promise to stay in the background and not take over?' he asked.

'Do you even know how to do that?'

A flash of indignation ran through him. She didn't know him at all.

'Yes, I do.' One of his strengths was helping up and coming young chefs learn the trade. It was the basis of his very successful cooking show. 'I'm happy for you to cook, Olivia, and I'll offer advice if you ask for it.'

'I don't want you to stand and watch over my shoulder and wait for me stuff it up.'

'You make it sound like I want you to fail. I don't. I can see how important this dinner is to you and I want to help.'

She lifted her arms then let them drop to her side. 'You saw me in the kitchen today. I'm useless.'

'You're not useless.'

'I'm okay with cooking meals for me and Scarlett and Nan, but I have no idea how to cook for two hundred people. I'm terrified I'll stuff it up and let Sally and Les and everyone else down.'

'You won't stuff it up if I'm right beside you.'

She stopped chewing her bottom lip. 'You promise you won't let me make a fool of myself.'

'Promise.' He smiled.

'Okay.'

'Can I ask you something?'

She gave him a tiny nod.

'The counsellor said one of biggest issues is we never really talked about our feelings. We just exchanged information. Do you think that's true?'

She dipped her head and mumbled, 'yeah, probably.'

'Why?'

'You were too busy.'

'I was never too busy for you.'

'It felt like you were.'

'I'm sorry.'

'You know, Jack, if we're being truthful, I'll tell you why I stopped talking.'

He waited.

'You always made me feel second best.'

He frowned. 'What?'

'I lost count of the social engagements you cancelled at the last minute because of an emergency at the restaurant or a change in the filming schedule or because your parents wanted you to help them. I know you loved me, but not enough to make Scarlett and me your priority.'

Other than offering an apology, he had no idea what to say. 'I am so sorry you felt that way.'

And he was sorry she'd buried her feelings for so long. But at least now she was talking. It was a good place to start.

'From the moment we met, I was happy Olivia, and nothing changed. You have to believe that.'

'You might have been happy.' She screwed up her nose. 'But I wasn't. Not at the end anyway.'

'I'm sorry I was blind, but honestly I never realised our happiness was so one-sided.'

A thousand emotions crossed her face until all that was left was sadness. The girl he'd fallen in love with, the girl he'd once been able to talk to about anything, was gone. In her place was this sad, hurt woman. If she couldn't get past the anger and resentment she held, there was no hope for their marriage. The counsellor had warned him that was a possibility. A possibility he'd ignored.

'Since we're being so honest, can I ask *you* something?'

His heart lurched and he braced himself. 'Sure. Anything.'

'After I left, did you try to get back with Chelsea?'

'No!'

'But you saw her.'

He had no idea how she knew but he wasn't going to lie or pretend he hadn't had dinner with his former fiancé. His relationship with Chelsea had always been a sore point between them because Olivia couldn't understand why they'd remained close friends after their split.

'Yes, I did. We had dinner together.'

She flinched as if he'd poured salt onto an open wound.

'You know Chelsea's married.'

'That doesn't mean anything these days.'

Wow. He couldn't believe she'd think he'd ever be unfaithful to her. 'She called *me*.'

'Why?'

The question hung between them, almost visible. She stared at him, unblinking, waiting for his reply.

He exhaled heavily. 'I didn't cope after you asked for a divorce. I drank a lot. Too much. Anything to dull the pain and pretend it wasn't happening.' He'd thought he'd lost everything and was rapidly spiralling out of control. 'Chelsea told me I needed to see someone and get help. So I did.'

'You didn't sleep with her?'

He blinked. 'What? No! Who told you that?'

She bit her lip, looked away. 'Maddie.'

He swore and thumped the table with both fists, causing Olivia to jump. 'What did she tell you?'

'That I'd barely left Australia before you got back with Chelsea. She showed me pictures from tabloid magazines of the two of you together and said you were sleeping with her.'

He shot to his feet. 'She said what? No! That did not happen.' He stared down at Olivia. 'If you believe a word of what she said, then clearly you don't trust me at all.'

Olivia stood and glared at him. 'I told you I didn't trust you.'

'Was I ever unfaithful to you during our marriage?' They were both shouting now, eyeballing each other.

'How should I know?' she snapped. 'They say lots of women have no idea their husbands are having affairs.'

He sat down again, clenched and unclenched his fists and tried to slow his breathing. He deliberately lowered his voice even though they were the only two people in the empty restaurant. 'Let me say it once, and let's be clear. I was never once, *not ever*, unfaithful while we were together.'

Olivia sat too. 'And afterwards?'

'I told you, I had dinner with Chelsea. That's all. I spent the entire dinner showing her photos of Scarlett, and she could see I was still in love with you.'

The fire was gone from Olivia's eyes.

'I was always so jealous of Chelsea. I could never understand why you broke things off with her for me.'

'Are you joking? Chelsea and I had a good time together, but we should never have gotten engaged. I never loved her like I love you.'

'Why would Maddie lie to me?'

He exhaled heavily. 'Maddie hinted once that she wished she'd found someone like me. She even suggested she'd keep it on the down low if I wanted to have an affair. Maybe she saw her chance when you walked out. When I told her I'd been to see Chelsea and Chelsea had suggested I ask you for a second chance, Maddie probably couldn't take it.'

'Yet you didn't sack her? Why?'

'Because she's good at her job. I just kept my distance. The last time I saw Maddie face-to-face was months ago. We email, phone or text and that's all. I can show you my phone if you want.'

'You don't have to do that.' Silence descended. This was not how he'd pictured the evening to go.

He scratched his jaw. 'Something I don't understand. Why were you and Maddie even talking to each other?'

A pained expression came over Olivia's face. 'I thought she was my friend. I didn't have anyone else and I didn't know who to trust. She seemed so nice. I guess because I was already unhappy in our marriage, anything negative she said about you, I wanted to believe her.'

He reached across the table for her hands and was surprised when she didn't jerk away. He gently rubbed the back of her hands with his thumbs. 'I am so, so sorry Olivia. For everything. For not being around. For not talking to you. For not supporting you.

For—'

'I'm sorry too, Jack,' she said, interrupting him.

She softly squeezed his hands and the slight pressure sent a surge of warmth along his arms and into his chest. His throat tightened, stealing his breath and for a nanosecond, he allowed himself to hope.

Once again, he was filled with an intense longing to kiss her, but he'd learned his lesson the day before. Taking any advantage of the tiny bridge she'd built between them would no doubt push her further away again.

He squeezed her hands again then loosened his grip, letting her go. 'I should have realised how unhappy you were. I wish I'd been better at listening.'

She shook her head and when her eyes opened, they brimmed with unshed tears. 'I think we both made mistakes.' Raw emotion filled her voice. 'I'm as much to blame as you.'

She looked away to wipe the tears from her eyes.

'Thanks for telling me now how you feel, Liv. I truly wish I'd known a long time ago.'

A tiny nod.

'The only way we can make this work is if we talk.'

'Okay. I'll try.'

His heart pounded and joy rushed in. She'd agreed to give him a second chance. Okay, so maybe not in so many words, but he'd take her "I'll try" as a step forward in the right direction. For now, he couldn't ask for more than that.

Chapter 13

Olivia brushed away her tears. Knowing the truth about Chelsea was good, and a huge relief, but it didn't mean she was about to do an about face and change her mind and give Jack a second chance. At least not yet. There was a lot of hurt between them but at least they'd talked—properly for once—and although there had been raised voices, the air felt clear for the first time in forever.

She checked her watch and stood. 'Crap. Look how late it is. We need to check the kitchen.'

Jack followed her, his eyes widening as he took in the top of the line appliances. 'This is great,' he said. 'It's huge. So much space.'

'It's only two years old. You should have seen it before when I used to come down to help. It was less than half the size. Sally said it's really workable now.'

'Does Sally normally cook for the dinner on her own or does she have help?'

'She's always had lots of volunteers. Once people hear what's happened to Aimee, it will be all hands on deck. I guarantee this place will be packed with people tomorrow, all offering to help however they can. I need to know what Sally had planned or it will be chaos.'

'That's why we're here now?'

'Exactly. Sally's really organised, so she'll have lists and notes in her day planner. I'll look at what she's done already, then I'll tackle the items on her to-do list. She usually sets people up at different stations and gives them their own tasks to do.'

'What would you like me to do?'

Unsure where to start, she looked around for inspiration. None came.

'Do you know what Sally was planning in terms of a menu?' he asked.

She didn't, but she could guess. It was basically the same every year. 'Turkey for the main meal of course. Roast potatoes and vegetables. Sometimes she made soup for a starter and she used to always make this incredible traditional fruit pudding for dessert. I'm not sure if she still does.'

'Have the turkeys been defrosted? That's a good place to start.'

'I'll check.' She darted into the walk-in cool room, found the unfrozen turkeys and breathed a sigh of relief. She also found brown paper sacks of potatoes, boxes of cauliflower and broccoli and a large plastic bag of carrots. No puddings, but she found blocks of butter, trays of eggs, and bottles of cream.

She returned to Jack and reported what she'd found.

Jack grabbed a notepad and a pen and swung himself up on a bench. 'Why don't we have stuffed turkey with gravy, potatoes in cream, honeyed carrots and steamed broccoli and cauliflower in a cheese sauce.'

She was already salivating. 'That sounds perfect.'

'Someone can make the stuffing, someone can peel the carrots, someone else can do the potatoes and others can cut up the cauliflower and broccoli.'

'What about the soup though?'

'Did you see any pumpkins in the cool room?'

She shook her head. 'Not at this time of year.'

'What about leeks?'

'Not that I saw.'

'Could you buy them at the local supermarket?'

'I guess. They may not have enough but we could go into Niagara Falls—they'll have a bigger supermarket—and it's only fifteen minutes away.'

'Perfect. Why don't you make a list of what needs to be done at each station and tape it to the wall. I'll check the pantry for ingredients for the stuffing and write out some instructions for the gravy and the cheese sauce for the cauli. Okay?'

'Okay. Thanks, Jack.'

He smiled. 'My pleasure.

They got to work and a little under an hour later Olivia had seven A4 sized lists stuck on the walls above the different workstations dotted around the kitchen. She detailed what prep needed to be done—as per Jack—and what time the veggies needed to be put on.

Standing back, she surveyed their handiwork and thanked Jack once again. 'It would have taken me hours to do this on my own and honestly I wouldn't have known where to start. Thank you for helping and not taking over. I feel like we worked on this together.'

He put an arm around her shoulder and gave her a quick sideways hug that melted her insides. 'We did work together.' He planted a sneaky kiss on her temple and her heart went into overdrive. 'And now it's time to head home.'

She cast her eye around the kitchen. 'Are you sure there's nothing I could do now?'

Standing behind her, he steered her by the shoulders out the door into the restaurant. 'I promise you'll have plenty of time tomorrow. Just follow the lists.'

She chewed her lip. The pressure to succeed felt enormous and she wondered if Jack ever experienced that same pressure when he cooked. She'd never given it much thought before but it was possible once the lights and cameras were on, he felt the same burden she felt now.

'It's going to be great, Olivia. Trust yourself.'

She blew out a long breath. She didn't trust herself, but realised she was beginning to trust Jack.

After switching off the heaters and lights and locking the doors, they headed home. It was cold and while they were inside it had snowed but the sky was clear, and the stars were out.

'Did you like living in Australia?' Jack asked.

'Yeah, I did. It's a great country.'

'I sense a "but".'

She needed to tread carefully. Scarlett was born in Australia and her lawyer had told her Jack had every right to ask for shared custody. However, with his work life, the logistics would be almost impossible. But she had to face the fact that one day Jack might want Scarlett closer than Canada.

'Canada has always been home.'

'What about Noosa? Did you like living there?'

'It was alright in winter, but the summers were awful. Far too hot.' She screwed up her nose, remembering the humidity. 'The people got to me too.'

'What do you mean?'

'I understand what it's like living in a place that relies on tourism, but Noosa was off the charts—different from what I'm used to here. It was full of all these beautiful try-hards. I couldn't stand the way everyone ambled aimlessly up and down Hastings Street or sat in cafes, people-watching all day. I never felt a sense of community in Noosa. Never found people I could connect with.'

'I'm sorry.'

Another apology. 'I tried to connect. Really. But you have no idea how hard it was to find real friends once they knew I was married to you. They either wanted me to invite them around for dinner parties hoping you'd cook for them, or they wanted to see where we lived. Everyone wanted to be able to say they knew you, that they were friends with you.'

She'd hated the way people trampled over her to get to Jack, so she put up walls very early in their marriage.

'It was hard work. And when you started spending more time in Melbourne and less time at home with me, the invitations and phone calls quickly dropped off. I realised very early that people didn't want me, they wanted you.' Even admitting it aloud brought back the pain of rejection and of never feeling good enough.

'Do you think Scarlett remembers Australia?'

'Yeah. She often talks about the beach.'

It was true. Scarlett pined for the warmer weather, the bush and the beach.

Jack's phone rang. He pulled it from his pocket, glanced at it then at Olivia.

By the flush in his cheeks, no prizes for guessing who it was or what it was about. Work.

She quickened her pace to give him privacy, but it was impossible not to hear his end of the conversation.

'Maddie. Hey. What's up?'

His eyes didn't leave her face.

'Yes, I am…yes, she is…' A pause. 'I haven't checked my emails yet. I haven't had a chance…yes, I know I've been here for two days already, but I've been busy…' A longer pause. 'How urgent is it? What do they need?' He exhaled heavily. 'I can try.'

Olivia was so used to this. Interrupted conversations, interrupted dinners, interrupted sex. His phone—and Maddie—seemed to rule his life. She increased her speed. She knew what would happen. Once he was off the phone, he'd look at her, puppy-dog-apology-eyes and tell her he was so sorry, but he had to do a, b, c, or d. She could hear him already. "Sorry Olivia, they need me".

It happened so often she finally realised whoever needed him was always more important than she and Scarlett were. As much as she wanted to believe he'd changed, the proof was right in front of her. Work came first. It always would.

'I'll look at it later, Maddie. Email me what you need, I'll review the plans and get back to you.' He ended the call and pocketed his phone. 'Sorry, Olivia.'

She held her breath, waiting for the excuses to start rolling.

'As you know, unlike *Harbourside*, *Atlas* doesn't close over Christmas. And something's come up in Melbourne. Looks like we may have to delay the launch date of *Globe*.'

She kept walking.

'Olivia.' He caught her arm and pulled her to a stop.

'I meant what I said. I've changed. I'm not going to work while I'm here with you and Scarlett, but it's going to take a while for Maddie to get the message that I'm on holidays and I'm not to be contacted. Everyone else knows to leave me alone.'

She frowned. 'You told them not to contact you?'

He nodded. 'I have good managers in place. It's time I trusted them to do their jobs without me looking over their shoulders.'

He looked and sounded genuine, but time would tell. She'd place a bet that the moment they were home, he'd make some excuse to go to his room. Then he'd pull out his laptop and work until all hours the way he used to, leaving her to sit and watch television alone and go to bed on her own.

'I know work is important to you and—'

Jack put up a hand to interrupt her. 'You and Scarlett are more important than my work. You always have been. I was just lousy at showing it. I thought by working hard and setting up a great future for us, when the time was right, I'd be able to pull back and spend time with you guys without the pressure of needing to work. I realise I was wrong.'

Hot tears formed out of nowhere. He'd often said he worked to provide for her and Scarlett, but that line had always been part of the white noise. Now, for the first time, she heard him. Believed him.

'Are you crying?'

He took both her hands in his and leaned down so he could look into her eyes. 'Please Olivia, believe me. Don't cry.' He gently brushed a stray tear away with his thumb. 'I know I've done a lot of things wrong and I want to make things right. You were the best thing that ever happened to me. And when we had Scarlett, I didn't think I could be any happier.'

She started walking. 'It was so hard.'

He caught up to her. 'What was?'

The memories rushed in. 'Having Scarlett. You brought us home from the hospital and that night you went back to work. It felt like you didn't care. I had no friends, no one to call. I was alone in a new house in a new city and I didn't know a soul. I couldn't drive because of the C-section, I couldn't feed her because I was in so much pain and I couldn't even call you and ask you to come home. When you finally realised how tired I was, you hired a night nanny to help and had meals sent over from the restaurant. I think I cried more than Scarlett those first six weeks.'

'But you seemed to be doing so well. I had no idea.'

'I couldn't admit to how bad things were. Not even to myself. I was floundering, drowning. Luckily, I had a good GP. She put me on anti-depressants and linked me into a mothers' group. Scarlett and I somehow made it through the first twelve months in one piece.'

He took her hand. His fingers were icy cold. 'You had post-natal depression?'

She nodded.

'I am so sorry. I wish you'd told me.'

'I should have.' She hadn't told Jack because she'd been so excited to become a mother that admitting she felt like she was failing at motherhood and marriage merely deepened her feelings of inadequacy.

'I thought the best way for me to help you and Scarlett was earn more and get someone to help you at home. I know how tired you were, so I figured having meals sent from the restaurant was something I could do to help.' He squeezed her hand. 'I never considered it was doing the opposite.'

'It made me feel like you didn't trust me. I lost my confidence when I had Scarlett, then I felt like you lost your confidence in me too.'

'Oh, Liv. It was the opposite. I had so much confidence in you that I never stopped to ask if you were doing alright.'

They walked in silence until they arrived back at the house.

'Why did you stop going to that mothers' group?' he asked, as he pushed open the front gate.

'Most of them went back to work and it slowly fizzled out. I caught up with them every now and then, but it wasn't the same. They were either planning their next babies or they were back at work focusing on careers. I had nothing. I didn't have a job and we hadn't talked about having another baby.' She swallowed. 'When one of the girls said you were out so much you were probably having an affair, I stopped seeing them.'

'I wasn't having an affair.'

'You were having an affair with work.'

He dipped his head. 'Fair call.'

'Maybe I should have said something in those early days when I was really struggling. But you were working so hard getting *Atlas* started and you had your commitments with the network. I didn't feel as though I could give you all my problems too.'

'I wish you had.'

'Yeah. Maybe we wouldn't be where we are now.' She found a tissue in her pocket and blew her nose. 'Sorry. I usually hold it all together but seeing you again has blown the lid off. Everything I've bottled up for so long has come out.'

'I'm glad it has. I only wish we'd talked about this years ago. Tonight has been an eye-opener, that's for sure.'

Regret grabbed her by the throat and squeezed tight. Jack's sincerity was starting to melt her heart and little by little the pain of the past felt like it was easing.

He took both her hands in his. 'Liv, I'm okay if you're not ready to give me another chance as your husband.'

She held her breath. What was he going to say?

'But can we at least be friends?'

She gave a tiny nod and he pulled her into his arms and held her, offering her nothing but support and comfort—two things missing from her life for years.

Chapter 14

The house was silent when they entered, dark except for the lights on the tree. The lounge room was warm and magical. Jack expected Olivia to make an excuse about being tired and head straight for bed. Instead she offered to make him a hot chocolate. Despite being dog-tired, he said yes.

After handing him his drink, she sank into the couch and curled her feet under her. 'Want to watch a movie?'

Without waiting for his reply, she pointed the remote at the screen.

Fighting off another wave of fatigue but refusing to surrender to it, he tossed the extra throw cushions on the floor and took a seat next to her on the couch.

'Sure. What do you want to watch?'

He took a sip of his drink while she scrolled through the Netflix menu.

'Remind me to give you the Wi-Fi password so you can check your emails later and reply to Maddie.'

'Not tonight. It can wait until tomorrow.'

She glanced at him. 'Really?'

'Yeah. I told you, I'm on holidays. They can wait. So can

Maddie.'

'Your call.'

For the next hour and a bit, they watched some Hallmark Christmas movie with a title he was unlikely to remember tomorrow. In truth, the only reason he could keep his eyes open was Olivia's proximity to him. Halfway through the movie, she changed position, propping herself up with cushions and resting her crossed ankles over his thigh the way she used to sit when they watched movies together before Scarlett was born. It took all his strength not to massage her feet. She used to love it when he did that.

When the movie ended, Olivia sat up and smiled at him, and this time it reached her eyes.

'Thanks for everything tonight, Jack. I'm glad we talked.'

'It was long overdue.'

She got off the couch and straightened all the cushions. 'So? Friends?'

He nodded. 'Yeah. Friends.'

She leaned down and gave him a light peck on the cheek. 'Goodnight. Sleep well.'

Jack sat for a long time staring at the twinkling lights before going upstairs to bed.

He fell asleep filled with hope.

*

The next morning Jack woke, feeling refreshed and ready for the day. He'd slept better than he had in years. Fresh optimism burst through him when he thought about how well things had ended last night. It wasn't much—a tiny kiss on the cheek—but it was the first time Olivia had made the first move. Sure, she'd declared it was just a kiss between friends, but they had to start somewhere. Even the knowledge he hadn't checked his emails from Maddie like he'd promised didn't dampen his good mood.

He padded downstairs in socked feet and found Joan in the kitchen at the stove.

She turned around when she heard him come into the room. 'Good morning Jack. How did you sleep?'

He had a strange sense of Groundhog Day.

'Really well. Where's Olivia and Scarlett?'

'Olivia dropped Scarlett over to a friend's house for the day. She said to tell you when you woke that she'll be back to pick you up at ten, unless you want to head over to the restaurant later than that.'

'Ten sounds good.' That would give him time to check his emails. He looked around for a clock. He'd forgotten to charge his phone and had no idea of the time. 'What's the time now?'

'Ten to.'

'To what?'

'Ten.'

'What?'

Joan chuckled. 'Olivia said she turned in around eleven after the movie. Did you sit up longer than that?'

'No. I fell asleep the moment my head hit the pillow.'

'You've slept almost eleven hours. Must have needed it.' She forked two pancakes onto a plate and pushed it towards him. 'Eat.'

'I'm not hungry.'

Without asking, she poured thick maple syrup over the pancakes. 'You will be later. Trust me, when Olivia gets going, there won't be time to stop for a break. You have a big day ahead of you.'

'I need to shower and get ready before she comes back to pick me up.'

'You have plenty of time. Won't hurt the girl to eat some breakfast herself.'

Half an hour later, after he'd showered and shaved—and laughed while watching Joan force Olivia to eat a plate of pancakes—they headed back to the restaurant.

Inside, the lights were blazing and the room toasty warm, lit by the gas fire. There was an enormous log fire he hadn't notice last night, but the hearth was empty. Nearby was a box of decorations. A woman was decorating the mantlepiece.

'What time did you get here this morning?' he asked.

'I came down after eight and turned everything on, and then took Scarlett to her friend's house.'

'Thanks for letting me sleep in.'

'We tried to be as quiet as we could. I figured you probably have stayed up late working after the movie.'

He shook his head. 'After you went to bed, I wasn't far behind you. I fell straight to sleep.' He could hardly believe it himself. It usually took him a few hours and a few drinks to wind down. 'I want to know what you put in that hot chocolate.'

She chuckled. 'I told you the jetlag would get you. Was the bed okay? Were you warm enough?'

'Apart from the fact I'm about a foot too tall for a single bed, it was fine.'

She put a hand to her mouth. 'Sorry, Jack, I never thought about you not fitting into a single bed. You can sleep in my bed tonight.'

Warmth shot right through him and he grinned.

She elbowed him in the ribs. 'I'll sleep in the spare room.' She turned away, but not before he caught the cute blush on her cheeks. 'Right. Let's get to work.'

Her attempt at a businesslike tone didn't fool him but now wasn't time to push any harder. He still had eight days to go.

'What do you want me to get started on?'

'I don't know.'

'How about I make the stuffing?'

'Okay. I'll start on the potatoes.' She pulled out her phone, fiddled with it for a second and soon had it connected to a blue tooth speaker. 'Is it okay if I play music? I thought some Christmas songs would get us in the spirit of the day.'

He didn't usually like to have music on in his kitchen and Olivia knew that, but this wasn't his kitchen and he wasn't in charge. He smiled at her. 'Great idea.'

If it was another test, he hoped he'd passed. 'I'll go and see what Sally has in the pantry if that's okay with you?'

'Go ahead.'

He returned a few minutes later, his arms full. The pantry was well-stocked, and he'd found everything he needed to make stuffing. He dumped the ingredients on the bench and stopped to look around. He loved cooking and was normally totally in his element in a kitchen, but today he felt like he was caught in a rip. He was out of whack because he wasn't in charge and he had to keep reigning himself back and making sure he didn't take over. This was Olivia's show.

He had to hand it to her. She might be freaking out on the inside about preparing a meal for two hundred people. But on the outside she was as cool as a snowman. Humming along to the tunes blaring through the sound system, she worked as if she didn't have a care in the world. He knew her well enough to know she was putting on an act.

He continually caught himself watching her. For someone who had no confidence in the kitchen, she appeared to be totally in control. He'd bet she was good at her job.

As she moved around the kitchen, he imagined her in a hospital, in scrubs, moving around a patient's room. Filling them with confidence with her calmness and her ability to get the job done seamlessly.

He knew she had no catering experience, so he was staggered she'd agreed to plate up two hundred meals, especially after admitting how scared she was. That took guts and he was crazy proud of her. He made a note to remind her she was doing a great job. She had no hospitality background or experience, and she was out of her element, but she was a natural.

He had both hands shoved inside his third turkey when he

heard whistling.

'That'll be Connor,' Olivia said, looking up from the potatoes she was peeling on the other side of the kitchen.

A broad-shouldered man in an oversized khaki camouflage snow jacket filled the doorway. He entered the room, eyes on Olivia. He hadn't yet spotted Jack.

'Hey, lovely Liv, I heard you're in charge today. What do you need me to do?'

His smile was a little too wide, his tongue hung out a little too far and he reminded Jack of an old dog at an animal shelter, hoping he'd be the next one to be adopted. Jack bristled when Connor greeted Olivia with a kiss on the cheek. Then Jack was further irritated when she didn't appear to try to deflect his slimy lips. Whoever this Connor guy was, he was a complication Jack hadn't anticipated.

Olivia smiled at him. 'Hey, Connor. Thanks for coming in early.'

'No problem. I've got my truck parked out the side. I went and got a load of firewood. Les rang me and said they were running low and he'd forgotten to stock up.'

'Great. Thanks. I saw the woodpile but didn't have time to think about it.'

'Once I've unloaded the wood, I'll start setting up the tables for you.'

'Thanks. I appreciate it.'

'Anything for you.'

Jack cleared his throat and Connor turned and saw him. 'Hey, man.'

'Jack, this is Connor Davidson. He owns one of the local cafes and he'll be making coffees tonight. Connor, this is Jack.' She hesitated. 'Scarlett's dad.'

'Ah, right.'

Connor nodded a greeting, but didn't smile, and his eyes darkened. If Connor was a dog, his hackles would be up. Jack wondered what Olivia had told Connor about him.

'You're the ex, right?'

Jack chose to ignore that. 'G'day mate. I'd shake your hand, but—' He pulled his hands from the turkey and put them in the air. Breadcrumbs and onion and herbs and spices fell to the floor.

'Nah, you keep doing what you're doing. Olivia tells me you're a famous chef back in Oz.'

'I have my own restaurant, yes.'

'Two restaurants. And his own cooking show,' Olivia said. Jack was pleased to note the hint of pride in her voice.

'Yeah, well, no cameras here, so it'll be interesting to see if you can perform.'

Jack wanted to deck the guy. Instead, he smiled politely and stuffed the final bird. He wiped his hands on his apron, put the turkeys in the ovens and adjusted the temperature. The plan was to cook them first, cut them up, then reheat the meat after the scalloped potatoes were cooked.

'Jack's made a special stuffing for the turkeys and he's going to do something incredible for dessert,' Olivia told Connor.

Jack stared at her in surprise. He didn't recall offering to do dessert. Then he remembered they'd talked about the missing Christmas puddings and he'd promised to think of something. He hadn't given it another thought.

'Wait until you taste Jack's pavlova. It's like nothing you've ever eaten.'

'That right?' Connor looked at him. 'Sounds like the pressure's really on. Hope you can take the heat in the kitchen.'

Jack waited to see how many more clichés the guy could throw. When there were no more forthcoming, he lifted a shoulder. 'No pressure.'

He was lying. There was definitely plenty of pressure now. This dinner couldn't be a flop or everyone would blame Olivia and he wasn't going to stand by and let that happen. It was time he showed her what he was capable of.

He headed to the pantry to see how many eggs Sally had, while he calculated how many pavlovas he'd need to make to feed two hundred people. And cream. Did he have enough cream?

'Wanna give me a hand with the firewood?' Connor called out.

Jack groaned inwardly. He knew what game this jerk was up to and he wasn't falling for it. Still, he'd told Olivia he was happy to help with whatever needed doing and having wood for the fire was important. 'Sure,' he replied.

'I'll wait outside,' Connor said, stomping off.

'Douche.' He whipped the apron over his head and laid it on the bench.

'Sorry, Connor can be like that.'

'I'll show him.'

'It's not a competition, Jack.'

He heard her warning tone and chose to disregard it. 'Might not be to you.'

She rolled her eyes. 'In the office on your way out, there's a cupboard behind the door. In there, you'll find thick work gloves. You'll need them. Don't do anything stupid. Connor's strong.'

'And I'm not?'

She gave him a quick onceover. 'Unless you've been hitting the gym over the last eighteen months, then I'd suggest you're not as fit as you'll need to be to keep up with Connor.'

'I'll be okay.'

'Please don't do anything stupid and hurt yourself. I need your help in here more than I need firewood chopped.'

What an idiot. Olivia needed him. Connor did not. Still, he had offered to help the bloke. He stood, vacillating.

Olivia flicked a head towards the door. 'Go and help him first.'

'You sure?'

'I'm okay in here for now.'

Half an hour later, they'd emptied the back of Connor's

oversized truck and the woodpile was stocked high. He'd kept up with Connor, but he knew he'd pay for it tomorrow. Already, every muscle ached. Other than running, he wasn't used to this type of physical labour.

Connor pulled off his gloves and shoved them in his coat. Jack's own jacket was ruined, the thin nylon ripped to shreds by the wood, duck down feathers flying in the breeze. He'd worry about that tomorrow.

'What's the deal with you and Olivia?' Connor asked, leaning against his truck.

'No deal.' *And none of your business.*

'What are you doing here then?'

'Spending Christmas with my daughter.'

'Right.'

'What are *you* doing?'

Connor frowned. 'What do you mean?'

'You know she's still married?'

Connor puffed out his chest. 'Not what she told me.'

Jack ignored the comment. 'We finished here?' He didn't wait for Connor's reply. 'Because I've got real work to do inside.' In truth, he wanted to go inside because the cold air was biting him through his thin coat, but he wasn't going to let Connor know that.

The brawny man eyeballed him. 'No. We're not finished.'

'Yeah, mate, we are.' Jack turned on his heel and walked away.

Chapter 15

With Jack outside, Olivia went back to peeling potatoes and tried to ignore the rhythmic thump of wood against wood as the two men restocked the woodpile. The sound accelerated as if they were seriously competing to see who could go the fastest. Typical. And so annoying. Connor's attention was impossible to ignore at the best of times, but today he'd taken it up three notches the moment he'd met Jack.

She sighed. At least Jack's presence would discourage Connor.

Olivia had almost finished peeling the last potato when she heard soft footsteps outside. She looked up to see her best friend Lexie, takeaway coffee in one hand, shopping bags in the crook of the other elbow. Even with her hands full she somehow managed to pull off her cap revealing a thick springy mass of tight black curls.

'Hi, Lex.'

'Hey.' Lexie dumped her shopping bags on the bench.

'Thanks for bringing me coffee.'

Lexie screwed up her face. 'Sorry. Hands were full.' She took a sip from her cup and sighed. 'Tastes good.'

'Tease. I thought you were working today.' Olivia worked with Lexie in the Intensive Care Unit at the Niagara Falls hospital.

'The unit was quiet. They offered me the day off. I had a ton of shopping to finish so I said yes.'

'Did you hear about Les and Sally's daughter?'

Lexie nodded. 'As soon as I heard you were going ahead with the dinner, I came down to see if I can help. Has there been any news on the baby?'

'I had a text early this morning from Sally with a photo. They had a bit of a scare, but Aimee and baby are fine despite how early she is. Twenty-eight weeks. They've named her Hope.' She handed Lexie the phone and her friend squinted at the screen.

'Man, that's a tiny baby. It's amazing how they use all the same equipment we have in ICU, but in miniature size. I take my hat off to the paediatric team. I couldn't do it.' She gave the phone back. 'What time did you get here this morning?'

'Early. I'm okay now but I'll need all the help I can get this afternoon if I want to have dinner on the table by six.'

'I'm more than happy to help. Where's my little princess?'

'She's at Beck's place playing with Noah.' Beck was a friend Olivia had made through Scarlett's child care centre.

'Nice one.' Lexie drained the last of her coffee and rolled up her sleeves. 'Want me to start cutting the potatoes?'

Olivia handed her a knife. 'In slices please.'

'Not going to roast them this year?'

'No, we're having them au gratin this year.'

'Very fancy.' She began slicing the potatoes. 'Any idea who the mystery hunk is outside with Connor?'

Olivia pulled out large roasting pans and put them on the bench next to Lexie so she could start layering the potatoes. 'Scarlett's father.'

The knife fell from Lexie's hand and clattered on the tiled floor. 'I'm sorry. What? Did you say Scarlett's dad? *That's* Jack?'

Olivia nodded.

'He's hot.'

Olivia felt a flush creep up her neck. 'He might be hot, but you know as well as I do that he's not on the scene.'

Lexie bent down to pick up the knife. 'Ah, I hate to point out the obvious, Liv, he's outside stacking wood. I'd say he's definitely on the scene.' She waved the knife. 'What's the deal and why didn't you tell me he was coming?'

'I didn't tell anyone.' Olivia took the knife from Lexie, went to the sink and washed it before handing it back. 'He wants to get back together.'

Lexie's mouth dropped open.

'Keep slicing.' Olivia pointed to the potatoes. 'I'm already running behind schedule and I need to start on the other veggies.'

'I can cut while you talk. Details. Now.'

By the time Olivia had finished filling Lexie in, there was no sound coming from outside.

'What are you going to do?' Lexie asked.

'If you'd asked me yesterday, I would have said I'd tell him to go jump.'

'But today?'

'Today, I don't know,' Olivia conceded. 'We talked for hours yesterday, cleared up some things.'

A lot of things.

'And you're starting to wonder if he's not as bad as you've made him out to be?'

Olivia inspected her fingernails. 'He says he's changed.'

'What do you think?' Lexie asked.

Olivia looked up and sighed. 'I think he's telling the truth. He's different.'

'Hmm. You're not over him.'

'I know. I thought I was, but—'

'Just because you're not over him isn't a reason to get back with him.'

Olivia smiled. That was why Lexie was her best friend. She

understood Olivia's turmoil. 'Exactly. I don't know if I can. I certainly know I can't go back to the way things were.'

'What are you going to do?'

'That's the problem. I don't know. He's only here until New Year's Day, then he'll go back to Australia.'

'You always said you loved Australia.'

'I can't, Lex. I can't go back to the life we had. We never saw him. It's not fair on Scarlett.'

'And what; you think it's fair on Scarlett now? She has a father she hasn't seen in twelve months. At least if you were in the same country, even if Jack is as busy as you say he is, he can see a lot more of Scarlett than he does now.'

'But I have a support network here that I didn't have in Australia. I have you and Beck and Nan and Paul and Sally and Les. One of the reasons I left was because Jack was never around. If I go back and things are the same as the way they were, that's not fair on Scarlett or me. I have to do what's best for her.'

'I get that. But I'm not sure being separated from her dad is the best thing long-term.'

Olivia chewed her bottom lip and stared at her friend. Lexie had a point. A good point. She knew well enough what it was like not having parents. It was only going to get harder to figure out custody issues the older Scarlett got. What if she wanted to live with Jack instead of her?

Boots stomped on the doormat and moments later Jack entered the room. His face was flushed, his eyes shining. The black fabric of his jacket was shredded to pieces, but he looked . . . happy. Yeah, he looked genuinely happy.

He smiled and something zinged in the air between them. Her breath caught and she looked away but not before seeing the smile on his face. Yeah, he'd sensed it too. Something in her had shifted last night.

Lexie didn't wait to be introduced. She walked over to Jack, beaming, her teeth white against her dark chocolate skin.

'Hi, honey. I'm Lexie. Olivia's best friend. Don't be surprised if she's never mentioned me. She never mentioned you either.'

Jack shook her outstretched hand and laughed. 'Nice to meet you, Lexie.' He glanced at Olivia then back to Lexie. 'I guess Olivia has filled you in now?'

'She has. She says you want to get back together.'

'Lexie,' Olivia warned with an eye roll. Lexie had zero filter.

Jack shot Olivia another look. 'Yeah. Yeah, I do want us to get back together, but right now I'm settling for us working on our friendship.'

'Hmph. If she says yes, sounds like you'll need to make some changes in your life.'

'Big changes. Yes. Yeah, I know,' Jack stammered.

'Good.' Lexie rubbed her hands together. 'Right. Glad we have that sorted. Now. Apparently you're some sort of celebrity chef. Sorry I've never heard of you, but I don't tend to watch cooking shows. Are you up for this?'

'This?'

'The community meal. I presume you're here to weave your magic.'

'Actually, no. I'm here to help Olivia, if she needs me.'

'Oh listen, honey, she needs your help. I've volunteered at this event for years, and it can turn into a zoo at a moment's notice.'

Jack looked away but Olivia caught the smirk on his face.

'*Lexie,*' she warned.

'What?' Lexie raised her eyebrows. 'It's true. You need help. You can't be expected to do this on your own.'

'I'm not on my own. I asked you to help and by this afternoon this kitchen will be swarming with others.'

Lexie shrugged. 'Still, you need someone in charge. I vote for Jack.'

'I didn't ask for your vote.'

Lexie checked her watch. 'Is that the time? Oh gosh. I have to get to the supermarket before it closes.' She passed the knife to

Jack. 'Looks like you're on veggie duties. But watch out, if you don't do it right, she'll let you know about it.'

Lexie grabbed her coat, flung it over her arm. She kissed Olivia on the cheek, waved to Jack and disappeared.

'Sorry about that,' Olivia said after the door had closed behind her. 'Lexie is a whirlwind.'

'She seems nice.'

'She is. She's amazing. She's like family to Scarlett. We work together at the hospital and she's become one of my best friends.'

'I must remember to thank her properly if I see her again.'

'You will. She'll be back later. She won't be able to help herself. In case you didn't notice, she likes to keep her nose in other people's business. I guarantee she'll want to hang around and check you out.'

'Keep me in line.'

'Yeah, that too.'

'What do you need me to do?'

Olivia checked her watch. 'Crap. I need to get these potatoes in the oven.' But first she needed to cut the onions and mince the garlic and melt the butter.

Lexie forgotten, Olivia's heart sped and her mind raced. How much milk did the potatoes need? And did they have enough cream? And what type of cheese would melt best so the top of the potatoes would be perfectly browned?

'Olivia.'

She looked up. 'What?'

'Stop.'

She exhaled loudly. 'I can't do this.'

'You already are. And you're doing a great job.'

She frowned at the unexpected compliment and the kindness in his tone. She'd never seen him at work in the kitchen, but for some reason she'd presumed he'd be a tyrant. One of those chefs who barked orders and instructions and berated his staff. She couldn't be more wrong. What she'd seen so far here was the total opposite.

'You okay?' he asked gently.

'Fine,' she lied.

He washed his knife and lay it down on the bench. 'All right, where are we up to?'

She wiped her hands on her apron and exhaled loudly. 'To be honest, I have no idea. It's all too much. I don't know what to start on next. The other vegetables. The desserts.' She picked up the master list and scanned it. It was already two o'clock and they hadn't even set up the restaurant yet. 'The turkeys are on.' She ticked that off the list. 'Potatoes peeled.' Another tick. 'I guess I should—'

'Guess you should stop while I make you a cuppa and something to eat. You haven't stopped all day.'

She glanced up at him. 'But I can't. There's still so much to do.'

'And hours left to get it done.' He took her by the arm and gently pulled her out of the kitchen and sat her in a chair near the fire. They had the empty restaurant to themselves. 'Sit. I'll make you a sandwich.'

Even though he only touched her sweater not her skin, the contact sent heat travelling up her arm and through her body. When their eyes connected, she felt it again, that tiny spark. She was once again hit with the knowledge that despite how unhappy she was *in* her marriage she was equally unhappy out of it, if not more so. And last night had cleared up so much of the misunderstanding she'd allowed to come between them.

He was back moments later with a simple ham, lettuce and mustard sandwich for both of them, a cup of coffee for himself and a peppermint tea for her.

'Tell me more about this community meal,' he said, between mouthfuls.

'It's been going for years. As long as I can remember. One of the local churches started it, but it outgrew their premises and Les and Sally offered to run it. They've hosted it for the last ten years. The churches and organisations like Zonta and Rotary get together and fundraise. They provide money to buy the food, but the bulk of the actual work on the day is done by Sally and the volunteers.'

'And anyone can come?'

She nodded. 'It's for anyone who doesn't feel they belong ,or for anyone who doesn't have family to spend Christmas with. You'll see the very poor and the very rich sitting side by side eating the same meal. Finding out that despite how much money they have in their wallet, deep down, they have something in common. A desire to be part of a community.'

'And it's free.'

'Totally free.'

'Amazing.'

'It is. The churches have a combined choir and they put on a small Christmas nativity play for the kids. Last year I heard they used a real baby to be baby Jesus and they even had live animals. Scarlett would have loved to see that.'

'And you used to come here as a kid?'

'Every year. Nan was on the committee.'

'I can see how much it means to you.'

'It does mean a lot.'

'You know, seeing you here has shown me a different side of you. I don't want this to come out the wrong way.' He rubbed his jaw. 'I've seen a more vulnerable side of you here.'

She blinked.

He exhaled. 'I know I'm not going to say this right, so hear me out. Last night we talked a lot and I went to bed thinking about what you told me. There was so much I could have said yesterday but I was reeling from some of the things you shared. I always thought you were so self-sufficient, so capable. Able to cope with everything. When you moved to the other side of the world to join me six weeks after we met, I thought you were the bravest person I knew. Every time I suggested we do something, you were always up for the challenge. Then you gave birth to Scarlett and I was in awe of you. The whole labour thing, then breastfeeding on no sleep. Was there nothing you couldn't do?'

She frowned. Where was he going with this?

'I didn't think you needed me, Liv. I thought you could manage without me. And I wanted you to need me. I wanted you to ask me to help you. I wanted you to crack a little bit, to be vulnerable, to show me that you didn't have it all together.'

She frowned. 'But I didn't. I don't.'

'I know, I know.' Jack rushed on. 'I can see that now. I can see you put on a mask and pretended everything was okay. But at the time I believed you didn't need me, so I let myself get tied up with work and I found people who *did* need me.'

A cold feeling dropped into her stomach. 'Did I push you away?'

He tugged at his sleeves and leaned in. 'No. You are *not* to blame.'

The intensity of his words came as a surprise.

'I should have asked how you were doing, asked if you were coping, asked if you were happy.'

Drawing a deep breath, he took both her hands in his. 'Liv, I know I've already told you, but I want to say it again. I still care for you, deeply. I know you're okay with us being friends, and I said I was okay with that. But truth is, I really want you to give me another chance to be your husband.'

She swallowed. After all he'd done—and hadn't done—after all the hurt they'd caused each other, there was still something there. It was small, but it was something to build on. But she still wasn't certain if it was enough for her to give him the second chance he was so desperate for. They sat, gazing at each other until she lost all sense of time.

A cough interrupted them, snapping the connection between them. They jumped as though they were a pair of kids about to share their first kiss.

Connor stood in the doorway with an older couple Olivia didn't recognise.

He removed his hat and had the grace to look embarrassed that he'd interrupted something. 'Mom and Dad offered to help.'

Feeling like her face was on fire, Olivia strode over to the couple, hand outstretched. 'That's awesome, thank you. I'm Olivia.'

Connor's father shook her hand firmly. 'Steve. And this is my wife, Angela. Connor said you could do with some help down here setting things up for tonight.'

'I've called a few friends from my bible study group,' Angela said with a smile. 'They're on their way.' She removed her coat, pulled an apron from her bag and slipped it over her head. 'Point me in the right direction and let me know what needs doing.'

Olivia risked a glance at Jack. The poor guy had shared his soul and they'd been interrupted before she'd had a chance to respond. She expected to see a scowl on his face, but he was smiling, eyes bright.

She needed time to process everything he'd said, but there was one thing she didn't need time to think about. It was time to admit defeat and ask for help.

She gave him her biggest smile. 'Jack? Would you mind helping me please?'

He returned her smile. 'I'd love to. Tell me what you'd like me to do.'

She chuckled. 'I want you to take over this whole thing and make it happen. I am totally out of my depth, in over my head, drowning.'

His smile broadened. 'It would be my pleasure.'

'This is Jack,' Olivia said, introducing him to Steve and Angela. 'He's a chef.'

'The food's in good hands then,' Steven said. He gazed around the restaurant. 'But by the look of this, we have plenty of work to do out here.'

'We do,' Olivia agreed. 'Come on, I'll show you what needs to be done.'

For the next two hours, the front door opened and closed as people arrived to help. The event preparation turned into an event of its own. Olivia ducked into the kitchen every so often to check on Jack. He had every volunteer in the room eating out of his hands.

It was good to watch him in action in his own environment. He was kind, friendly, helpful, encouraging and fun. He engaged with everyone in the room, moving from person to person, smiling and laughing, organising, tasting. Exactly the way he was portrayed by the cameras. She'd always presumed everything about Jack was scripted, but if what she was seeing was true, the man in the kitchen was, in fact, the real Jack.

At one point, Jack appeared bearing a plate of warm chocolate cake and everyone stopped for a quick break before getting stuck back into setting up.

By four o'clock they'd finished setting up and decorating the venue. The volunteers headed home to get changed before coming back again to help serve the guests. When the room was empty, Olivia looked around and released a satisfied sigh.

She found Jack alone in the kitchen. She caught him with his finger in his mouth, eyes closed, having obviously just finished licking a bowl.

She coughed, and his eyes opened. He flashed a guilty smile.

'What are you doing?' she asked.

'I had to taste the chocolate sauce. Make sure it was okay.'

Olivia chuckled. He'd always had a sweet tooth. 'What's the sauce for?'

'I'm going to drizzle it over the pavs.'

'Sounds good. Is it your original recipe?' Early in their marriage he'd perfected a chocolate sauce that she used to love served warm over vanilla ice cream.

He nodded.

Heart pounding, she walked around the bench and took the bowl from his hands. Memories flooded in. 'Can I have a taste?'

He held the bowl out and she took it from him and ran her finger around the edge, scooping up the sauce. Bringing it to her lips she closed her eyes, savouring the familiar dark chocolate taste.

'Mmm. Amazing.'

'Taste okay?'

She dipped her finger back in the bowl. 'Just like I remember, maybe even better. It's been a while.'

'It has been a while.'

She handed him back the bowl and he took it to the sink and washed it out.

'Thanks for everything you did today, Jack. I appreciate it.'

He turned and smiled. 'I enjoyed it. It's been a fun day.'

She smirked. 'Fun, eh? Even your wood stacking competition with Connor was fun?'

He laughed. 'I had something to prove.'

'Looks like we both had something to prove today. I bet you'll regret it tomorrow.'

'There's not a chance I'll regret anything about this day. You've done a great job, Liv,' he said, suddenly serious. 'It's going to be a great dinner tonight. A huge success.'

'Thank you.'

'No. Thank *you*. For everything.'

Chapter 16

If Jack was a praying man, he would have thanked God with every fibre of his being for the glow in Olivia's eyes when they left the restaurant. It had taken every ounce of his self-control not to gather her in his arms and kiss her when she ran her finger around the edge of the bowl and brought his chocolate sauce to her lips. His breath quickened and he felt warm all over at the memory. She clearly had no idea how sexy that was.

Emotion swelled in his chest and clogged his throat. Olivia was softening, showing small signs that she might be prepared to give him another chance. He didn't want to rush her, but his time was limited. Everything in him wanted to get down on one knee and start over, but the timing had to be right.

They walked back to the house side-by-side and Olivia stunned him again by tucking her gloved hand into the crook of his arm. An icy wind pushed them along but despite his shredded coat, he barely felt it. The warmth emanating from her was enough to ward off any chill. Not even the fact he still hadn't checked his emails and replied to Maddie like he'd promised wasn't enough to spoil the moment. With any luck he'd be able to log on later tonight after the dinner. Until then, he was ignoring the notifications that kept popping up on his phone.

'It's going to snow again tonight,' Olivia said as she released his arm and pushed open the front gate.

He glanced into the dark, cloudless, star-filled sky. He didn't know much about snow but he presumed it formed in clouds like rain. 'How can you tell? Is that some Canadian thing? I've noticed the weather is the first thing everyone talks about.'

She chuckled. 'I checked the weather app. And yes, you're right, we do talk about the weather, especially this time of year.'

Olivia inserted the key in the lock and they'd barely stepped foot inside when Scarlett threw herself at Jack, bypassing Olivia. Jack swept their daughter up in a hug then deposited her on the ground again.

'What happened to your coat?' Scarlett asked, fingering the ripped fabric. She looked up at Jack, eyes wide. 'Was it a bear?'

Jack chuckled. He was tempted to make up a big story. 'No. Turns out my Australian jacket isn't really good enough for a Canadian winter.'

Scarlett's face fell. 'Oh.'

'Everything ready for tonight?' Joan called out.

'It sure is,' Olivia replied. 'Jack did an amazing job.'

Hearing the pride in her voice, his heart swelled. He pulled off his boots and tossed his ruined coat on top of them before following Olivia into the lounge room and going straight to the fire to warm up. He was soon joined by Scarlett. When Olivia warned her not to stand so close, she obeyed, inching forward, but she stuck like glue to his side. Jack hadn't realised how much he'd missed his daughter. Jack wanted to savour every moment he had with Scarlett before his return to Australia.

But as much as he longed to spend time with his daughter, he also needed Olivia to himself. His Christmas present for her was a night's accommodation in Huntsville where he'd arranged a dog-sledding experience, something Joan assured him Olivia had never done. Joan and Paul had willingly agreed to look after Scarlett so they could get away for the night. He wasn't sure how he'd go convincing Olivia it was a good idea, but he figured with Joan and Paul in his corner, his chances were high.

'Thanks for looking after Scarlett this afternoon. I didn't realise it would take us so long,' Olivia said.

As Jack sank into the couch he looked closely at Joan. She looked a little tired, but it was clear how much joy she took in looking after Scarlett. A joy Jack wanted to get back into his own life.

'What time are you heading back to the restaurant?' Joan asked.

'Jack?'

He blinked. 'Sorry, what did you say?'

Olivia looked to him with a questioning gaze. 'What time do we need to go back?'

'We don't need to be back there until after five. Everything is done, but if you want to start serving just after six, I'd like to be there at least half an hour beforehand.'

'I'm going to have a shower then.'

After Olivia had disappeared up the stairs with Scarlett in tow, Joan cleared her throat. 'Jack? You okay?'

He shook his head to clear it. 'Yeah. I was thinking about what I'm going to do if she won't come home with me.'

'Baby steps, Jack. Don't worry about tomorrow until tomorrow comes.' She smiled. 'At least she's not angry with you all the time now.'

'A definite improvement,' he agreed. He scratched his jaw. 'But she'll never leave Canada. Never leave you. I saw the way she was today at the restaurant. She loves being part of this community, and everyone adores her. She has her job here, her life, everything.' Everything but him, but he wasn't yet convinced she wanted or needed him any longer.

'I feel so bad that you're left to look after Scarlett so often.'

'It's my pleasure. She's a darling girl and I love taking care of her.' Joan's smile broadened.

'Does Olivia know about the house yet? About you and Paul?'

Colour tinged Joan's cheeks. 'Not yet. We've decided to tell her everyone on Christmas Day.'

'Do Paul's kids know?' Paul spoke fondly of his sons, daughters-in-law and grandchildren.

'Not yet but I'm sure they'll be thrilled for both of us.'

'As Olivia will be.'

'I hope so, Jack. I hope so.'

'Sounds like we're both hoping for similar things.'

'It does,' Joan agreed.

'Any news from Les and Sally?'

'The baby was born very early this morning. A little girl they've called Hope. She's in the neonatal intensive care unit at Mount Sinai and has a long road ahead of her. Sally and Les are going to stay in Toronto with Aimee for as long as it takes. Aimee lost her husband six months ago, not long after she found out she was pregnant.'

'Tough gig.'

'Very.'

'What's going to happen to the restaurant?'

'Nothing. It's always quiet this time of year. I imagine they'll re-open in the summer. Or they'll sell up and stay in Peterborough.'

He checked his watch and was startled by how much time had slipped by. 'I'd better take a quick shower.' He turned to head upstairs and bumped into Paul coming in from the mudroom. 'Sorry. I didn't hear you come in.'

'Back door,' Paul said, pointing. 'Easier for me to walk across the yard and that way Joanie doesn't have to get up and answer the front door.' Paul winked at Jack.

Jack smiled. Paul and Joan made a great couple.

'I'll drive Joan to the restaurant later. It's a bit hard for her to walk that far now. We can bring Scarlett in with us if it makes it easier for you and Olivia.'

Jack hesitated. The gleam in Paul's eyes suggested he and Joan had hatched a plan to ensure Jack and Olivia had as much alone time as possible. He was about to agree that it was a good plan when Scarlett interrupted from the top of the stairs.

'I want to go with you and Mummy.'

In the lounge, Joan laughed. 'I don't need my sight to see the look on her little face.'

Scarlett had her hands on her hips, looking adorably cute with her stubborn frown. Like her mother.

'You can come with Mummy and me. I'm going to have a shower then we'll head out.' He couldn't resist tickling Scarlett as he walked past.

He showered quickly, with the sound of Scarlett's giggles ringing in his ears.

Twenty minutes later he helped Scarlett into her coat and mittens. Such a simple act, but it felt massive. Without even realising it, he'd let Olivia do everything for Scarlett because he assumed Olivia didn't need his help. Rather than asking what she needed or wanted from him, he'd subconsciously made those decisions for her. Now was his chance to make it up to her. If she'd let him.

He reached for his wrecked coat and sighed. The duck down stuffing was coming out of the sleeves and front.

'Do you want to borrow Granddad's coat?' Olivia asked.

He tilted his head and looked up at her. 'Are you sure?'

In answer, she pulled the coat from the hanger and passed it to him. 'It'll probably swim on you, but it will be warm.'

He thanked her as he slipped his arms into the sleeves.

She reached into the cupboard and pulled out a box from the top shelf. 'Grab some gloves and a hat too. I'm sorry I only just realised you didn't have gloves or a hat. You must have been freezing. Why didn't you say something?'

He wanted to remind her that she'd initially baulked at him

borrowing her grandad's gear, but it wasn't necessary. He rifled through the box and found a pair of thick gloves and an ugly Christmas beanie with deer antlers. Tiny bells hung from the tips of the antlers.

Olivia laughed. 'I'd forgotten that was in there. I bought it for Grandad one year as a joke.'

He pulled it over his ears and shook his head.

Scarlett giggled.

'Right then, are we ready?'

'You can't wear that. What will people think?'

'Who cares?'

Her eyes widened. 'If someone recognises you and takes a photo, you'll look stupid.'

'I don't care who sees me, Olivia. It's Christmas and I'm in Canada with my family. If I dress up in an elf suit and someone wants to snap a photo of me and post it on social media, they can go ahead. Who knows, the publicity might be good.'

She didn't look like she believed him.

Stepping out into the moonlit evening, it felt totally natural to take Scarlett's mitten-clad hand in his. Olivia took Scarlett's other hand and they walked along the freshly-shovelled footpath swinging Scarlett between them, her laughter echoing through the cold night. The frostiness had disappeared from Olivia's expression, replaced by smiles and laughter that changed her whole face. Joy mixed with hope swelled in his chest and knotted in his throat. This is what he'd always wanted, a proper family. He'd lost it once, and he was desperate to get it back for more than ten days.

They arrived at the restaurant too soon. He could have walked around town for two hours just to spend more time with her.

Once inside they shed their outer wear, Scarlett found her friend, Noah, and disappeared. Jack soon lost sight of Olivia as she got caught up greeting people and playing the role of hostess. He headed into the kitchen and found everything in order. If he could bottle up whatever these volunteers had, he could open restaurants around the world. They had passion, enthusiasm and great attitudes. And every one of them raved about how special Olivia was and how much they loved her.

No wonder she was happy here. She had family, friends, and a job she enjoyed. She had people around her who loved and valued her, and made her feel needed and special. She'd found a community here, in total contrast to the isolation she'd experienced back in Australia.

No wonder she'd been so unhappy there. It took a lifetime to grow roots like this, and he'd asked her to abandon those connections and replant herself wherever he wanted to work next.

Once again, he was struck by how impossible his task was. He couldn't see why she would give up all of this for him, even if he could convince her he'd changed. It wasn't fair of him to ask her to leave all this behind.

Joan's advice rang in his ears—not to worry about tomorrow, but tomorrow was almost upon him. And as far as he could see, it didn't look much different from today.

He was coming to understand why Olivia had left him. They'd shared the same surname, the same bed, the same address and they had a child. But while they'd been physically intimate, there'd been little to no emotional connection. Despair sagged his shoulders and threatened to weigh him down, but he forced himself not to think about it. Tonight he would focus on the community meal and when he woke tomorrow, he'd worry about the rest of the week.

The next time he stuck his head out of the kitchen he was amazed at the sight that greeted him. The room was packed and not a single seat was spare. There had to be over a hundred people in the room. His gaze found Olivia's and he gave her the thumbs up sign.

'Ready,' he mouthed.

She nodded, picked up a glass and fork and tapped gently until she had everyone's attention. It took a while for everyone to hush, then the music dropped in volume so Olivia could be heard.

'I want to thank everyone for coming.' Her voice was clear, strong and sweet. 'As most of you know, Les and Sally's daughter Aimee went into labour early and they had to do an emergency caesarean. I've spoken to Sally, and she asked me to tell you all that Aimee is doing well. The baby, Hope, isn't out of the woods yet, but she's in excellent hands. Sally and Les also asked me to thank the volunteers for stepping up and helping to make this event happen tonight.'

There were murmurs of "hear, hear" and "amen" among the guests and volunteers.

Jack didn't take his eyes off Olivia. She looked so in control and self-assured standing in front of the crowd. But now he knew there was another side to her, a side that didn't know how to ask for help.

'Tonight wouldn't have happened without the incredible help from the community.' She took a moment to smile and look around the room. 'Many of you here came in today to help us set up.' She glanced towards the kitchen. 'I know there are at least half a dozen volunteers in the kitchen working hard to make sure we enjoy this meal. Can we take a moment to thank them?'

The crowd burst into cheers and claps and whoops.

'I'd especially like to acknowledge one special man.'

Jack's heart stilled for a second before it started beating again, much faster.

Olivia beckoned for him to join her. 'Everyone, this is Jack Carter. Most of you won't have heard of him, but if you Google him, you'll discover he's a renowned executive chef. He runs a Michelin-starred restaurant in Australia, and he has his own television show.'

The murmuring increased and Olivia waited for it to die down.

'I personally watched Jack prepare tonight's meal, and let me say, you're in for a special treat. He's taken our annual community dinner to the next level.' She put her arm around his waist and pulled him close. 'What you also may not know is that Jack is Scarlett's dad.' She paused, smiled at him. 'And he's my husband.'

She stood on tiptoes and kissed his cheek and he had to stop himself from touching the spot where the warmth of her lips lingered.

'Please put your hands together and thank Jack.'

He gave a little wave and for the first time ever, felt a wave of embarrassment sweep over him. The dinner wasn't about him. It was about the community. And it was about all that Olivia had achieved.

After the clapping slowed, Olivia indicated a young man seated nearby. 'Before we eat, Pastor Brad is going to say grace. Then I'll call you by table to come to the servery window and receive your meals. Enjoy your dinner, and Merry Christmas everyone.'

As Brad prayed, Jack dashed back to the kitchen to supervise. He needn't have bothered. The volunteers had everything under control

The evening wound down around eight-thirty. When Jack tracked down Scarlett, he found her playing with a group of older kids. He picked her up and a fierce protective love filled him when Scarlett wrapped her arms around his neck.

'I reckon it's past your bedtime, sweetie.'

'I'm not tired.' Scarlett stifled a yawn.

'Yeah, me neither.'

He hoisted Scarlett onto his hip and found Olivia in the kitchen chatting to a group of women including her friend, Lexie. They stopped talking as soon as he came in and Olivia blushed. He didn't have to be Einstein to know he was the topic of conversation.

'Do you want me to take Scarlett home?' he asked.

'Would you mind? I'll be hours here cleaning up.'

'I'll put her to bed and come back and help if you like.'

'No, it's all good. We've got it covered.'

He struggled with a mix of guilt and pleasure. He was happy to care for Scarlett, and he was thrilled that Olivia trusted him to take their daughter through her nightly routine. But he felt bad about not staying to help clean up. And he felt worse at the knowledge that once Scarlett was in bed, he'd have to tackle his emails. He knew he was in for a late night but didn't want Olivia to know he planned to work. He didn't care if he had to pull an all-nighter, if it meant he was awake to see Scarlett's face when she realised Santa had been overnight.

'We can take Scarlett home,' Paul said, appearing in the kitchen with Joan on his arm.

Scarlett gripped Jack tighter around the neck and latched onto him like a monkey, wrapping her legs around his waist. 'No. I want Daddy to take me home.'

Jack looked at Olivia. It was her decision.

'It will be good for Scarlett to have Jack tuck her in,' Olivia said. 'And tomorrow is a big day. She'll be up earlier than usual.'

'You and Jack take Scarlett home, Olivia,' Lexie said. 'I don't need to be up early. I'll help clean up here.'

'There's no rush to put the tables back,' Paul said. 'Sally and Les won't be re-opening. As long as the kitchen is clean and any leftovers are stored, you can come back after Christmas and do what needs to be done.'

'You're right,' Olivia agreed, removing her apron and placing it on the bench. 'Such a shame, this might have been our last ever community Christmas dinner.'

Nan tucked her arm around Olivia's waist. 'I know, sweetheart, but sometimes one door has to close so you'll look for a window.'

Chapter 17

It didn't take long for Scarlett to fall asleep. The house was quiet, and Olivia was straightening up presents under the tree when she overhead Jack on the phone in the next room. The walls of the old house were paper thin, and Jack probably had no idea she would hear every word of his side of the conversation. His first call was obviously to his parents, wishing them a merry Christmas.

'I fly out New Year's Day,' she heard him say. There was a long pause. 'Yes, I know that's a lot of time off work at this time of the year, but I needed a break.' Another pause. 'I don't care what Maddie told you. It's none of her business.'

Olivia pictured him running his hands through his hair.

'I'm not coming back early, Dad. No. I can't.'

Olivia held her breath.

'It can't be that urgent.' Another long pause, then he swore loudly. 'Are you flipping kidding me?' He let out a sigh. 'I can probably swing it and come home a few days earlier but I'd promised Scarlett I'd be here until New Year's Day . . . yes, she will be upset . . . okay . . . see if you can buy me a few extra days and I'll be there.'

He ended the call and Olivia quickly made herself busy in case

Jack came in and realised she'd overheard his side of the conversation. She filled Scarlett's stocking with gifts from Santa and took a bite out of one of the cookies Scarlett had left on the mantle. She tipped half of the milk into the sink and returned the glass to the table near the fireplace. Breaking off chunks of carrot she scattered it near the fireplace along with blades of grass. Finally, she sprinkled some black powder on the floor and using one of Grandad's old boots, making a sooty footprint. Satisfied Scarlett would believe Santa had visited while she slept, she checked the doors were locked and headed upstairs.

There was a faint light glowing from under Jack's bedroom door.

After brushing her teeth and getting into her pyjamas, she lit her favourite Christmas candle. As the room infused with the scent of orange, cinnamon, nutmeg and lime, she sank back into the pillows and tried to read. It was hard to concentrate on the words on the page. Her mind kept circling from what an amazing night it had been, to what she'd overheard during Jack's phone call.

The reality was, Jack would return to Australia. He'd go back to his restaurant empire and sixteen-plus-hour days. Sure, he'd told her it was all for her—that the lifestyle he was building was for her and Scarlett, but he didn't seem to get that wasn't what she wanted. She would be happy in a little house in the suburbs if it meant they got to see him every night.

Of course that was her dream, not Jack's.

The day he'd told her about his plan to open his first restaurant in Noosa she been excited for him. He'd been jubilant and champagne-popping-exhilarated about the future and she'd imagined they'd go forward together. But she hadn't fully grasped how much time it would take, or the hours he would spend away from home as he built up his business. The harder he worked, the more successful he became, the lonelier she felt.

She closed her book. There was no point trying to read when her mind was racing. Jack could tell her how much he'd changed, but with the Melbourne restaurant opening soon, the workload was only going to escalate. Jack would get caught up with promotional appearances and forget about her and Scarlett stuck at home. And from what she'd overheard in his conversation with his father, Jack needed to get home sooner than he'd planned. Which meant, despite his assurances to the contrary, nothing had changed.

She heard a door open and the floorboards creak. A moment later there was a light tap at her door.

'Liv. You still awake?' he whispered.

'Yeah.'

Her door opened a crack and he stuck his head in.

'I thought you'd gone to bed,' she said.

'I couldn't sleep.'

'Me either.'

He entered the room wearing nothing but boxer shorts and a T-shirt. Seeing him wear so little made her shiver and she pulled the covers up around her chest. He must be freezing.

'I went to the bathroom and saw your light on.'

Jack sat on the end of her bed and reached for the book she'd been attempting to read. The candle flickered as he moved.

'Any good?'

She shrugged. 'I haven't taken in a single word.' It was the latest bestseller, a gift from Lexie. She was mid-way through the third chapter and if asked, wouldn't have been able to remember what the story was about or who the main characters were.

Without a word, Jack made himself comfortable beside her, propping himself up against the headboard, using all her extra pillows. Despite how little he wore, warmth radiated from him. He opened the book where she'd placed her marker and scanned the page as if figuring out where she was up to.

She snickered. 'Are you going to read to me?'

A smiled played across his lips. 'It puts Scarlett to sleep. I thought it might help you.'

'I doubt it.'

He started to read. *"Hannah hadn't slept well."* He paused. *"Usually, the endless roar of the waves lulled her immediately to sleep, but not last night."* He stopped reading. 'Did you like the sound of the waves when we lived in Noosa?'

Their house had overlooked the water. 'Yeah, I guess I did.' Until he'd asked, she hadn't given it much thought.

He kept reading and she snuggled down under the blankets and closed her eyes. He read slowly, with his on-camera voice. His tone was warm, the cadence calm and soothing.

She lost track of time and only woke briefly when he turned out the bedside light, blew out the candle and whispered, 'sleep well, Liv.'

She wasn't sure, but she would have sworn he'd also said, 'love you'.

*

Olivia woke the next morning to the sound of Scarlett's feet hitting the timber floorboards in the bedroom next to hers. It was still dark, so she rolled over and tried to pull the covers tighter around her neck. But something locked them in place. She opened her eyes and sat bolt upright.

'What are you still doing here?' she hissed.

Jack blinked his eyes open and looked around as if confused. 'I'm sorry. I must have fallen asleep.'

At least he wasn't under her covers, he was on top of them, but he'd pulled up the quilt from the end of the bed to keep himself warm.

She lowered her voice. 'You shouldn't have stayed all night.'

'I fell asleep, Olivia. I'm sorry.'

'Well, you need to go back to your room now. I don't want Scarlett to find you in here.'

The bedroom door creaked open.

'Too late,' Jack murmured. A grin played across his face. She

164

rolled her eyes; she'd forgotten he was a morning person. He always woke bright and bubbly.

'Mummy and Daddy wake up! It's Christmas.' Scarlett threw herself on the bed and bounced.

Olivia moaned when she received an accidental knee in the bladder.

'Has Santa been yet?' Scarlett asked, still bouncing.

'Why don't we go downstairs and find out?' Jack said, throwing his legs over the side of the bed.

'What time is it?' Olivia asked. She needed coffee, stat.

'You probably don't want to know.'

'It is after six at least?'

'One-minute past.'

She groaned. 'Give me a chance to go to the bathroom and get dressed, then I'll come down.'

Scarlett tried to drag her out of bed by the hand. 'Don't get dressed, Mama. We have to hurry.'

Jack pulled her back. 'Let Mommy go to the loo while you go and put a dressing gown and ugg boots on otherwise you'll freeze.' He led Scarlett back to her room.

Five minutes later everyone sleepily gathered together under the tree, even Joan. Jack had put on sweatpants, a hoodie and a thick pair of socks. Outside, white flakes swirled in a continuous stream, lit by the streetlights. Judging by the amount of snow on the ground, it had snowed steadily all night.

Olivia lifted the largest present, wrapped in silver, and passed it over to Scarlett. She squealed with delight when she pulled off the paper and found a red plastic toboggan.

'Can I use it now?' she asked.

'No.' Olivia chuckled. 'Maybe after lunch.'

'Thank you, Mama.' She threw her arms around Olivia's neck and planted a sloppy kiss on her cheek.

'Sledding on Christmas Day is a tradition,' Olivia explained to Jack. 'Every year before Mom died, we'd go out to the hill behind the cottage at the lake and sled until our lips turned blue.' She smiled at the memories. 'Granddad had this antique timber sled that used to belong to his dad. It had metal runners and a steering bar. Man, that thing got up some speed. It's a wonder I never had any broken bones.'

'Are you talking about Robert's sled?' Joan asked from the other side of the room. 'I think that old thing is in the garage somewhere.'

'Maybe we should pull it out,' Jack suggested.

'Maybe.' It was a pity he wouldn't be sticking around long enough to learn how to use it.

Half an hour later, Scarlett had pulled out all the presents from her Santa sack leaving wrapping paper and plastic and ribbons strewn around the room.

'Christmas really is for kids,' Jack said, helping Olivia bundle up all the paper.

'Absolutely,' Joan agreed. 'I wish I could see her face, but I can hear the joy in her voice.' She smiled at Jack. 'I'm so glad you're here for this.'

'So am I.'

'Can we go sledding now?' Scarlett asked, trying to balance the toboggan on her head.

Olivia smiled at her. 'No. We have to wait until it stops snowing. Maybe after lunch.'

'What if it snows all day?' Scarlett asked.

'Then you can go tomorrow.'

'But what if Daddy's gone tomorrow?'

Olivia's head snapped up to look at Jack. Had Scarlett overhead Jack's phone conversation last night?

'Daddy said he has to go home early. I heard him.'

Olivia's good mood evaporated. She was devastated for Scarlett.

This was exactly what she'd been dreading. She looked at Jack, waiting for him to give an answer. It wasn't her job to let their daughter down again.

'There are plenty of days for me to take you sledding, sweetheart. I promise.' The lie rolled off his tongue, but Scarlett seemed satisfied with that answer.

With a fresh ache in her chest, Olivia stalked off to the kitchen. It was only a matter of time before he'd announce he was leaving early.

An undercurrent of tension and frustration swirled around her. Pulling out a frying pan she banged it on the stove with more force than was necessary. She then went to the fridge and took out bacon and eggs and ingredients to make a cooked breakfast. It was one of their family traditions—a big breakfast then a late Christmas Day lunch.

She opened the packet of streaky bacon and tossed the strips into the pan. They sizzled as they hit the butter. The ache in her heart formed a knot in her gut. The invisible threads that had drawn them closer over the past three days were starting to fray exactly as she knew they would.

She felt angry and betrayed and annoyed with herself for thinking she could trust him again. As always, his assurances that they could make their marriage work were a bald-faced lie. Fairy-tale happy ever after endings didn't happen except in books. Families didn't always end up together. And no amount of wishing could change that.

Behind her, she heard Jack come into the kitchen and fiddle with the coffee machine. He was obviously unfamiliar with how to operate it, but she was too angry to help him.

Despite his promises, he'd reverted to type. Work came first.

Finally she couldn't keep a lid on her anger. 'You're leaving early, aren't you?'

He stopped playing with the coffee machine. 'Only a couple of days earlier than I'd planned.'

'When?'

'The twenty-eighth.'

'What's so important you have to go home early?'

'There's a major problem with the design of the restaurant. The architects can't come to an agreement with the builders. They want me to come home and sort the situation because the contractors are threatening to pull out. If they do, I won't be able to open the restaurant on time. That means financial penalties and a loss of wages for the staff I've employed. Maddie called Dad and he's gone to Melbourne to try and sort it out. That's why he called me. I'm the only one who can sign off on the final decision.'

Olivia heard everything he said. She understood how many people were relying on him. But it seemed that once again, she and Scarlett weren't on that priority list. 'When will it stop?'

He frowned. 'When will what stop?'

'Your drive to climb the ladder. Who are you trying to please, Jack? Your parents?'

'I'm trying to please *you.*'

She shook her head. 'If you truly believed that, we wouldn't be looking down the barrel of a divorce.'

'I'm here now. Doesn't that count?'

Tears pricked her eyes. 'Should it? You're here for a handful of days then you're leaving again. You're putting your career before your family because you have this driving need to prove something.'

'I'm not trying to prove anything. I merely want to support my family the best way I can. I'm setting up a life for us, a future.'

'A future Scarlett and I won't be in.' She lowered her voice in case Scarlett overhead their argument. 'I want a husband who would be there for me. Not just on Christmas Day, but every day. Scarlett deserves a hands-on dad, not a father figure who turns up for a week and hands out some presents. I don't want her wondering if she's going to see her dad again before next Christmas. We both deserve more than that.'

He didn't answer for a long time. 'Clearly my success isn't important to you.'

She turned to face him. 'No, it's not. You were important to me, but success? That means nothing.'

He exhaled. 'What do you want me to do, Olivia? Walk away from it all? It's my career. My life. I've put everything into opening this second restaurant. If it goes well, it will pave the way to opening in L.A. and London.'

Which would only take him even further away from their family. 'That's the problem, Jack. It's *your* life, not *our* life.'

She turned back to the pan and removed the bacon, laying it down on paper towel to drain. She was furious at herself for being tempted into giving him another chance. He'd almost convinced her he'd changed, and she felt so stupid now the truth was out.

As she cracked eggs into the frypan, she heard him sigh again. Too bad. He could sigh all he wanted, it didn't change the facts. He was leaving again, going back to Australia to expand his empire. Filling up his life with everything but his family. Hurt billowed and built inside her, coming from a deep dark place she'd kept hidden for years. Swallowing hard, she tried to push it back down, but it kept rising.

She slid the eggs onto a plate and slammed the frypan back onto the stove. What a fool she'd been to trust him, to believe he'd changed. She should have listened to that internal voice, the one that knew his work would interfere and he'd choose his career over a life with her and Scarlett. She filled her lungs and held her breath, struggling to contain her hurt. Trying to control the tears which were threatening to explode.

'We have all day tomorrow to spend with Scarlett,' he said. 'Let's make it count.'

She let out a shuddering breath and shook her head in disbelief. 'And that's enough for you is it? One day playing with your daughter?'

The light in his eyes dimmed. 'I'm sorry, Olivia. I don't know what to say or what to do.'

Then he hadn't been listening. She'd opened herself up to him, told him what she wanted for Scarlett and herself. If he didn't know what to do, there was no hope for either of them.

'What did you expect, Jack? That you could waltz in here for all of five minutes and everything would be normal? That we'd be one happy family?'

'I don't know. I guess I hoped you'd see that I've changed and give me a final chance.'

'I already did. You blew it.'

A stab of searing pain between her ribcage caught her off guard. Was this what a broken heart felt like? She put a fist to her chest. All the snippets of happiness she'd allowed herself to feel started to dissolve. She'd been foolish to think he would love her enough to stay, enough to put her first.

What about me? She wanted to scream at him. *Aren't I enough?* If only he could set aside his career, his dreams for her and Scarlett, maybe things would be different.

She'd made a huge mistake trusting him and letting him back in their lives. What a fool. A fool to think he'd changed. A fool to think they wanted the same things. A fool to think a second chance was possible.

Anger pushed heartbreak aside and she tossed the pan into the sink and walked out of the kitchen scrubbing at her tears and trying to hold back the sobs. She wasn't going to let him crush her again.

Chapter 18

Despite their earlier argument, Olivia managed to bury her animosity towards Jack, for Scarlett's sake. As a result, the rest of the day went smoothly. In the presence of her family she was relaxed and chatty and seemed to be thoroughly enjoying herself ,but she was quieter than normal and when she smiled it didn't often reach her eyes. If only she hadn't overheard his conversation with his parents. If only he'd had time to come up with an alternative to cutting his family time short.

Later that afternoon, after eating far too much of Joan's superbly cooked roast, Jack gazed around everyone sitting at the table. Olivia was laughing at something Paul was telling her. Scarlett had her paper hat sitting crooked over one eye and was playing a game of cards with Paul's teenage grandchildren, Toby and Max. Joan and Peter, one of Paul's sons, were giggling over silly jokes from their Christmas bonbons. And Peter's wife, Hannah, was breastfeeding their new baby, Lila. There was so much love and life in the room. Exactly the way Christmas was supposed to be.

Paul's other son, Tom, leaned across and poured Jack another drink. 'How have you enjoyed your first white Christmas?'

'It's been the best Christmas ever,' he said, without a shadow of a lie.

'We have two Christmases,' Tom's wife Debbie said. 'The community dinner on Christmas Eve then a family lunch on Christmas Day. I love it. So much food.'

'It's a Schmidt family tradition,' Tom said. 'Dad's family are from Germany, so Christmas Eve is always a big deal for us.'

'It's a good tradition,' Jack agreed.

He glanced across the table at Olivia. She'd always wanted to make a fuss of Christmas and he could never understand why. Growing up, his own parents had been busy over the holiday period, working, just as he had. Christmas was a busy time in the hospitality industry and taking time off wasn't an option. Seeing Olivia here now, surrounded by family, the fire roaring, candles burning, snow falling outside, he realised what she'd missed out on all these years by being in Australia with him.

They used to celebrate by exchanging gifts early on Christmas morning—gifts he'd piled high under their plastic tree—and eating a light brunch. He'd head off to work around eleven, coming home again briefly in the afternoon to see Scarlett before heading back to the restaurant again where he'd work until closing. Most years, by the time he came home at night, Olivia was sound asleep.

'What about you, Jack? Do you have any family traditions?' Debbie asked.

He shrugged off a bitter laugh. 'Other than work you mean?' He couldn't remember the last Christmas Day he hadn't worked. 'No. I could tweet my family traditions and there'd be characters to spare. Work hard. Be successful. Make money.' There wasn't much more than that.

'That's sad.'

'Yeah. It is.' He didn't realise how much he'd missed out on until this Christmas. Seeing Scarlett and Olivia flourish as they shared family traditions made him all too aware of how sterile his own Christmases had been with his family.

'What about you guys? Any other family traditions I need to know about?' He directed the question to everyone but hoped Olivia would be the one to answer.

She closed her eyes for a second before opening them again. They shone brighter than the lights on the tree. 'Every year we go down to the local church and pick out our tree. All the decorations you see are antiques and each year we add a new one. That's what I bought Nan.'

A knife twisted in his gut as he realised how much he'd taken from her, and how little he'd given in return. If Olivia agreed to go back to Australia with him, he'd make sure they brought some of the traditions with them. Or maybe they could create some new ones of their own.

Sadness clawed at him as he watched his dream of a second chance with Olivia die before his eyes. Because of his lifestyle, Olivia and Scarlett had missed out on so much. They weren't a religious family, but there was something about observing the Christian traditions that was special. After lighting a candle before lunch, Paul had said a short prayer and read the Christmas story from an old family bible. After that, they'd pulled apart crackers, placed paper hats on their heads and passed around plates of food. No wonder Olivia loved Christmas. And the look on Scarlett's face as she opened each present had been priceless. Jack would remember it and cherish it forever.

'It's time for a toast,' Paul said, lifting his glass high. 'Does everyone have a drink?'

Glasses were hastily refilled.

'I propose a toast to my Joanie,' Paul said.

She smiled up at him. 'Neighbours and friends for almost twenty years.'

'On that. We have an announcement to make.' Paul put a hand on her shoulder. 'I've asked Joan to marry me.'

Jack glanced at Olivia. Her mouth was open in a large O.

'Olivia, I can't see the look on your face, but I'm sure this has come as a surprise to you,' Joan said. 'Please be happy for us.'

'I had no idea,' Olivia said. She looked around the table at Paul's family. 'Did you all know?'

Peter and Tom shook their heads. Clearly it was news to everyone.

'Wow. That's great. I didn't see that coming. You've surprised me.' Olivia stood and went around the table to give them both a hug. 'I'm happy for you. I really am. I'm just shocked. When are you going to move in, Paul?'

'Actually, love, I've asked your nan to move into my place. It's on one level and it will be easier for both of us as we get older.'

Joan found Olivia's hand. 'I'm leaving my house to you and Jack.'

Olivia's head snapped around to look at him. Her eyes flashed. 'Did you know that?'

He nodded.

'I told him, sweetheart,' Joan said.

'And you didn't tell me?' Why did it feel like everyone was betraying her trust?

'I'm telling you now.' She patted Olivia's arm. 'Now sit down and let's finish the toasts so we can enjoy dessert. I heard a rumour there's leftover pavlova and some of Jack's famous chocolate sauce.'

Olivia returned to her seat, face flushed. He wished he could tell what was going on in her head.

Paul leaned down and kissed Joan on the cheek. 'Here's to the next twenty years, darling.'

'My turn,' Thomas said, standing and holding his glass aloft. 'I propose a toast to my adorable wife who next year will be holding a new member of our family.'

Everyone cheered and for the next few minutes chatted about Debbie's pregnancy.

'Your turn, Jack,' Paul said, when the commotion died down.

Jack raised his glass but didn't stand. 'Here's to clean slates, fresh starts and new beginnings.' He didn't care how clichéd he sounded; he meant every word. Not that Olivia believed him, judging by sense of betrayal he could see in her eyes. At least this time it seemed to be directed at Joan more than him.

'Daddy, Daddy.' Scarlett waved a Christmas cracker at him. 'There's an extra one. Pull it with me.'

'But I already have a hat.'

'It doesn't matter.'

Jack inserted two fingers into the end of the bonbon and found the thin strip of cardboard.

Face screwed in concentration, Scarlett grasped the other end of the cracker with both hands. 'Ready. Set. Go!'

As it popped, the paper wrapped token flew into the air and landed on Jack's empty plate. He unwrapped the token and flattened out the piece of paper to read the joke.

'Why are Christmas trees so bad at knitting?' He waited. 'Because they're always dropping their needles.'

Everyone groaned.

'I've got one,' Max called out from the other end of the table. 'What's the name of Santa's rudest reindeer?'

'That's easy,' Toby said. 'Rude-olf.'

More groans.

'Here's a good one for you, Jack,' Hannah said. 'What do you get if you cross a snowman with a shark?' She paused, looked around and grinned. 'Frostbite.'

Jack joined in the laughter.

'What did you get?' Scarlett asked, pointing to the token that had fallen out of the cracker.

Jack picked it up. It was a silver ring with a large "diamond" that would have been at least two carats had it been real.

Scarlett's eyes widened. 'You should give it to Mummy. She doesn't have a ring like everyone else.'

The room suddenly constricted around him and he found it

hard to breathe. Everyone's eyes were on him, even Olivia's. He passed the ring over the table and watched as she swallowed nervously before putting on her biggest smile and slipping the ring onto her ring finger on her right hand.

'No, Mama, that's the wrong hand.'

Scarlett pulled the ring off and put it on her left hand. Olivia smiled indulgently and made a show of admiring her "diamond" ring.

'Thank you, Scarlett, it's beautiful.' She dropped a kiss on her head.

'Don't thank me. It's from Daddy.'

Olivia met his eyes and he had a sinking feeling he knew what she was thinking. She was remembering the tiny package she'd mailed back to him with her engagement and wedding rings inside.

But he was remembering his proposal. They'd only known each other for six weeks but he'd been a hundred percent certain she was the one for him the moment they met.

The night before she was due to leave Aireys Inlet and continue her trip around Australia, he'd dropped to one knee in the sand at the beach and proposed. At the time, he didn't even have a ring. He was about to start a job and she was about to return to Canada. But they let their hopes and dreams of a future colour the reality in front of them. They were so crazy-in-love it blinded them to how different they were. They were so young they didn't understand that a successful marriage took hard work and compromise. Something he'd been very bad at doing.

A smile laced with sorrow formed on Olivia's lips. 'Thank you, Jack. It's just what I needed. The best Christmas present ever.'

She glanced away, but not before he saw her blink back fresh tears.

She was wrong. The best Christmas present ever was still in a little blue velvet box in his carry-on luggage.

'Let's go into the lounge room and open some presents,' Paul declared, pushing back from the table. 'The dishes can wait.'

Scarlett's eyes widened when she saw the pile of presents under the tree. '*More* presents!' She clapped her hands together with glee, dropped to her knees and shuffled as close to them as she could. 'I want the biggest one.'

'Why am I not surprised?' Jack said with a laugh.

He found a spot on the floor and while he waited for everyone to choose a present from the pile under the tree, he took a moment to have another look around the room. It was hard to swallow around the lump that continually formed in the back of his throat. He didn't want this day to end.

Surprising him, Olivia sank onto the carpet beside him and handed him a standard sized envelope, a cardboard tube and a couple of smaller gifts, all expertly wrapped. He felt a stab of embarrassment that his present was wrapped in simple brown paper. He hadn't even thought to tie a ribbon around it.

'Just something little,' she said.

'And this is for you.' He too, passed her an envelope and a small wrapped box.

She flashed him a brief smile as she looked at the envelope. 'I hope we haven't bought each other the same thing.'

'I'm sure we haven't.' One hundred percent sure.

'I'm sorry we argued earlier.'

'That's okay. I can understand why.'

'I didn't want you to ruin Christmas for Scarlett.'

'I get that.'

'I'm glad you're here,' she said softly. 'I want you to know I really appreciate it. This has meant the world to her.'

It would make him even happier if it meant the world to Olivia too.

He let a beat pass before speaking again. 'I'm glad I'm here,' he replied. 'With both of you.' He turned the envelope over in his hands. 'This has already been the best Christmas ever and I feel like it's only just begun.'

Scarlett ran over and landed between them. 'Open your present, Mama. I want to see what it is.'

'Go for it,' he said with a grin. 'Rip it open.' He knew she wouldn't.

Olivia carefully removed the wrapping and removed a box containing the coconut and lime hand cream she always used.

'Thank you, Jack. I'm almost out.'

'Open your present, Daddy.'

He heard his phone ringing in the other room where he'd left it at the table. He gave Olivia an apologetic look. 'Sorry, I should have turned that off.'

It stopped ringing, then started again straight away.

He pushed himself up off the floor. 'I should take it. Might be my parents.' Though that was unlikely. They probably wouldn't give him a second thought on Christmas Day until after lunch, then they'd screw up the time difference.

Olivia followed him into the dining room. The phone stopped ringing. He picked it up, glanced at the screen and frowned. Three missed calls from Maddie.

'Your parents?' she asked. There was a sharp tone in her voice.

He shook his head, turned it to silent and slipped it back in his pocket. 'Not urgent. It can wait.' He went back into the lounge room, sank back down onto the carpet again, and leaned his back against the couch.

Scarlett was on the other side of the loungeroom begging Paul's grandchildren to help her with the Lego Jack had given her. The set was probably a bit too advanced for her, but everyone he'd asked said girls were into Lego these days. Judging by the look of delight on her face when she'd torn off the wrapping paper, she was thrilled with the gift.

Olivia sat beside him, cross-legged, and hugged a throw cushion to her lap.

'Open your other present,' he said, handing the envelope to

her.

His heart hammered in his chest and his mouth went dry. He had no idea how she would react to his gift, but he had a feeling she wasn't going to be as ecstatic as Scarlett was with her Lego.

Rather than giving her more "things", which she'd made it clear she didn't want, he'd arranged a night away in a tiny house on a secluded lake half an hour outside Huntsville on the edge of Algonquin Park. It was advertised as the ultimate in romantic luxury getaways—so remote they would have to snowshoe to get there. After an intimate dinner for two cooked by their hosts, they could ice skate on the frozen lake. Hopefully, if the weather co-operated, they might even be able to see the Northern Lights. He'd organised a private dog sledding tour for the following day.

'You first,' she said, holding out her gifts to him.

'Which one?'

She shrugged. 'You choose.'

He took the envelope and slid a piece of card out of it. It was a dinner reservation for two on New Year's Eve at a restaurant overlooking Niagara Falls.

'I'm sorry, Olivia.'

She shrugged. 'I'm sure I can get a refund.'

The other package he opened contained a *Roots* beanie and a gorgeous pair of leather gloves. Both practical and stylish.

She passed him the cylinder and he opened the end and pulled out a canvas.

'It shouldn't be too hard to have someone stretch it onto a frame back in Australia,' she explained.

He unrolled the canvas and stared in surprise at the stunning artwork that depicted two loons on a lake. It was almost ethereal, and he loved it. He knew enough about art to know it was worth a lot of money. 'It's gorgeous. Thank you. I love it.'

'The artist is local. If you have time before you go home, you might like to pop into her store and meet her.'

'I'd like that.'

She offered him a smile and his heart started beating erratically again. It was now or never. 'Your turn.' He handed her his envelope.

Olivia pulled out a sheet of paper and her lips thinned. Her brow furrowed as she read the words he'd written on the card, explaining his gift.

She finally looked up at him, eyes wide. 'I don't know, Jack.'

He could see the struggle in her eyes and his stomach went into freefall. He felt like he was walking on ice that might break without notice. He'd made space for Olivia in his heart and he thought she'd moved in, but now he wasn't so sure and he regretted overstepping the mark again. He understood why she was so torn and wished there was something he could do to convince her to trust him.

'I . . . I . . . can't.'

'Please,' he begged softly. 'It will be good for us to get away. Alone. Time to talk and think.'

'What am I supposed to do about Scarlett?' she whispered, glancing over to where Scarlett sat. No one was else was paying them any attention. Everyone was busy showing each other what they'd received or helping Scarlett with her new Lego.

'Joan and Paul will look after her. I've already arranged it with them. It's just one night.' He kept his voice low.

'But she wants to see you. That's the whole reason you're here. To spend time with her.'

'No, Liv, that's not the only reason I came,' he said softly.

She blew a strand of hair away from her face. 'I don't know,' she repeated.

'One night,' he repeated.

'Separate beds?'

'Sure. We can sleep in separate beds.'

He didn't like lying to her, but he was desperate. He'd seen photos of the room and there was only one bed—a king-sized bed with views over the lake. But if getting her to agree to join him there meant he had to sleep on the couch, that's what he'd do.

She exhaled slowly. 'Okay.'

'Thank you,' he whispered.

He reached for her hand and gave it a squeeze. She squeezed back once, and it was almost enough to reignite a flame of hope. He searched her eyes and was again struck with an overwhelming urge to take her in his arms, But he held back even though it nearly killed him.

Tears welled in her eyes and her lip trembled. He frowned. He hated that she was crying. He moved closer and put an arm across her shoulders and felt her stiffen. He didn't care if anyone was watching them and this time, he wasn't letting her go. 'Hey, don't cry.'

'I don't know whether I'm ready for this.'

He repeated Joan's words, whispering them in her ear. 'Baby steps, Liv. One step at a time. That's all I'm asking.'

She pushed herself to her feet and left the room.

He gave her a moment before getting up and following. He found her in the kitchen, clasping his envelope in her hands.

'You okay?'

'This is all so overwhelming, Jack. I invited you here for Scarlett. I had no idea you still had feelings for me.' She waved the envelope in the air. 'This is the last thing I expected.'

'I should have said something sooner, but it wasn't a conversation I could have over the phone.'

Her shoulders sagged. 'I guess not.'

'The past few months have been really hard for me. I was desperate to see you, but I didn't want to come to Canada until you asked me. Until I knew you were ready.'

'Scarlett's your daughter. You could have come and visited any time.'

'I know. You made it clear I can see her anytime I want, and I appreciate that. But I wanted the timing to be right for you, too.'

She stayed silent, watching him.

He groped for the right words to convince her that all he wanted was to start again, and gave up the struggle. She was listening to him but not hearing what he was trying to say, and it was almost killing him.

'Can I give you a hug, Liv?' He begged her with his eyes.

A second passed, then, wordlessly, she stepped into his open arms. He held her tight, closed his eyes and said a silent prayer. She stood as frozen as an ice sculpture to begin with, but slowly she thawed. As she relaxed, he pulled her closer and inhaled the peppermint fragrance of her shampoo. He could have stood like that forever. They stayed wrapped around each other, listening to the muted chatter coming from the other room.

Eventually she pulled away and looked up at him, eyes wide, pupils dilated, cheeks flushed.

'I'm trying, Jack.' She dipped her head down again and her hair covered her face.

With two fingers, he gently tilted her chin. 'I know you are.' He smiled. 'Thank you.'

Removing the envelope from her hands, he placed it behind him on the table. Taking both her hands in his, he leaned forward and pressed a tender kiss to her lips. Not enough to take her breath away but hopefully enough to stop more fears from tumbling from her mouth and shadowing her eyes.

Chapter 19

Jack's featherlight kiss stole the air from Olivia's lungs and it took her a moment to catch her breath. She hadn't planned on a kiss when she stepped into his arms. Her legs shook and her heart hammered. Struggling to stay standing, she leaned against his chest and felt the furious pounding of his heart beneath his shirt and sweater.

How was it possible to feel frustrated and confused and angry and yet so deeply attracted to him at the same time?

Jack rested his chin on the top of her head and pulled her close. 'I'm sorry. I had no right to do that without asking your permission.'

As he spoke, she felt his breath move across the top of her head.

'It just felt so natural. So right.'

So right. When his lips had brushed hers, her spine had tingled in the exact way it had when he'd kissed her the first time, all those years ago. And like then, Olivia had wanted to kiss him in return.

She also wanted to cry, shout, laugh, and scream.

Instead, she covered her face with her hands. Since Jack's arrival her heart felt like it was doing an extended bungee jump and she wanted to get off. They stood in silence for a moment and she wondered how she was going to navigate the next twenty-four hours. Her brain was muddled, whether from the intensity of her feelings for him or something else. She shook her head, hoping for some clarity in her thoughts, but none came.

'This is so complicated, Jack. You're leaving to go back to Australia in three days and then what? Where does that leave us? You, me and Scarlett?'

Once he was gone it would be up to her to put on a brave face for their daughter and pick up the normal rhythm of their lives again. Olivia wasn't sure she could do that after the upheaval of the last few days.

Jack pulled her back into a hug and she fell against him again. His arms tightened around her chest and she felt him shrug, heard him exhale. 'I honestly don't know.'

'I'm not sure it's worth us going away to Huntsville. Perhaps it would be better to stay here. For Scarlett's sake.' And she had her own heart to think about too. If she gave herself fully to him, there was no turning back. Not without a lot more pain.

'I'd really like us to go away. It's only one night and it will be good for us to spend some time alone. Even if you don't want to stay married, at least we'll know we've tried.'

She pulled back and tilted her head to look at him. 'I don't want to lead you on, Jack.'

He stroked her cheek. 'You're not.'

'And if I say it's over, you have to accept it's over.'

He gave her a wry smile. 'Okay.'

She knew he was lying. She could see it in his eyes. He'd never accept it was over.

'Come on.' He took her hand and put some enthusiasm in his voice. 'It's stopped snowing. Let's take Scarlett outside and try out this new toboggan of hers.'

'Will you tell her we're going away tomorrow and that you have to leave earlier than planned?'

He nodded. 'Yeah.'

'Expect tears. Scarlett will be gutted.'

'Despite what you may think, I'm not exactly thrilled about it either, Liv.'

*

Much later that afternoon, when it was growing dark, they headed inside, numbed and chilled from the crisp air. Paul's family had already said their goodbyes and Joan had disappeared to her room. Seconds after crashing on the couch in front of the fire, Scarlett was sound asleep. Olivia covered her with a quilt and tucked it around her. She wouldn't let her sleep for too long or she'd have trouble falling asleep tonight, but a quick nap would do her good.

'Cup of tea?' Jack asked.

'I'd actually love a hot chocolate please.'

'Sure.'

He returned with two steaming cups, a plate of leftover dessert, two forks and a grin. 'Not sure if you're hungry.'

She clutched her stomach and groaned. 'I couldn't eat another thing.' She accepted a fork from him. 'But I'll give it my best shot. Thanks.' She leaned over and took a spoonful of cake from the plate in his hands and brought the chocolate ripple cake to her mouth.

Joan entered the room on Paul's arm. 'Glad I caught the two of you alone. I have something I need to say.'

'Scarlett's here too,' Olivia warned Nan. 'She's asleep.' Gentle snores rose from the couch.

'Precious child. It's been such a big day for her.'

'Jack said you and Paul are happy to look after her while we go away for the night tomorrow,' Olivia said.

'We'll be fine,' Paul said. 'No need to worry, Olivia.'

'If not—'

Joan put her hand up. 'Wait Olivia. Hear me out.'

Olivia put the fork on the plate, sat up straighter and stared at her grandmother.

Joan stood in the centre of the room, all five foot of her, with her hands on her hips.

'I'm an old lady and that means I get to speak my mind. You two are dancing around your issues and it's time to stop. You need to get away, talk and sort things out. In my opinion, the two of you have something very special. My advice is to find it again because let me tell you, neither of you will be happy until you do.' She pointed a finger in Jack's general direction. 'You need to have a long hard think about your future. Not what *you* want, but what Olivia wants. What Olivia and Scarlett need. You have to stop thinking as a single man and think as a family man.'

Olivia watched him swallow, nod and mumble an 'okay.'

'It's not enough to come to Canada and ask Olivia for a second chance then ruin all your good intentions by proving you haven't changed.'

'But—'

'Don't argue. I overheard you two quarrelling earlier and I understand you've decided to go back to Australia early because of work. Have a long think about that, Jack. Is that demonstrating you've changed?'

She glanced over at Jack again. He looked as shocked as she felt. She'd never heard Nan speak with so much force or put things so bluntly.

'And Olivia...'

Olivia's stomach churned as if she was sitting in front of the school principal, in trouble for something that wasn't her fault.'

'I've already had words with you. You need to communicate with Jack. He doesn't have a crystal ball. It's time you learned to speak up for yourself and be honest about how you're feeling. But not in an angry way.'

Olivia chewed on a fingernail and kept her mouth closed. She didn't know where to look.

'So, tomorrow morning you're going to get up nice and early and drive to Huntsville. Time together, alone, is what you need. Okay?'

'Okay,' they mumbled in unison.

Joan and Paul walked out, leaving them both sitting there, mouths ajar.

After a minute of absolute silence, Olivia started to giggle. 'Remind me never to get on her bad side.'

Jack started to laugh too. 'I didn't know she had one.'

'Until now, neither did I.'

'Well, you heard her,' Jack said. 'Time together alone is apparently what we need.'

They needed more than that, but it was a good place to start.

Chapter 20

They woke early, ate breakfast with Scarlett, and left as the sun was starting to paint the sky a pale yellow. Scarlett took the news of Jack's early return to Australia better than expected. Perhaps because Jack promised he'd be back again as soon as the new restaurant was open. He'd also promised Scarlett a trip to Australia to see real koalas again.

They took Olivia's car because it was equipped with snow tyres and was safer on the roads than Jack's hire car.

Olivia drove the first hour or so and once they were through the usual bottleneck around Toronto, they pulled over in Barrie, grabbed a coffee and swapped drivers. The highway was clear of snow and, being Boxing Day, there wasn't much traffic. Barrie to Huntsville was only another hour or so of driving.

The lakeside scenery was stunning, and Jack oohed and aahed as they went around every bend in the road. They'd seen people out on the frozen snow-covered lakes, walking, cross-country skiing and skating. On one small lake, they saw a group of around twenty young people playing ice hockey.

'What are they?' Jack asked, pointing to little buildings on the ice.

'They're ice fishing huts.' On frozen lakes all across the country, the huts appeared every winter. They were havens for people who found meaning in sitting for hours hoping to catch a fish. Olivia couldn't think of anything more boring.

'It looks like a little ice village shanty town.'

She chuckled. Many of the huts were built in backyards in the summer using scrap materials. Some of the larger ones looked like little houses and even had propane heaters inside them.

They continued the drive and with her favourite music playing softly through the car speakers, and the sun shining warmly through the window Olivia felt sleepy. Jack was content to keep up an easy-going conversation and was equally happy with longer gaps between topics.

At one point, as she felt herself drift off, Jack reduced speed.

She shifted in her seat and opened her eyes. 'Why are we slowing down?'

'I'm not sure but I think that car up ahead has stopped.'

Olivia squinted. 'Accident?'

'I don't know.'

She peered through the front windscreen. 'Could be anything. We're far enough north that a deer or moose may be walking across the road and the cars might have stopped to let them through.'

'Really?'

So far they hadn't seen any live animals, but there had been a lot of roadkill.

She narrowed her gaze and made out two cars slightly off to the side of the road, one of them facing the wrong way. Her pulse accelerated and her mouth went dry.

'Crap. It *is* an accident. Stop the car, Jack. Let me out.'

He'd barely pulled on the handbrake before she had her door open. She sprinted along the side of the road, pulling on her coat as she ran. Going automatically into nursing mode, she scanned the accident scene as she drew closer. She heard Jack behind her, panting as he chased her.

She slowed and Jack skidded into her. She put an arm out to stop him from running past her. 'We need to check the scene first. Make sure there's no danger.'

It appeared there were only two vehicles involved in the head on collision. Steam hissed from the crushed radiator of the small sedan. The massive pickup truck appeared undamaged other than a shattered windscreen.

Olivia was no expert, but it looked as though the pickup had drifted across the divide and into the wrong lane.

Two other cars had pulled over ahead of her car. As Olivia and Jack approached the pile up, the driver's door of the car furthest away from the accident opened and an elderly man struggled out from behind the wheel, slipping on the snow.

'I've called 911,' he yelled out.

'Did you see it happen?' Olivia asked as she strode over to him.

He shook his head. 'I just got here. I don't think it happened that long ago.'

The driver of the second car got out. The Asian man stared at the mangled wreck, and he appeared to be in shock. He must have seen it happen.

'Are you okay?' Olivia called out to him. 'I'm a nurse. I'm here to help.'

She'd said those words time and time again and it was true. She'd become a nurse to help people and support them in their time of need, but she'd never found herself in a situation like this.

The man looked dazed. 'Chinese,' he said. 'No English.'

'Okay.' Olivia gave him a smile. It was unlikely he'd be able to assist.

She hurried over to him and indicated he should get back in his car, keep the engine running and the heater on and wait. Inside, she saw four frightened faces, all of them elderly Chinese. None of them seemed to speak English, so she gave them an encouraging smile and shut the door.

She ran back to Jack who was still standing with the old guy. Jack wasn't moving and his face was whiter than the surrounding snow-covered paddocks. He looked like he wouldn't know his first name if she'd asked him.

She gave him a little shake. 'Jack, I need you to go to my car and drive it closer. In the trunk there's blankets and a basic medical kit.'

'Shouldn't we wait for the paramedics?' His voice wobbled.

'It could take them half an hour to get here. We can't wait. I need to check if there are any fatalities, then check for injuries. I'm going to need your help.'

He still hesitated and she gave him a little shove in the direction of the car. 'Go.'

He finally moved.

'I'm a nurse,' Olivia said the elderly man. 'My name's Olivia. That's Jack, my husband. Do you think you'll be able to help us?'

The man nodded. 'Name's John. Forty years in the army.'

'Brilliant.' That meant he'd follow instructions as well as keep a clear head. 'Can you watch out for traffic and make sure the paramedics can get through?' The last thing she needed was rubberneckers getting any closer and blocking the road.

'Done.' He marched off and she almost expected him to snap her a salute.

Jack returned with the first aid kit banging against his leg. His arms were loaded with blankets and coats. Smart man. The sun was gone now, and thick clouds were coming in fast, dropping the temperature and bringing with them the smell of freezing rain. She glanced up. The last thing they needed was a storm.

'Let's go,' she said to Jack, taking the bag and a blanket from him.

She heard shouting from the larger vehicle and Jack veered that way.

'Jack. No.'

He froze and turned to look at her.

'If he's shouting, he's alive. We need to check the other car first.'

They approached the smaller car and what Olivia saw filled her with trepidation. The single occupant was a young female and she lay slumped forward, trapped by the airbag. Gift-wrapped presents were strewn everywhere. Olivia checked the back seat and saw no child's car seat or anything to indicate there were any passengers. One good thing.

Her feet crunched on broken glass as she got closer to the mangled wreck of the tiny sedan. Miraculously she was able to open to the driver's side door. She took the girl's arm, pushed up the sleeve of her coat and palpated for a pulse. It was weak and thready, but it was there. She glanced at the girl's face. She barely looked like she was out of her teens.

Olivia gently eased the girl back from the steering wheel, aware that in doing so she was potentially causing more injuries to her neck or spine, but she needed to protect the girl's airway. She grimaced at the deep gash on the girl's forehead that extended from her right eye and disappeared in her hairline. There was blood everywhere, running down her face. Her eyes were closed, and she was unresponsive. But at least she was breathing. And she had a pulse.

Olivia forced herself to switch off from the carnage laying across the road. Filled with the weight of responsibility, she couldn't afford to stop and think about what had happened or whose fault it was. She simply had to focus on what was in front of her.

'Jack, go and check the other driver.'

She heard him move off.

Olivia did annual Advanced Life Support competencies as part of her hospital training. But she'd only done CPR once and that was in the controlled environment in the hospital where she and the team had everything needed to perform a resuscitation.

Thankfully, because of medicine and machines and manpower, that patient had lived. Unless help arrived soon, this young woman wouldn't be so lucky.

Fingers shaking—partly from the cold and partly from the adrenaline coursing through her—Olivia unzipped her first aid kit. She found a wad of gauze, removed the plastic wrapping off a bandage and donned a pair of rubber gloves. The bleeding head wound was most likely the least of this girl's worries, but applying some pressure to it would stop the bleeding. Olivia tightly bandaged the woman's head until it looked like she wore a turban. Finding another wad of gauze, she upended a bottle of water she found in the car onto the gauze until it was soaked and using that, wiped blood from the girl's face. Her skin was the colour of glue.

The girl hadn't moved and she was slumped in the seat. Knowing she needed to keep her neck as straight as possible, Olivia grabbed two boxed Christmas presents of similar sizes. Placing them on either side of the girl's head, she wrapped a large bandage around her forehead, using the boxes and the headrest to fashion a neck brace of sorts. It was crude, but it would stop her from slipping further down the seat and possibly keep her neck aligned.

Rifling through the first aid kit she plucked out the pen torch. The girl's pupils were sluggish, and her skin already felt far too cold. Olivia unfolded the reflective space blanket and wrapped it around the girl as carefully as she could, checking for any other visible injuries like bleeding or broken bones. Without X-rays and CT scans it was impossible to tell what else was wrong internally.

She found a stethoscope in another zipped pocket of the first aid kit and had a quick listen to the girl's chest. Heart sounds were there, but they were slow and irregular. It also sounded like only one side of her lungs had any air entry. Had she punctured a lung? Tension pneumothorax? The possibilities slipped through Olivia's mind and caused a wave of heat-induced stress to swamp her. It was freezing cold but sweat still ran down the centre of her back.

Unfortunately, until help arrived, there was nothing she could do but rely on her training and hope for the best.

She wrapped her stethoscope around her neck and rocked back on her heels. Slushy snow started to fall. Taking a deep breath, she glanced over to see Jack striding purposefully towards her, face flushed, eyes dark.

She stood. 'Is he okay?' She could still hear the other driver yelling.

Jack exploded with a string of swear words. 'I'm not a doctor obviously, but there's nothing wrong with him physically as far as I can tell. But judging by his breath, he's a dozen times over the legal limit. And the way he's yabbering on? Probably drugs too.'

'Idiot!' Olivia growled. 'I'd better take a quick look at him. Did you see any other passengers?'

'No, he's on his own.'

The snow was falling heavier now, and the road was quickly carpeted in white, covering the broken glass from the smashed cars. Other vehicles had pulled up and people were out of their cars asking if they could help.

One woman in a bright red jacket jogged over. 'My name's Christine. I'm a trauma and emergency doctor from St Michael's in Toronto.'

Thank you, God.

'The driver is a young female,' Olivia said. 'Alive, but she's unresponsive. Airway is open, she's breathing but it's shallow. I can only hear air entry in her right lung. She has a pulse but it's thready and heart rate is irregular. Pupils are equal but very sluggish. She has a very deep head wound and I've applied pressure to stop the bleeding. I can't feel any other injuries and she doesn't appear to be bleeding anywhere else.'

'You a doctor?' Christine asked.

'Nurse. ICU. This is way out of my comfort zone.'

'Sounds like you've done an amazing job.'

'Thanks.'

'Can I borrow your stethoscope?'

Olivia handed it to her. 'Keep it.'

'What about the other driver?'

'Very much alive and kicking.'

Out of the corner of her eye she saw the driver of the pickup get out of his car and stagger away from the scene.

'Hey!' she shouted. 'Stop!' Olivia took off, feet slipping in the icy snow. She yelled at him again. 'Stop! Jack! We have to stop him. He can't leave the scene of an accident.'

Hearing her shouts and realising what was happening, two young men got out of a car and ran like quarterbacks towards the driver, tackling him to the ground. He landed with an oomph as the air left his lungs. Moments later, they hauled him to his feet. Pinning his arms behind him, they frog marched him back to his truck to wait for the police.

Sirens sounded and someone cheered. It may have been her.

It felt like hours later, but was only minutes, when two ambulances and a fire truck appeared. Not long after that, the police arrived and soon a slow parade of cars passed the accident scene to continue their journeys.

After giving the police officer a quick rundown of what had happened and leaving her number, Jack and Olivia were free to go too.

They stumbled back to her car and when Jack offered to drive, she didn't complain.

For the next ten minutes, neither of them spoke—each of them trapped in their thoughts. She kept playing through the accident scene in her mind, hoping she'd done the right thing and hadn't caused any further injuries. The paramedics had assured her she'd done great, but there was no promise the accident victim would pull through. She tried to ignore the nervous knot tightening in her stomach. Some poor parents were probably waiting at home for their daughter to show up with Christmas presents. So sad.

'I could use a coffee,' Jack said finally. 'And something to eat.'

Olivia checked the map on her phone. 'We're only forty minutes away from Huntsville, or we can stop ahead in Gravenhurst. It's about fifteen minutes away.'

'As long as there's a Tim Hortons.'

Olivia felt a smile form on her lips, the first one in a while. Jack had become addicted to their Tim-bits donuts. 'There's always a Tim Hortons.'

'Decision made. I need a coffee, and you look like you could use a hug.'

Chapter 21

Jack was in awe of his wife. While he'd stood at the edges of the accident scene, frozen, shocked, uncertain of where to start and what to do, Olivia hadn't hesitated. She'd jumped straight in, calm and totally in control of the whole situation. Even the paramedics and police had complimented her on a great job.

After leaving the accident scene, they'd driven nearly ten minutes in unbroken silence and for that whole time his head had been full of swirling thoughts.

His desire to further his career and achieve personal success had thwarted Olivia's own dreams and aspirations. When he'd first met her, she'd just finished her first year of nursing but when she moved to Australia to be with him, she hadn't been able to transfer her registration and get work straight away. The nursing board had strict rules on overseas trained nurses working in Australia and by the time she got all her paperwork in order ready to apply, they moved to Queensland and she had to start the whole process all over again.

Life got busy with the restaurant and when she fell pregnant with Scarlett she stopped talking about wanting to work. He never thought to ask whether she'd wanted to go back to work, assuming she'd want to be a stay-at-home mum.

As it turned out, he'd been very wrong. She hadn't wanted to stay at home fulltime looking after Scarlett but with him so absent, she didn't have the time or his support to get her Australian registration. The moment she and Scarlett had returned to Canada Olivia had evidently gone straight back to work. He was smart enough to see she clearly excelled at her job and loved it.

He slowed as they came to the outskirts of Gravenhurst and spotted the Muskoka Road turnoff and a Tim Hortons. The snow continued to fall; so heavy now it was hard to see the other side of the road. The drive had taken all his concentration, and he wouldn't truly relax until they arrived in Huntsville.

They got out of the car and he hustled around to Olivia so he could pull her into his arms for the hug he'd promised her. She offered no resistance and he held her tight and long before letting her go.

'You were amazing out there, Liv,' he said as he took her by the hand and led her inside.

If anyone had ever suggested he'd be excited about drinking coffee from a donut shop started by a former Toronto Maple Leaf's hockey player, he would have laughed. It was almost impossible to describe the love affair Canadians had with the brand. It was as quintessentially Canadian as maple syrup, hockey, Molson beer and poutine.

Not that he'd ever say it aloud, but it was simply a fast food restaurant, not dissimilar to a Wendy's or Burger King and the coffee was dreadful, but it was hot and strong and right now that was precisely what his body needed.

The restaurant was empty except for two people behind the counter. Tinny Christmas music played through the speakers and a fake gas fire burned in an equally fake brick fireplace.

Olivia rubbed her face and he noticed a tightness around her eyes.

'I hope I did the right thing moving that woman,' she said.

That explained her silence in the car. She was worried.

'The paramedics said you did everything right,' he assured her.

'But what if I injured her neck? What if moving her caused permanent damage? I had no way of knowing if her spine was injured and I could have made it worse.'

'You had to make sure she was breathing.'

At the accident scene he'd overheard Olivia explaining her actions to the police and paramedics. He'd also heard the praise they heaped on her for staying calm and for triaging so effectively.

'They said the way you made that neck brace was genius.' He pulled her close for another hug. 'You did a great job and should be proud of yourself. I know I'm proud of you.'

'Thanks, Jack.'

While she went to the bathroom, he placed their order, collected their meals and found a seat.

'I don't know how you do what you do,' he said after taking a bite of his toasted sandwich and a sip of hot coffee. 'I can't stand the sight of blood.'

'We all have things we're good at. I can't even cut onions without crying and you've seen my baking skills.'

He chuckled. 'Remember that time I came home and found you cutting onions wearing swimmer's goggles?'

She laughed. 'I'm hopeless in the kitchen.'

'You're better than you think. You were all over it at the community dinner and Christmas lunch was awesome. That turkey was cooked to perfection.'

'That was all Nan's doing. I only helped.'

As they ate, their conversation flowed easily. Whether deliberate or not, they steered away from talking about the accident.

'It puts everything into perspective doesn't it?' Olivia asked after she'd thrown away her rubbish and wiped her hands.

'What does?'

'Seeing an accident like that. Tomorrow someone might wake knowing they're never going to hug or kiss or talk to their daughter again. It's so sad. Makes me want to hug Nan and Scarlett close and not let go.'

'It is sad,' he agreed. He touched her on the arm. 'Do you want to go home? If this has been too much for you, we can turn around.'

She shook her head. 'No. The weather is closing in and the roads will be dreadful. Best thing we can do go to Huntsville and find our accommodation before it gets dark.'

As they left the restaurant with a box of "Timbits", he held the door open for her. 'Are you okay to drive? That snow is pretty heavy, and you have far more experience on the roads than me.'

'Yeah, that's fine.'

He passed her the keys.

As they turned onto the highway, Jack had texted the hosts of the Air BNB he'd booked to let them know they were running late because of the accident.

For the next forty minutes they chatted amicably and arrived in Huntsville a little before one o'clock.

The crossed the historic swing bridge onto main street.

'There it is,' Jack said, pointing out the window to the Algonquin Outfitters store on his right. 'That's where we have to go to get our gear. Looks like there's parking behind the store.'

'Okay. There's not much traffic so I'll drive to the top of the hill then turn around and come back.'

The street was lined with two storey buildings that looked like they were built in the early part of the last century. As quaint as the town was, it seemed to be thriving, as Jack hadn't spotted any empty storefronts.

'Nice place,' he said, craning his head left and right. He spotted a brewhouse, a chocolatier, lots of clothing shops and giftware, homeware and furniture shops that all looked very high end judging by their window displays. 'You been here before?'

Olivia shook her head. 'I haven't, but I wouldn't mind coming back here in summer if I could afford to. Muskoka is to Toronto what the Hamptons are to New York. There's a lake not far away that has a row of cottages that they call "Millionaire Row". Rumour has it that Kate Hudson has a place up here. So do Tom Hanks, Goldie Hawn and Steven Spielberg.'

Olivia reached the top of the crest of main street and turned around.

'What's with all the murals everywhere?' he asked, as he spotted yet another large abstract painting on the side of a building.

'It's an outdoor gallery of around a hundred murals replicating the art created by a group of Canadian artists called The Group of Seven. Huntsville has around thirty paintings all displayed on exterior walls of businesses and public buildings not just here in Huntsville but in Lake of Bays and the Algonquin Park region.'

'You're like Miss Wikipedia with all this information.'

Olivia chuckled. 'We Canadians are proud of our cottage country and our heritage. I'd also planned to major in art at college before I decided to go into nursing so I'm very familiar with the work of these artists.'

He looked at her in surprise. 'I never knew that.'

She shrugged. 'I think there's a lot about me you don't know.'

Olivia turned into the narrow laneway and parked the car behind the store. It wasn't snowing, but the clouds hung so low over the lake it was almost hard to see the trees on the other side of the water.

'What should I do with my bag?' she asked.

'Morgan said to meet her here.' He checked his phone. 'She'll be here in about five minutes.' They'd get fitted with snowshoes first then follow Morgan to her place leaving their car there. From Morgan's it was a twenty-minute walk to the cottage which was all part of the experience. He'd memorised all the instructions in the email confirming his booking. Morgan and her partner would then take their bags and stuff to the cabin on their snow mobile.

'Sounds good.' Olivia pulled on her beanie and a pair of gloves and zipped up her coat. 'It's going to be cold out there.'

He got out his phone again and checked the weather app. 'Wow. It's minus sixteen.'

Olivia chuckled. 'And that's not with wind chill.' She gave him a nudge with her elbow. 'You're the one who wanted this Canadian winter wilderness adventure. I hope you know what you're in for.'

She got out of the car and the wind whipped in, chilling him instantly. He put on his own brand new beanie and gloves and made a dash for the store while pulling Robert's coat around him.

While they waited for Morgan, Olivia wandered around the store, returning to the counter with a men's coat, three pair of men's socks, gloves and a beanie. 'You'll need this for the dog sledding tomorrow.'

He frowned. 'Oka . . . ay. Why?' He thought he'd packed more than enough suitable clothes but clearly not.

'Did you bring thermals?'

He shook his head. He was seriously under-prepared.

She disappeared and returned shortly with a pair of thermal tights and a long-sleeved T-shirt and placed them on top of the other stuff.

'You'll need all this too,' she said.

'Your granddad's coat is fine,' he said. But still, he fingered the thick material of the heavy coat she'd placed on the counter. It was a nice-looking winter jacket. Not that he'd have any use for it in Australia.

'It's old, it's not waterproof and doesn't fit you properly. This will be much more suitable, especially for dog sledding.'

She pulled out her credit card to pay, but he took it from her. 'You're not paying for all this.'

'Consider it a gift. Part of my Christmas present.' She snatched the card back and passed it to the guy at the counter.

Jack didn't argue. He had Olivia's bank details and would

easily transfer money into her account later.

As their purchases were being placed into bags, a young woman approached them, wearing a broad smile.

'You must be Jack and Olivia. I'm Morgan.'

'G'day.' Jack thrust out his hand. 'Great to meet you.'

Morgan shook his hand, then Olivia's. 'Great to meet you guys too. You're Aussies, eh? That's so cool. Where are you guys from?'

'Queensland.'

'Niagara-on-the-Lake .'

They spoke at the same time.

A confused look crossed Morgan's face.

'I'm Canadian,' Olivia explained. 'Jack's Australian.'

'Oh, my bad. When Jack said he was coming here with his wife, I assumed you were both Australian.'

He didn't reply, unsure what to say. After a night in the little cabin in the woods, he hoped they'd still be married, and not heading towards divorce.

Morgan quickly recovered. 'Right. Great. I see you've got lots of warm clothes. You're gonna need them, that's for sure.' She turned to Olivia. 'What about you?'

'I have plenty of snow gear but I realised Jack won't have ever experienced temperatures like this and I figured he probably needed some more layers.'

'Good thinking,' Morgan said. 'Come on, let's head downstairs and get you fitted for snowshoes. They've forecast a massive dump of snow later tonight so best we get you to the cabin while it's still light. Have you ever snowshoed?' she asked Olivia.

'Yeah. Plenty of times. Obviously Jack hasn't.'

'How 'bout dog sledding?'

'Never.'

'Man, you're gonna love it. Just remember not to let go.'

Ten minutes later the two of them were fitted with hired snowshoes, and they were back in the car following Morgan to her place.

They pulled up outside a white two-storey farmhouse. Smoke curled from a chimney and lights blazed in the windows. Jack handed Morgan their bags and she loaded them straight into a little trailer attached to the snowmobile.

'You guys might as well strap on your snowshoes and head off.' She handed Olivia a laminated map. 'Taylor and I will head out to the cabin shortly. She's inside getting your food ready. It'll take us about ten minutes on the skidoo and it should take you about an hour to hike there if you keep up a good pace. Jack said you're both runners and pretty fit so you'll be fine. The trail is well-marked but stick to it, or you'll get lost, especially if it starts to snow again.' Morgan laughed. 'Last thing we need is to send out a search party.' She looked them over quickly. 'Looks like you've got enough layers for walking now but, tomorrow you'll need to rug up. It's gonna be minus twenty tomorrow plus wind chill. And on the dog sleds, it'll feel colder than that, especially if the sun's out.'

Jack listened, nodding, but his head spun. He was certain he'd heard her correctly. She'd said minus twenty. Was that some kind of joke? And he had no idea what she meant about it being colder when the sun was out. Surely if it was sunny, it would be warmer. That made logical sense. He didn't have time to ask because Morgan had taken their bags and walked off.

Olivia was already expertly attaching her snowshoes and adjusting the straps over her knee-length boots. Hands shaking, he followed suit, glad he had an old pair of Robert's well-worn boots. They were warm and comfortable.

'What did Morgan mean about it being colder when the sun is out?' he asked.

'Do you want the scientific explanation?'

He shook his head.

'Basically, it has something to do with the sunlight exciting the cold air in the first foot or so above the ground. That causes the cold air to mix into the atmosphere. This mixing drops the temperature of the air at thermometer level.'

He stared at her like she'd spoken another language.

She laughed. 'Trust me. After years of living through winter I can assure you that you should never think a sunny day means it's warm out.'

Morgan returned and gave him a quick slap on the back. 'Good luck, eh. We won't see you until tomorrow afternoon when you're back from the dog sledding. If you need anything, you'll have to make do without it. There's no mobile coverage at the cabin, but I promise it's set up for everything you need. Tay and I will have the fire roaring by the time you get there.' She glanced up at the sky. 'If the weather stays like this, you might be lucky to see the lights. There's also a heap of different-sized skates at the cabin so feel free to use them. If the moon comes out, it's magical skating at night.'

'What happens if there's an emergency?' he asked, frowning. When he'd booked a remote experience, he hadn't realised it would be this remote.

'You either have to hike back here or light a fire and send up a smoke signal.'

He gaped at her. What kind of tourist operation was she running that didn't have proper emergency systems in place?

'It's not a problem. You'll be fine. Stick to the groomed trails, don't walk across a lake unless you know how thick the ice is, and keep away from the bears.'

He broke out in an instant cold sweat at the thought of bears. He tried to swallow. 'Right. Great. Thanks.'

'If you do spot a bear, remember not to run or climb a tree. And don't bother playing dead either. They're smarter than that.'

He looked from Morgan to Olivia with a frown. They were laughing at him. This was no laughing matter.

'She's joking,' Olivia said, barely able to contain her giggles. 'Bears hibernate in winter.'

Idiot. Of course they did. He pretended to wipe sweat from his brow. 'At least I don't have to worry about snakes. In Australia we have almost all of the world's most deadly snakes. And spiders too.'

Morgan chuckled. 'True. Anyway, sorry. Couldn't resist. In all seriousness, you might get some patchy mobile phone coverage out there but it's unreliable. There's an emergency radio at the cottage with clear instructions on how to operate it. As soon as the door to the cottage unlocks, it sends me a notification that you're inside. If you don't unlock the door within half an hour of the time, we expect you to get there, we send out a team to look for you. Trust me, we haven't lost a tourist yet.'

'Always a first time,' he muttered.

Suddenly the romantic Canadian wilderness adventure he'd planned didn't seem like such a great idea. He was a city boy and the idea of bears and forests and the possibility of falling through frozen lakes was not appealing at all. He glanced at Olivia who seemed to be taking it all in her stride. If anything, he'd never seen her look so happy. She was glowing.

'See ya tomorrow, guys. Have a great time, eh.' With a wave, Morgan went inside leaving them alone.

They hitched small packs to their backs and took off down the trail, their feet sinking slightly into the deep powder snow. It took Jack a while to get the hang of walking in snowshoes, but Olivia looked like she'd been born with them strapped to her feet.

Half an hour later they arrived in a clearing, out of breath and sweating. As they'd walked, each of them had to keep stopping to take off layers. They'd wrapped their jumpers around their waists and stuffed their beanies into the pockets of their jackets. It was cold but tramping through the thick snow was harder than he'd anticipated.

Olivia looked back at him and smiled and his heart constricted. Her face was flushed from the cold and her eyes sparkled. And best of all, she looked so happy. He hadn't seen her smile like this for such a long time.

'Isn't this amazing?' she said, doing a little spin in the snow. 'There's nothing better than being outside in the wilderness. Listen to that.' She tilted her head back and closed her eyes.

He listened. Heard nothing.

'Can you hear it?' she said. 'That's the sound of silence. It's amazing. So quiet it feels like it's closing in around you.'

'That's a good way to describe it.'

'Come on, let's keep going.'

For the next twenty minutes he followed Olivia through the snow watching the way her backside moved in her ski pants and wondering how he was supposed to keep his hands off her tonight.

Dragging his eyes away, Jack took in his surroundings. Tall, skinny pine trees extended as far as he could see in all directions. Someone had marked the path with reflective strips attached to the trees, so it was easy to follow, thank goodness. The idea of getting lost out here held no appeal.

In front of him, Olivia stopped and looked up, tilting her head right back.

'Wow.' Her breath came out in a plume of steam. 'Isn't this gorgeous?'

The clouds parted and rays of late afternoon sunlight pierced through the gaps between the trees. His breath hitched. *She* was gorgeous.

She started walking again and he called out to her.

'Olivia, stop for a second.'

She stopped and turned around. 'What is it?'

'Can I take your photo? You look stunning in the middle of all these trees.'

She hesitated for a second and he saw two spots of colour appear on her cheeks. 'Okay. Sure.'

He pulled a glove off with his teeth, fumbled in his pocket for his phone and snapped a few photos before his fingers froze off. She stamped through the snow back to him and leaned close to view the pictures on the screen. Her hair brushed his hand and his skin tingled. Suddenly he forgot how cold it was.

'They're great photos, Jack. Great scenery.'

He laughed. 'I'm not looking at the scenery. I can't take my eyes off the subject.'

She nudged him with her hip, but he saw the smile of pleasure on her face, and it lit his insides and warmed him through.

Olivia took his phone from him and held it up high in front of her. Leaning towards him she said, 'smile' and snapped a selfie before he'd had a chance to think.

It was his turn to look at the screen. 'Ugh. My eyes are closed. Can you take another one?'

She handed him the phone. 'Your arms are longer than mine. You take it.'

He angled the phone and they both smiled up at it. He snapped a few photos and they laughed as they pulled funny faces and he kept clicking. He leaned down and kissed her lightly on the cheek, quickly hitting the button on his phone and hoping he'd managed to capture the moment.

Olivia pulled back in surprise, but she giggled and her eyes were glossy and she was smiling. Good signs that he hadn't overstepped her boundaries again.

'Show me that.'

He held the phone so they could both see it.

She leaned close again. 'That's a nice photo of us. Can you send me a copy later?'

'Absolutely.'

Before he pocketed his phone, he took another look at the photo. It wasn't "nice", it was spectacular. He'd snapped the kiss as a ray of sunlight sliced through the trees behind them, creating a striking halo effect. But what he really noticed about the photo wasn't the sun or the trees or the snow. It was the way it had caught Olivia's smile when he kissed her.

Hope bloomed in his heart that maybe, just maybe, his plan

would work.

'Come on, let's keep going. I want to get there before that sun sets completely.'

Ten minutes later they arrived in a clearing and stopped side-by-side, mouths open in wonder. Across a small frozen pond was a tiny timber log house nestled amongst towering fir trees. Smoke curled from the stone chimney and lights lit the two windows either side of a bright red front door.

It looked even more charming and romantic than it had in the photos online, and Jack's heart raced.

'It's beautiful, Jack. How'd you find it?' she asked, with an awe-filled voice.

'Google.' He'd spent hours poring over reviews on Trip Advisor.

'It's so pretty. It's perfect.'

'Come on, let's go inside and check it out.' This time he led the way, hoping the interior was as beautiful as the outside.

He wasn't disappointed.

The cabin had a compact kitchen at one end of the cabin with a little nook to sit and enjoy the views over the pond in the middle. Up a set of steep stairs was a tiny loft, where a king-sized mattress took up almost the entire space under a sloping roofline. Olivia hadn't said a word about the lack of two beds and he wasn't about to bring it up. Downstairs at the other end of the cabin was a large bathroom.

Smelling something amazing, he went over to bench, lifted the lid on the slow cooker and inhaled deeply.

'You hungry?' he asked.

'I am, but it's still early. Why don't we have a quick wander around while it's still light, then we can eat.'

'Sounds like a plan but you said you were hungry, so let me find you a snack first.'

He opened a few cupboards and found a container filled with homemade chocolate chip cookies. He lifted the lid, took out two cookies and handed one to Olivia.

'Thanks, Jack.'

After putting their outerwear and boots back on, they headed back outside. A quick circle of the frozen pond only took ten minutes. In that time, they spotted two deer and dozens of animal tracks in the snow. When they got back inside, he stoked the fire using logs from the stack of firewood Morgan and Taylor had left for them on the little front porch.

While he took care of the fire, Olivia found a bottle of wine and some freshly baked, still-warm banana bread under a tea towel. She poured two glasses, lathered the passionfruit-infused butter onto the banana bread and brought it over to Jack in the little seating nook. They curled side-by-side on the couch and drank their wine in silence until the sun slipped down behind the trees and the first star appeared.

Olivia put her hand on his arm and let out a long sigh. 'Thank you, Jack. This is *just* what I needed.'

Her hand burned through his jumper to his skin and when she leaned a little closer, her perfume invaded his senses, stirring desire deep within him. He wanted to kiss her senseless and never stop, but he willed his body into submission. No point ruining the moment because he was having trouble keeping his hands off her.

'I could stay here forever,' she said, offering him a warm smile. 'It's magical, isn't it?'

He smiled back. It was magical. And the total opposite of all the places they'd ever visited on holidays. All these years he thought he'd been giving her everything she ever needed and now he could see how far off the mark he was. It seemed all it took to make Olivia happy was a cabin in the woods, a simple log fire, a glass of wine and a sunset over a frozen lake. If only he'd known that six years ago maybe they could have avoided so much heartache.

He entwined his fingers with hers and a frisson of need stirred deep in his gut. He caught her gaze and felt the pull of attraction like a magnet between them. His body strained for her touch. He could only hope she felt it too. He wanted to take her up the little stairs and make love to her in that massive bed, but he wouldn't unless she was ready.

He squeezed her hands. 'You are so beautiful.'

A blush swept up her neck and she dipped her head, hiding her face with her long hair.

He released her hands, cupped her cheeks and ran one thumb slowly over her bottom lip feeling it quiver beneath his touch. He'd missed this so much—the special moments when it was only the two of them.

Her breath hitched and her eyes widened and when she pulled back a fraction, he knew he had to let her go.

He pushed himself up from the couch. Arousal had shot through him the minute he'd touched her lips and he'd seen the desire in her eyes. He wanted to make love to her right there on the couch in the little nook overlooking the frozen pond. He wanted to feel the softness of her skin again.

'Fire needs more wood.' He reached for the bottle of wine. 'And your glass is empty.'

He poured her another glass, then went outside to get more wood. It was like taking a much-needed cold shower.

Chapter 22

By the time the first star made its appearance and Olivia was onto her second glass of red wine she started to relax. It had been a long and emotional day. Not just with the car accident but the long drive to get here. Somehow, the view of the sun setting behind the trees made the harrowing day worth it. And surprisingly, sitting in the peace and quiet enjoying the moment with Jack made it even better. She couldn't remember the last time she'd enjoyed his company so much.

Jack got up to stoke the fire and stir the stew. From her seat in the nook she watched him. Her impression of him had changed in the last few days. There was something different about him. He was still a charmer, but he'd mellowed or something. She couldn't put her finger on what it was, but it was definitely there, lurking under the surface.

He'd been amazing today, supportive and encouraging and loving. It was the first time she'd ever felt like he was putting her first.

Jack turned off the lights so they could watch the stars as they came out, and joined her again on the couch. They sipped their wine in contented silence.

She wasn't sure how to broach the subject of sharing a bed yet. It seemed petty to make Jack sleep on this couch in the nook, when the bed in the loft was so huge. But if she agreed he could sleep with her, she was possibly sending the wrong message. They'd had an amazing afternoon and evening together, but she was a long way from reconciliation. A long way from wanting to sleep with him again. Wasn't she?

This was the most romantic place they'd ever stayed in. And in the early days of their marriage, they'd stayed in a lot of beautiful places. It was more than magical. The blazing log fire, the cute cottage, and the stunning frozen pond outside. Not to mention the long snowshoe walk in the fresh air to get here. The whole picture combined to undermine her defences and gently erode the feelings of hurt and anger Olivia had clung onto for so long.

'Don't let the sun go down on your anger.'

The little voice in her head sounded remarkably like Nan.

Olivia had a right to be angry. She just wasn't sure it was serving a purpose anymore.

The trouble was, she didn't know how *not* to be angry. Night after night for the past few years she'd fallen asleep, fuelled by hurt and a burning fury towards Jack for causing her pain. Anger became bitterness which, if left unchecked, would have quickly turned into hate if she'd allowed it.

Then, like a lightbulb going on inside her, Olivia understood what her problem was. She had no peace in her heart because she was filled with anger. And fear. Fear of being hurt again. Shivering, she pulled the throw rug off the back of the couch, wrapped it around her shoulders and stared out the window.

The question was, could she do it? Could she risk trusting Jack again and give him another chance?

She rested back in the soft couch cushions, tucked her feet under her and took another sip of her wine. Beside her, Jack lay sprawled out, eyes closed. She watched him doze and flickers of suppressed feelings for him emerged. She turned back to the window and let out a soft sigh. Was she brave enough to admit she still had feelings for him?

A faint glow appeared over the trees in the east and when it turned a luminous white before expanding and taking on a slightly greenish cast, she gasped.

She shook Jack awake and he jerked, almost spilling her wine. 'What's wrong?'

'Look.' She pointed, putting down her glass. 'The Northern Lights.' At first, she'd thought it was the moon rising but the light wasn't still. It moved as though it had a life of its own. The ghostly glow swayed right, then left, undulating like a wave.

They sat, transfixed.

Jack edged closer and put his arm around her. 'Have you ever seen it before?' he whispered, as if talking out loud would make it stop.

She shook her head. She'd heard the lights described as mystical and moving, but no words were adequate to describe the show Mother Nature was putting on for them.

For the next half hour the lights blazed in the silent sky. In a perpetual motion of dancing, swaying bands of vibrant colours, they moved as if they were alive.

'I'll never be in awe of fireworks after this,' Jack said, when the colours finally faded. 'That was incredible.'

'The greatest show on earth,' Olivia agreed.

They stared out the window for the longest time, hoping the colours would return, but the heavens remained a black canvas. Clouds soon moved across the sky, blocking out the stars.

The last thing Olivia wanted to do was move, but the smell coming from the kitchen was making her stomach growl. Dinner wouldn't serve itself.

Jack moved first. 'I'll get dinner ready if you like.'

She looked at him in surprise. 'Are you sure?'

'I want to see what Taylor has cooked. It smells incredible.'

'It's a venison stew.'

'How do you know that?'

'Morgan left instructions pinned to the fridge. She said we need to steam the greens and put bread in the oven to warm through. There's a bottle of red wine she says will go perfectly with the stew.'

'Is that the wine we just polished off?'

Olivia chuckled. 'No, there's another bottle in the cupboard.'

'Do you want to try it?'

'Absolutely.' Her face felt flushed and she was borderline tipsy, but another glass wouldn't hurt if she drank it while they ate.

After they'd eaten the incredible stew and washed up, Olivia yawned. 'Is it okay if I take a quick shower before I go to bed?' It was only eight o'clock, but she was exhausted. She'd had enough wine to make her a little sleepy, and they had an early start planned for the morning. If she went to bed and fell asleep first she could avoid discussing the sleeping arrangements.

'You don't want to go outside for a skate?' he asked.

'We can do it tomorrow when we get back from the dog sledding.'

'Okay. Sounds like a plan.'

He took his glass of wine back to the little nook while Olivia went to the bathroom.

The cabin was small, but the shower wasn't. It was large enough for two people with floor to ceiling windows overlooking the little pond. An outside light perfectly illuminated the snow and beyond that, the forest of trees. She felt like they were the only people around for miles.

As she stripped off and stepped into the shower she thought back to the early part of her relationship with Jack. When they'd gone away, before Scarlett, they showered together, marvelling at the view while soaping each other's bodies. A tingle zapped through her and a wave of heat rolled over her skin. She shuddered and pushed the memories out of her head. The situation with Jack was complicated enough without her confusing the issue by thinking of happier times.

After towelling herself dry, she slipped into one of the thick white robes hanging on a hook behind the bathroom door and climbed the narrow steps to the loft.

Jack was in the bedroom, pulling clothes from his bag. He spun around when he heard her. 'Sorry, Liv. I thought you'd take longer in the shower. I dashed up here to get my trackies. I'll leave you to get dressed.'

He tried to slip past her. She moved to the right to let him pass and he moved left, and they bumped into each other.

He reached for her arm to steady her. 'Sorry.'

They were so close she could almost feel the heat coming off him. His eyes widened and she glanced down and realised the robe had come apart, exposing her cleavage. She wrapped the robe tighter around her waist causing it to hitch up higher, revealing her thighs. She made a mental note to tell Morgan they needed to invest in some longer robes, not these short ones that barely covered her backside.

Jack's eyes were on her legs. Her body tingled all over and fresh heat rushed to her cheeks. She smelled the scent of his aftershave and memories of the way he used to touch her flooded in. She closed her eyes to block them out, but it didn't work. When she lifted her lids, Jack was still staring at her, eyes wide, lips parted.

'God I've missed you,' he whispered. 'You have no idea how beautiful you are.'

A shiver shuttled down her spine, tightening her legs and making her insides liquefy. She gripped the robe tighter to her chest with both hands. For a second neither of them moved. Their eyes locked and before she had time to panic, he cupped the back of her head and pulled her close, kissing her firmly on the lips.

He pulled back and searched her eyes. 'Tell me to stop and I will.'

'Don't stop,' she whispered. Unable to resist him any longer, she pressed her mouth to his, gentle at first, then with more intensity as passion and memories of the past surged through her.

His hand touched her shoulder and she felt the heat of it through the fabric. Frustration surged and she wanted him to push aside the robe and touch her, skin to skin. It had been too long.

As his fingers worked through her wet hair, Jack ran slow, purposeful kisses down her neck pushing aside the robe so he could kiss her on the shoulder, then his lips moved towards the centre of her chest. She gasped at the feel of his whiskered cheek against her skin. She closed her eyes, let her head fall back and soaked up the sensation of his soft kisses. A small moan escaped, and she gave him a half-hearted shove back.

'I should get dressed.'

'No,' he murmured into the hollow of her throat. 'Stay like this. Please.'

'I'll get cold.'

'I'll warm you up.'

He kissed her cheeks, her eyelids, then made his way back to her mouth.

'You're so beautiful, Liv,' he said again. 'I've missed you, missed this.'

She closed her eyes and leaned towards him. She'd missed it too.

'Can I touch you?' he whispered.

She nodded and snagged her bottom lip between her teeth. Every cell in her body was crying out for him, but her brain was taking a while to catch up. And her heart was lagging a little further behind.

As if sensing her hesitation, he pulled back and looked at her. His eyes were dark, pupils large. 'Are you sure?'

She nodded again and smiled as relief flickered in his eyes. 'But go slow,' she cautioned.

'I promise.'

She closed her eyes and curled into his arms.

'Slip off your robe,' he murmured into her ear.

For a moment everything seemed to stop. Olivia couldn't breathe, couldn't think. And there was no room inside her to feel anything but the need to have Jack even closer.

Unhurriedly, she undid the tie on her robe and allowed it to fall to the floor.

Cool air touched her skin, but she didn't have a chance to get cold. Jack pulled his shirt over his head and pressed the warmth of his chest against hers. Her heart hammered against her ribs and her breath came in rough gasps. A part of her didn't want to do this, but the rest of her did. Very much.

Then her old fears rose up, threatening to spoil the moment. 'I don't know if I can do this yet,' she said, voice trembling.

'Shh,' he whispered in her ear. 'I promise I'll take it slow.'

Their lips met again, soft and tender. When Jack's tongue flicked hers, she felt her knees buckle. If he kept this up, she'd never want him to stop. As if sensing this, Jack took the first step. Reaching for her hand, he gently led her towards the bed.

*

Much later, when it was pitch black outside and there wasn't a sound except for the occasional popping of the logs in the fire, Olivia lay spooned in Jack's arms. She lay quietly, savouring the memories of what they'd shared, feeling the rise and fall of his bare chest against her back. She shivered slightly and pulled the covers over them.

Jack rolled her over to face him, resting his hand on the curve of her waist. 'You alright?'

She couldn't speak. She had no idea if she was alright. She closed her eyes, feeling the sting of tears and dipped her head to her chest so he couldn't see she was on the verge of crying.

'Liv.'

She sensed, rather than felt, the tension coming off him.

'It's okay,' she assured him, looking up into his eyes and brushing her tears away. 'I'm okay.' She smiled. 'They're happy tears.' *Sort of.*

His entire body relaxed. 'Thank God. I thought you were going to say you wish we hadn't done that.'

She smiled. 'Bit late now.' She ran a finger down his arm. 'Did you think this would happen when you booked the cabin? You and me. Making love again.'

He shook his head. 'Never in my wildest dreams.' Then he chuckled. 'Actually, that's a lie. I have been dreaming about this for a long time.'

Her gut tightened. This was a mistake. So much had happened in such a short time and she still wasn't sure she could trust Jack with her heart, yet she'd trusted him with her body. She wasn't sure what that said about her. The weight in her gut travelled upwards to her throat, squeezing hard. She unfolded herself from his embrace and felt the bite of cold as she moved away from his heat. She wasn't ready to say goodbye yet, but in forty-eight hours or so Jack would be gone, and she didn't know what would happen except that she and Scarlett would be in exactly the same place they were in now. A place that felt like limbo.

'It's okay.' He reached and stroked her face. 'I can see you're overthinking this.'

'It's what I do best.' Her brain was in overdrive, coming up with a trillion reasons why what they'd just done was the worst decision of her life. Making love with her husband didn't change the facts. He was still going back to Australia.

'I know what you're doing, Liv. You're pulling back. But don't. Please. We can make this work.'

She blinked at him. 'How?'

'I've been thinking a lot about us. Me. The restaurants. Our future.' His hand reached her shoulder and he gently squeezed. 'I guess if I'm going to give all that up, I need to know if you still have feelings for me. If you still love me.'

Olivia's heart slammed against her chest and for a second she wondered if she'd heard him correctly. Surely he hadn't said he was prepared to give it all away.

She held her breath and waited for the "but" but it didn't come. Her heart felt so full and yet empty at the same time. She now knew she couldn't live without him any longer, but she couldn't live with him unless they made changes. Radical changes. Was he prepared to do that for her?

He pushed himself up on his elbow to look at her. 'Are you okay?' he asked again.

No. She was confused and anxious and not sure whether to follow her head or her heart. Right now, she didn't even know which one was leading the way.

'What do you want, Liv?'

That was an easier question to answer. She wanted everything. She wanted the things they'd promised in their marriage vows. The parts about cherishing each other, trusting each other, building one another up and supporting each other's dreams.

She wanted them to be a family again, but she couldn't— wouldn't—risk Scarlett getting hurt. It was only going to get harder as she got older. Olivia knew that so well. She remembered how, not long after her mom died, Nan had spoken to her father and told him he needed to come back to see Olivia. She waited for him and he never came. The next day and the next, she waited again. On the fourth day she cried and after that, she forced herself to forget about her father. Even as a young girl, not much older than Scarlett was now, she'd known what it felt like to be rejected and she'd carried that with her into adulthood. It had been the worst thing ever, wishing so hard that someone would love her enough to stay.

She shivered, realising Jack's rejection of her had opened all the scars she bore from her childhood.

'Do you still love me, Liv?'

His questions snapped her back into the present. She took a deep breath. She did love him, but she wasn't sure that was enough. 'Yes but—'

He put a finger to her lips. 'But I need to make some changes.'

She nodded. Big changes. 'Scarlett and I deserve more than a tiny piece of you.'

'You do,' he agreed.

He reached for her hands, stroking the back of them with his thumbs.

'I know what you're going to say,' she said. He was going to tell her it was impossible for him to give up what he had in Australia. She dipped her head. 'Say it.'

His thumbs squeezed. 'I'm not going home.'

She sat up and looked down at him, not caring that the blankets fell away leaving her naked. She blinked at him and tried to find the right words. Was he serious about not going home? He couldn't possibly give the restaurants and his contract with the network up. She must have misunderstood.

She swung her legs out of the bed and reached for her clothes. She slipped her knickers on and pulled a long-sleeved T-shirt over her head.

'Liv.' He ran a finger down her spine.

She shook her head. She needed a second to process what he was saying. Her heart thundered in her chest.

'I want to make a home with you and Scarlett again and if that home is in Niagara-on-the-Lake, then that's where I'll be. I'm not letting either of you go again.'

She spun around and gaped at him. 'But what about Maddie? *Globe?* All your other commitments?'

'My family is more important. *You* are more important.'

Olivia gulped and her heart exploded with joy. She'd waited so long to hear him say those words.

'Thank you, Jack.'

He lifted the covers and patted the bed and she slipped back in beside him and rested her head on the pillow next to his.

His hand landed on her hip again and he tugged her closer.

'There's something else I've realised too. I'm embarrassed to admit this, but I've become like my parents. I worked so hard because I wanted to provide for you and Scarlett. I'd been taught by my parents that being a good provider meant having a big house and lots of money. That being able to give you things was a mark of my success as a man and as a husband and father. But the more I did that, thinking it would make you happy, the more unhappy you became. I didn't understand how I could try so hard and fail so badly. When I was at home, I felt like I didn't have a clue. At work, I felt in charge, in control. A success.'

Fresh tears stung her eyes at his painful confession, and she tried to blink them away. She owed him the same honesty. 'Actually, I wanted to talk to you about something too.'

'Yeah?'

She let out a shaky laugh. 'Since you arrived, I had some realisations of my own. I saw how bitter I've become. I was so angry with you, so frustrated at the way things ended, and I couldn't let it go. That anger festered until I was so bitter, I blamed you for everything. I'm really sorry, Jack. I've been so unfair to you. There were two people in our marriage, and we both have to take some blame. I had a narrow view of what a good husband should be, on what a successful marriage would look like and I need to make some changes too and meet you in the middle.'

'What are you saying?'

'I'm saying that if you'd like, I'm prepared to go back to Australia with you.'

He stroked her cheek and tucked a strand of hair behind her ear. 'What if we were to stay in Canada?'

It was her turn to frown. 'How could you make that happen? What about your obligations with the restaurants and television?'

He flashed her a smile. 'I made some calls and I happen to have inside knowledge about a little restaurant coming up for sale that needs a new lease of life. I also know there's a lovely house perfect for a family, and it's right next door to a wonderful older couple who love us very much.'

Tears filled her eyes. 'You want to buy *Harbourside?*'

He nodded. 'And I want to rename it. I want to call it *Home.*'

She shook her head in wonder, trying to take it all in. 'But what about *Atlas* and *Globe* and *The Chopping Block*?'

'That's why I employ good staff. *Atlas* basically runs itself anyway and I've been rethinking *Globe.* For some reason those doors are closing. Maybe the timing isn't right for Melbourne, or maybe the location isn't right.'

'You could open it in Toronto.'

He shrugged. 'I could.'

'And the show?'

'I'm committed to that for another year, but we film it over six weeks, so I'd need to go back to Australia for that, but then I'd be back home to you and Scarlett.'

Olivia's head felt like it was spinning. Everything she wanted and more and he was offering it to her without strings. She couldn't believe it. He was prepared to let so much go for her. He was prepared to make her and Scarlett his priority by building a life for them together. One that allowed him to pursue his passion while also giving her the chance to pursue her own dreams. It was almost inconceivable.

'Does Nan know?'

He shook his head. 'She doesn't, unless Paul has said something. He and I had a good chat on Christmas Day and he urged me to contact Les and Sally and ask what their plans were for the restaurant.'

So it was Paul who had sowed the thought. Bless him. He'd get an extra big hug when Olivia saw him next.

'And Les and Sue are keen?'

'At this stage we've had one brief conversation. There's a lot to consider, but if I'm not opening up in Melbourne, I have the time to focus on starting something here. It's going to take a lot of time and work, but at least I'll be home at night and I'll be around for you and Scarlett.'

She shook her head. 'I can't believe it.' It felt like she was dreaming.

'To be honest, I'm having trouble getting my head around it too. It's all happened so quickly, but it feels right. Like the doors are open. Like I said, it's not going to happen straight away and I'll probably need to go back and forwards for the next six months at least making sure things are in place.'

'Thank you, Jack.' She didn't know what else to say. He could take all the time he needed.

He kissed her on the forehead. 'Thank *you*, Olivia. Thank you for giving me a second chance.'

Chapter 23

When she finally fell asleep, Olivia was grateful for her physical and emotional exhaustion. To her surprise, she slept soundly. In fact, she couldn't recall the last time she'd slept so well.

Perhaps it was the fresh air, or the absolute quietness of the cabin or the amazingly tasty dinner they'd eaten the night before. Or the two bottles of red wine they'd shared. She smiled. Most likely it was the sex.

After making love, then talking about the future, they'd both been too buzzed to sleep, and too hungry. They ate the last of the banana bread while attempting to watch a movie which they abandoned a quarter of the way through because they couldn't keep their hands off each other. After taking a shower together and using up all the hot water, they talked some more, then fell asleep, limbs entangled.

She opened her eyes and rolled over gently so she could watch Jack sleeping. His mouth was open a little, enough that she could hear the soft in and out of each breath. One arm was flung over his head, the other rested on her hip.

The frown he'd worn since arriving in Canada was gone, making him look years younger—like the man she'd fallen in love with.

The familiar feeling of hurt pushed its way into her heart but it was gone so fast she wondered if she'd imagined it. After their conversation the night before, her fears no longer applied.

*

After a lazy start to the morning they had a cooked breakfast, then packed their bags ready for Morgan and Taylor to collect later that day, layered on their clothes and strapped on their snowshoes. The path to the dog sledding had already been groomed and it was well-signed. The instructions Morgan had left said it should take them around twenty minutes.

They arrived at the dog sledding camp just before eleven o'clock. Olivia was sweating after the quick walk, but she knew she'd be glad of all the extra layers later that morning. She wore merino wool thermals, three pair of socks, a long-sleeved T-shirt, a hoodie, a mid-layer jacket and a heavy, wind and waterproof ski jacket along with ski pants. She also had hand-warmers in each pocket, a polar fleece-lined toque on her head and a facemask ready to pull up to cover her mouth and nose. Jack had laughed at her when he'd watched her dress but when he'd stepped outside into the bright sunshine he'd yelped and come straight back inside and added another few layers.

A huge bearded man approached them. He was taller than Jack and twice as broad and in his padded snow suit, he looked bigger again. 'Morning. I'm Brad.'

'Hi. I'm Olivia. This is Jack.' She shook Brad's hand and tried not to wince.

He pumped Jack's hand firmly then strode off in a no-nonsense way, calling over his shoulder. 'Righto, let's go. Dogs are this way.'

Olivia and Jack raised eyebrows at each other, then jogged to keep up.

Through a gate, they entered a large enclosed area. To the left and right were dozens of dog kennels. Each one was separated from the other by about ten metres and each dog was chained to a peg staked in the snow. Most of the dogs sat calmly watching Brad, others ignored them, asleep either inside or on top of their kennels.

For the next fifteen minutes Brad gave a demonstration and explained the safety aspects of dog sledding, while Olivia and Jack shifted from one foot to the other and rubbed their hands together, trying to keep warm. As he talked, Leah, his partner, harnessed the dogs and attached them to the ropes leading from the sled. By now, the dogs, realising they were going to work, had started barking and howling. The haunting sound raised goose bumps on Olivia's arms.

'They do that because they love to run,' Leah explained, raising her voice so they could hear her over the racket.

Brad showed them to the sled. 'Right. What are the rules again?' he asked.

'Never let go of the sled,' they said in unison. He must have said it a dozen times.

'If you forgot anything I've said, don't forget that.'

They nodded. Olivia shivered nervously.

'What else?' Brad asked.

'Always keep one foot on the brake,' Jack said.

'And?'

'When we're going uphill, we have to help the dogs out,' Olivia said.

'Good. You got it?'

They nodded again. Jack squeezed her hand. She was too cold and nervous to squeeze his back.

'Leah will take photos of you with the dogs now if you like.'

'That'd be great, thanks,' Jack said.

They spent the next couple of minutes taking photos of each other with the dogs and Leah took a few of them together.

'Okay. Let's get going, eh?' Brad looked them both up and down and over. 'The first half hour of the run is uphill, so it'll be easier on the dogs if you drive first, alright?'

'Right.' Olivia pulled her facemask up, slipped her sunglasses on and ignored the fear coiling in her gut. Why had she imagined this dog sledding experience was going to be a relaxing scenic ride?

'Rule number one again?' Brad asked as he helped Jack into the sled and covered him in animal skins and extra blankets, tucking them around him then zipping up the canvas flap.

'Never let go,' she said.

'Even if you fall off,' Jack added.

Olivia didn't dare ask what would happen if she *did* let go.

'And no selfies eh? The only person to take photos is the passenger and I guarantee you'll be too cold to get your phone out. We'll swap at the halfway point and you can take photos then. Right. Good to go?'

Without waiting for an answer, he moved off to his pack of dogs and positioned himself on the sled.

'You doing okay?' Jack twisted in the sled to look back up at her. All she could see was his eyebrows moving.

Olivia nodded and chewed on her bottom lip. 'I think so.' She put her hands on the handlebar and tested the brake which was basically a giant metal fork that rested on top of the snow. When she pushed down on it, the fork clamped into the snow, slowing down the dogs. Apparently.

Sensing they were about to leave, the dogs' howling reached fever pitch, setting off all the other dogs in their kennels. The sound echoed up and down the valley.

Leah undid the safety lines and shouted to Olivia to release her foot from the brake. Olivia did as she was told and, with a small squeal of shock, they took off. Brad was already well ahead, and Olivia's pack of dogs were keen to catch up. As soon as they started running, the dogs stopped barking and howling. The sleds sped along in total silence, the only sound was the shhhh of runners gliding through the snow.

Brad had told them the names of the six dogs in their team, but in her anxiety, she couldn't remember any of them. All she did remember was each litter was named after letters of the alphabet.

The next few minutes was a blur of snow and trees. The brochures talked about the amazing scenery, but in her sheer hold-on-for-dear-life panic, she couldn't focus on anything other than what was in front of her. Six dogs, straining against their harnesses, desperate to run. It took all her attention to hold on, balance and breathe. And not to laugh when the dogs starting peeing and pooping as they ran. That was a talent in itself.

At first, she didn't dare look down at Jack. But after a while she got the feel for it and was able to relax enough to take in more of her surroundings. She looked down at the dogs, and they were magnificent to watch.

Unlike the huskies she'd expected to see from Disney films, these dogs were cross-bred. They were lean and incredibly strong and appeared to be a mix between a Siberian Husky, a Border Collie and an Alaskan Malamute. Brad had explained they looked so different from each other because the dogs were bred for characteristics, not breed standard. Sled dogs had to be athletic, adaptable to cold temperatures, have a desire to run and they had to have a good temperament. In top condition, the dogs had the capacity to run further, longer and faster than any other animal on earth.

They were definitely fast. Breathtakingly so. But somewhere between fearing for her and Jack's safety and blinking away the wind-induced tears streaming down her cheeks, she started to enjoy herself. On either side of the sled, untouched snow sparkled and danced in the sunlight that filtered through the massive pine trees either side of the freshly groomed trail.

They exited the pine grove and crossed a frozen lake. The change in landscape was so stark and the feel of racing between the trees one moment then sledding across the open expanse of lake was so different. The dogs' speed increased as they strained against their harnesses. Then it was back into the forest again. The wind was blistering cold, but she didn't care. She felt alive and vibrant, and so present in the moment. This was what she wanted her life with Jack to be about. Not the gifts he used to give her but experiences they could share together. She wanted to create memories like this, snapshots in time.

The terrain they slid through was smooth and Olivia relaxed enough to occasionally look away from the dogs. The land on either side of them was incredible. Trees so tall it was impossible to see the tops of them and snow so white and pure and untouched it felt like no one had ever been through here. They were on private land that backed onto Algonquin park. Brad had bought the property after one of his dogs was killed during a run by a testosterone-infused teenager on a skidoo. Two other dogs had been injured and had to be put down. Prior to having his own place, the dogs and ski mobiles had shared the same trails and it was too dangerous.

At one point Brad stopped and signalled for her to halt her dogs which she managed to do a safe distance behind his team, as he'd instructed.

'All good?' he shouted back.

'All good,' she replied with a thumbs up.

They took off again, travelling through a variety of terrain— from flat tundra, to some hills and climbs, across vast expanses of frozen lakes then through thick green forests. Clumps of fresh snow covered the branches of the trees, weighing them down. Away from the groomed path, it was so deep in places she was sure she would have sunk in it up to her neck.

The sky was a deep, cloudless blue and the sun shone, bathing the landscape in golden hues of morning light.

Olivia's thoughts wandered and it wasn't until they were hurtling downhill approaching a bend that she realised they were going too fast. There was no sign of Brad and his team. Her dogs, obviously keen to catch up with their kennel mates, were running flat out, their hot breath steaming as it hit the cold air.

'Slow down,' Jack shouted.

Olivia stood on the brake as hard as she could, but the dogs kept going.

'The brake, Liv. Stand on the brake.' His words carried in the wind back up to her.

'I am,' she yelled back at him. 'I can't slow them down.' Icy fear snaked down her back. She was losing control.

She either wasn't heavy enough to push the brake through the snow or they had too much momentum. Either way, they were out of control. As the dogs began veering to the left, she felt the sled tipping. In her confusion and fright, she automatically leaned the other way to counterbalance, remembering too late she was supposed to put all her weight on the runner, not the brake and let the sled right itself.

As realisation dawned that the sled was about to flip, it was already happening. Olivia had a short moment of freefall, followed by a choking sensation as her breath was ripped from her lungs and the dogs pulled her face forward down the hill. She used every ounce of strength to grip the bar and not let the dogs go, but it was no use. She tasted snow and closed her eyes. When she opened them again, she saw nothing but a wall of white. Her hands slipped from the bar and she lay face down in the snow, panting.

Then she heard Jack scream.

Chapter 24

It took Jack a few seconds to realise they were about to tip. His heart rate sped up and he flailed his arms like a kid who couldn't swim. He screamed for Olivia to slow down, but nothing was stopping the dogs. Branches flew past, slapping against the sled. They were off the track now, heading towards the trees and there was nothing he could do but hold on. Brad hadn't told them what to do if they tipped, other than not to let go.

The sled tilted on its side and one alarm bell after another sounded in his brain as the world tumbled. Then he was coughing up snow.

'Don't let go, don't let go.' He tried to shout but his words were muffled, and he had no idea if Olivia could hear him.

'I'm trying.' He heard the fear in Olivia's voice. He didn't dare turn around. If she was still holding on, the sled would be dragging her along the ground. He tried to see if she was alright, but he was on his side, trapped in the sled.

'NOOO!' Olivia's shout was a mix between a strangled sob and a muted cry.

The tree seemed to come from nowhere and before it slammed into the sled, he instinctively put out his arm to brace the fall. He heard the snap before he felt the pain.

He lay on his side in a pile of powder snow and a world of agony. He tried to move, and a cry exploded from him. White-hot, searing pain like nothing he'd ever experienced bit into him. He looked down at his right arm. Even with the layers of clothing he wore, he could see it was at a wrong angle. There was no question he'd broken it.

Tentatively he flexed and extended his other arm, then his legs, testing he hadn't broken anything else.

He struggled to sit and turn around to see if Olivia was okay, but the slightest movement made him see stars.

'Liv?'

No answer.

'Olivia!' he shouted.

He clawed around with his good hand for his phone. He needed to call someone but had no idea who or whether they even had reception this deep in the forest. Where was it? Had it been flung out when they hit the tree? Inch by inch, gasping with each painful breath, he dragged himself out of the sled. Crawling commando style, he headed to the tree line and collapsed in a thick bank of snow. A wave of nausea crashed over him. Ahead, still attached to their lines, the dogs looked like angels. The tree had halted their run and they stood patiently waiting to be released. Two of the dogs were asleep, curled into balls. Jack generally loved dogs, but at that moment, he could have throttled the lot of them.

Olivia.

He looked behind him and nearly fifty metres back there was dark mound on the ground. 'Olivia,' he shrieked. The sick feeling in his stomach intensified. 'Olivia!'

He saw the mound move and her hand go up. She waved and gave him a thumbs up. He exhaled in relief. She slowly got to her feet and staggered through the snow towards him. As soon as he realised she was okay, he collapsed back on the ground and nursed his broken arm in his lap.

There was no sign of Brad. He hoped he'd realise something was wrong and turn back for them. If not, they'd somehow have to right the sled, get back in and keep going. He didn't like their chances of making that happen.

Olivia stumbled towards him, whiter than the snow. 'Jack, are you hurt?' She fell to her knees next to him.

He nodded, biting down on his bottom lip. He needed painkillers.

'My arm.'

'Is it broken?'

He nodded. More pain filled every cell of his body. Another wave of nausea hit, and he gasped for air.

'Phone. Brad.'

She pulled off her mittens and gloves and searched her pockets until she found her phone. Wide eyes met his a second later. 'There's no coverage. I'm so sorry. This is all my fault.'

'Doesn't matter.' Right now he didn't care whose fault it was. He needed help before he passed out.

'Shall I run ahead and see if I can find Brad?'

'We're not on any track.'

Olivia scanned the area. 'What are we going to do?' Her voice rose a notch.

'Do you think you can get the sled upright again?'

'Even if I could, I don't think I should. It's wedged into the tree. That's the only thing stopping the dogs from taking off again.'

He shivered, partly because he was freezing and partly out of shock.

Olivia crawled across the snow to the sled and grabbed all the rugs and skins. She lay them on the snow and helped him sit on them, then carefully wrapped the others around him to keep him warm.

'Can I have a look at your arm?'

He shook his head. It was too painful to move.

'Can you wriggle your fingers at all?'

'No.' He wasn't willing to try.

The dogs started howling in unison, heads tilted to the sky. 'Do you think they're letting the others know something has happened?' Olivia asked, having to shout above the din.

'If they have, maybe I'll forgive them.'

She rested a hand on his shoulder. 'It's not their fault, it's mine. I got too confident, then I couldn't slow them down. I'm so sorry, Jack.'

'Don't apologise. It was an accident.' If anyone was to blame it was him. He was the one who decided dog sledding would be a good idea.

Seconds later, they heard barking moments before Brad's team of dogs came into view. She expected Brad to yell at her for losing control and letting go, but he took one look at the colour of Jack's face and went straight into action.

'Is it broken?'

Jack nodded. 'I think so.'

'Right. I need to unhook my dogs and get them turned around. That's going to take me a few minutes. Don't move.' He pulled out a walkie-talkie and radioed back to Leah requesting emergency services.

'Not planning on going anywhere.'

Jack and Olivia watched while Brad anchored the front dog before unclipping the lines from the sled and bringing the sled closest to Jack. He then turned each dog around and re-attached each one to his or her place on the line. Ten minutes later, after checking over every dog, he returned to Jack.

'You're going to have to get in my sled. Olivia, you'll have to drive this one home on your own. You okay with that?'

Jack looked at her. She'd gone white again. 'You can do it, Liv. Without my weight, it won't go so fast.'

'Keep both feet on the brakes the whole way. We'll take it

slow.'

Olivia nodded, but Jack could see she was petrified. When she stepped back on the sled, he was so proud of her. He had no doubt Brad would have to pry her hands from the handlebar when they got back to base because with a broken arm, there was no way Jack would be able to do it.

This time, they went much slower, but the pain in his arm was excruciating even with the slightest movement.

Brad leaned forward. 'The last bit is downhill, and I'll try to hold them back as much as I can, but they're going to fly.'

Jack nodded. He trusted Brad to keep the sled upright, but he feared for Olivia.

When they arrived, Leah came straight over and took hold of the dogs while Brad helped him out of the sled. Jack could barely stand. Heart in his throat, he turned to watch as Olivia and her team of dogs navigated the steep hill at a very sedate pace.

'Good job, Olivia,' Brad said, taking hold of one of the dogs. 'That last hill can be a bit tricky.' He gave her an encouraging smile. 'I've got the dogs. You can hop off now.'

Two paramedics headed over, lugging first aid bags.

'I take it you're Jack,' one of them said.

He nodded.

'Broken arm?'

'Hundred percent.'

'Think you can walk back to the truck?'

'Yeah.'

Jack didn't remember much after that. They helped him into the back of the truck and gave him something for the pain. Then they carefully cut away the layers of his clothing on his arm until he saw the end of his bone sticking through his skin. That's when he passed out.

He came to lying on his back, the sound of sirens ringing in his ears, then he closed his eyes again.

Chapter 25

It was nearly two o'clock when they arrived at the Huntsville District Memorial hospital. Because Jack was in so much pain, he was taken straight into the trauma bay and given more analgesia. Olivia hovered in the background and watched, twisting her scarf around her fingers. Finally, the nurse got another line in Jack's arm and once the Fentanyl hit, he stopped groaning and writhing in pain.

When he was more settled, he opened his eyes and looked around for her. She stepped in and gave his good hand a tight squeeze. 'You're going to be okay.'

He smiled. 'I know I am, because I'm in good hands.' He squeezed her fingers. 'Don't look so worried, Liv. It's a broken arm. I've had worse injuries surfing.'

'Does it hurt?'

'Not now. These drugs are goo-o-od.'

He was trying to joke, but she couldn't find the humour in anything. 'I'm so sorry.'

'Stop saying that. It was an accident.'

'But I didn't listen to Brad.'

'You *did* listen to Brad but there was nothing you could do.

These things happen. I was the dumb idiot who put my arm out to try to stop.'

'Reflex.'

'Exactly. A simple mistake. And once I'm patched up, I'll be as good as new.'

'But you won't be able to use your arm for six weeks at least.'

'Might be a blessing in disguise.'

He dozed off again and Olivia called Nan to tell her what had happened. She spoke to Scarlett too and explained she and Daddy would be away for another night. Scarlett was upset, more about Jack's broken arm than she was that they weren't coming home.

As Olivia hung up the phone, Laura, the doctor, appeared.

Olivia gently nudged Jack awake and carefully helped him prop his arm on another pillow.

'You've done a good job of it, Jack,' Laura said. 'Want to see the X-rays?'

'I won't have a clue what I'm looking at.'

Laura opened the laptop screen. 'Trust me, you won't need a medical degree to know what you're looking at.' She clicked on a button and the image appeared on the screen. She turned the laptop around for Olivia and Jack to see.

His mouth fell open. 'Crap.'

'Wow. Ulna *and* radius,' Olivia said, wincing. No wonder he'd been in so much pain. 'Nasty.'

'Very nasty,' Laura agreed, 'but at least it wasn't an open fracture.'

'He'll need surgery.' Olivia said, part question, part statement. She didn't deal with fractures in ICU, but she knew enough to know he'd need pins in his bones.

'Absolutely.'

'Today or tomorrow?'

'Normally I'd try to relocate the fracture now and leave surgery until tomorrow when the swelling settles a bit, but I don't like the look of those fingers.'

'Me either,' Olivia said. They were too mottled for Olivia's liking. She'd been doing her own neurovascular observations when no-one was looking, and was troubled that Jack had almost no sensation in two of his fingers.

'Hope you have nothing planned for the next few weeks,' Laura said to Jack.

Olivia glanced at him. Until last night she'd assumed he was still flying home tomorrow. Now she wasn't sure what his thoughts were.

'Sounds like I'll be taking a well-earned break.' He grinned at them. 'Pardon the pun.'

Olivia rolled her eyes and Laura laughed. 'It's the drugs,' Olivia said. 'He thinks he's funny.' She put a hand on Jack's shoulder. 'You won't be able to fly back tomorrow with your arm in a cast.'

'No flying,' Laura interrupted, her face serious. 'At least for forty-eight hours. And even then, I'd discourage it, especially a long-haul flight. You're at a greater risk of developing a blood clot.' She closed the laptop and signed some paperwork the nurse handed her then gave Jack an awkward left-handed handshake. 'All the best, Jack. Nice to meet you.'

'Thanks, Laura.'

'Guess the decision is made then,' Jack said after Laura was gone and they were alone in the cubicle. He looked up at Olivia with a cheeky smile. 'Do you want to be the one to break the news to Maddie and Mum?'

She shook her head. 'I'd rather not.' She'd rather walk ten kilometres barefoot and naked through the snow.

'That's okay. Do you have my bag? If you could pass me my phone, I'll call them now.'

She grimaced. 'About that. The screen is totally smashed. It must have fallen out of the sled when you fell.' She pulled it from the bottom of her bag to show him.

Jack laughed. 'This day keeps getting better.'

'It's fine. I'll make the calls. I think I still have Maddie's number in my phone. What do you want me to tell her?'

'The truth. I've broken my arm and don't know when I'm coming back to Australia.'

'She's going to be furious.'

'That's an understatement, but don't let her intimidate you. Tell her what's happened and that I won't be flying back tomorrow. When I'm up to it, I'll work out what I'm going to do.'

'What *are* you going to do?'

He gave a little shrug. 'If I needed a sign that the timing of this new restaurant wasn't right, this,' he pointed to his arm, 'is it, don't you think?'

'I suppose.'

An orderly appeared. 'Hey, man. How's it going, eh? I'm ready to take you to theatre.'

'Already?' Olivia asked. That was quick.

The nurse stuck his head back in. 'The ortho surgeon was called in to repair a fractured NOF and he's happy to add Jack to the end of his list.' He picked up the paperwork and shuffled through it. 'Have you signed the surgical consent form and filled in the admission paperwork?'

Jack laughed. 'Yes. Although it doesn't even remotely resemble my signature.'

'It'll be fine. Your wife verified all your details anyway, so we're good to go.'

The orderly unplugged the bed and pushed it into the corridor.

'Can I come with him?' Olivia asked.

The nurse shook his head. 'Sorry. Once we go through the elevators we go straight up to theatre. No visitors allowed.'

'That's okay.' She leaned over the rail of the bed and kissed Jack on the lips. 'You'll be fine, darling. I'll see you when it's over.'

He nodded and closed his eyes. All his bravado had disappeared and he'd turned a pasty shade of white She touched him on the shoulder. 'I love you, Jack.'

His eyes snapped open and the last thing she heard as he was wheeled out of the emergency department to theatre was, 'I love you too, Liv. Lots.'

*

After leaving Jack, she exited the emergency department and headed into the main part of the hospital to see if she could find something to eat and somewhere to sit and wait.

She had almost given up and figured she'd have to trudge down the hill through the snow to the nearby Tim Hortons when she heard someone calling her name. She looked up to see Morgan and another woman walking towards her, both wearing matching worried expressions.

'Hey, Olivia. This is Taylor. We heard what happened to Jack. Is there anything we can do?' Morgan asked.

'I don't think so, but thank you.' Seeing a friendly face was enough.

'We picked up your bags from the cottage and we have them in your car. Were you planning to drive back today?'

Olivia nodded. They had planned to go back to the cottage after the dog sledding for a late lunch and fit in a quick skate on the pond before driving back to Niagara Falls.

'Jack's in surgery now and he'll be in overnight. I imagine they'll discharge him first thing in the morning.'

'Come and stay with us,' Taylor said. 'We have a spare bedroom at the farmhouse.'

'Oh, I couldn't impose. I'm sure I can find a motel.'

'I doubt it. This time of year, everything's usually fully booked. We'd offer you another night at the cottage, but I don't think you'd want to be so isolated and on your own that far away.'

'No, I couldn't.'

'So stay with us,' Taylor said.

'Are you sure?'

Morgan nodded.

'I'm happy to pay you for an extra night.'

Taylor flicked Morgan a look and Morgan smiled at her, then gave Olivia an apologetic look.

'When Tay heard I'd rented the cottage to you and Jack, she was so excited.'

'I've watched every episode of his cooking shows,' Taylor interrupted, 'and it's my dream to visit Australia one day. I'd be happy with a photo of the two of us together.'

Olivia laughed. 'I'm sure Jack will be more than happy to oblige.'

'Are you hungry now?' Taylor asked.

Olivia nodded. She hadn't eaten since breakfast and it was nearly four o'clock. Part of the dog sledding was an included lunch and they'd missed that.

'How long will he be in surgery?'

'Hard to say. A couple of hours at least then he'll be in recovery.'

'Do they have your phone number?'

Olivia nodded.

'Why don't you come back to our place, have something to eat, grab a shower and get changed then come back to the hospital when Jack's awake,' Morgan suggested.

It was the perfect plan and Olivia graciously accepted their kind offer.

Chapter 26

Three hours later, Olivia headed back to the hospital. Jack was out of theatre and the surgery had been straightforward. The surgeon had called her and said he expected Jack would be discharged first thing in the morning as long as his pain was under control. He suggested it wasn't worth coming back that night to see Jack as he would likely be sleeping off the anaesthetic, but there was no way Olivia would be able to sleep herself until she'd seen with her own eyes that Jack was okay.

She also wanted to bring him his bag. While he was in the emergency department, he'd kept asking for it. Along with some toiletries, she'd thrown his sweatpants, a T-shirt and a hoodie into it, knowing he would be more comfortable in his own clothes than a hospital gown.

She perched on the edge of an uncomfortable chair in the dim light of his hospital room waiting for him to come out of recovery. It was morning in Australia now which meant it was time to call Maxine and Maddie.

With a fortifying breath she scrolled through her phone and found Maxine's number. Probably better to start with her first, then Maddie. Before chickening out, she hit the button to make the call, jiggling her leg while the phone rang and rang. She was about to hang up before the call went to voicemail when it was finally answered.

'Hello?'

She swallowed. Apparently she was no longer in her mother-in-law's contacts list. 'Um. Hi, Mrs. Carter. It's Olivia.'

There was a long pause. 'Hello.'

She waited for Maxine to ask how she was, ask about Scarlett, or say "Merry Christmas" or something, but she got nothing. She knew Jack's parents didn't like her, but she hadn't expected Maxine to be so rude.

She licked her lips. 'Jack asked me to call you. He's okay,' she rushed on, 'but he's had an accident and broken his arm. He's in hospital in Huntsville.'

There was a long silence, whether because it was an international call or whether Maxine was figuring out what to say.

She blew out a short breath. 'I told him not to bloody-well go skiing. It's too dangerous.'

Olivia pictured her mother-in-law shaking her head, rolling her eyes and taking a sip of her wine. She'd never seen Maxine without a glass in her hand.

'He's going to be fine,' Olivia said. *In case you're wondering.* 'We were dog sledding actually, not skiing, and I—'

'When is he coming home?' Maxine interrupted.

'Actually, um, that's the thing.' Olivia cleared her throat. 'He's not allowed to fly.'

'Why on earth not?' Maxine spluttered.

'Because of the cast. For the first forty-eight hours at least. It can be dangerous if his arm swells. After that, the doctors said—'

'Tell him to call me tomorrow.'

Olivia stared at the black screen in her hand in disbelief.

'Right. Okay. I'll pass on your love to him and ask him to give you a call. Lovely to chat to you, Maxine. Bye.'

Cow.

Her hands shook as she scrolled through her contacts and found Maddie's number. She still found it hard to believe she'd once thought of Maddie as a friend.

Unlike Maxine, Maddie answered on the first ring.

'Olivia! How are you?' she drawled. 'How's Jack? I haven't heard from him in days. I've been trying to call him and he's not replying to my emails.'

After her call with Maxine, Olivia didn't waste her time trying to soften the blow. 'Jack's broken his arm and he's in hospital.'

'*What*? What happened?'

'He and I were dog sledding and—'

'You were what?' Maddie's voice rose.

'Dog sledding.'

'I heard what you said. What I want to know is why the two of you are out galivanting around *dog sledding*, when he's supposed to be working on the menu for *Globe.*'

Olivia gritted her teeth. 'He's fine, by the way.'

'I'm sure he is. Put him on.'

'He's still in recovery.'

Maxine exhaled heavily and Olivia pictured her lighting her first cigarette of the day and blowing smoke above her head. 'You're flipping killing me here Olivia.' Gone was any pretence at politeness.

'Do you know if he's checked his emails? I've had to change his flight time again. I had him booked on a flight out of Toronto on the twenty-eighth, but the airline has cancelled the flight and I can't get him out of there until the next day.'

Maddie made it sound he was stuck in hell.

'Actually,' she said, putting on her sweetest voice and wishing she'd Facetimed Maddie so she could see her reaction. 'Jack's not allowed to fly.'

The pause was so stretched Olivia wondered if Maddie had hung up on her too.

'For how long,' she asked finally.

'They haven't said, but it could be six weeks. Or longer.' She bit her lip to stop the smile from forming. It wasn't technically a lie. The doctors did say it was better if he didn't fly.

Maddie swore. 'Does he have any idea how much this is going to affect everything? Not just the opening of the restaurant. He's supposed to start filming for *The Chopping Block* in two weeks. He can't do that with a broken arm, can he?'

Olivia opened her mouth to reply but Maddie kept talking.

'Does he have a cast?'

'Yeah.' *Yes, he has a cast. He's broken his arm!*

'I guess we can hide it.'

'Probably not. It's above his elbow. Oh, and it's his right arm too which means cooking is out of the question until its healed, and the cast comes off.' He wouldn't be able to hold a knife or a frypan or do anything other than supervise.

Maddie swore. 'This day just gets worse and it's only started. I hope he realises how much I'm going to have to do to cover for him. He has contractual obligations and the network could easily cut his show or even sue him for breach of contract. Are you sure he can't fly home?'

Olivia repeated what Laura and the surgeon had said about travel.

Maddie let off another string of swear words. 'People are relying on him, Olivia. If he's not here at least by the beginning of January, we might as well kiss the *Globe* deal goodbye. The contractors are already running weeks behind on set-up and if he keeps delaying decisions the investors are going to start asking questions, or worse, pull the pin on the whole thing.'

Olivia wasn't sure how to reply. Jack had basically told her he was happy to lay down his plans for the *Globe* but it wasn't her place to break that to Maddie. That was Jack's job. Assuming he wasn't going to go back on his word and what they'd talked about last night at the cottage.

'Tell him I'll call him tomorrow.'

Olivia stared at the black screen for the second time in five minutes. If she was Jack she wouldn't put up with people like Maddie in her life.

Duty done, she slid the phone back into the pocket of her jeans and thought about what Maddie had said. If Jack didn't go home, he was potentially letting so many people down. And it wouldn't be his fault, it would be hers for keeping him here.

She stared down at her feet and reminded herself she hadn't asked him to stay, he'd offered. But worry flickered through her. If he woke up from surgery and she told him what Maddie said and he changed his mind, she didn't know how she'd cope.

She thought about all the amazing moments they'd shared over the past few days. It had been a whirlwind! Jack's help in the kitchen at the Christmas dinner. Jack at the table on Christmas Day, laughing and getting involved with her family. Jack on Christmas morning playing with Scarlett. And how many times did he trudge up that hill again only to chase Scarlett down on her sled? If he changed his mind and left now, there was no way she could give him another chance.

A dull ache settled over her like a blanket. Jack *had* to go back to Australia. As much as she wanted him to stay here with her, he had to honour his commitments. It was as simple as that. She blinked back tears. It was so unfair. Why was it that as soon as they'd discovered how much they still loved each other, work won?

A thought popped into her head and wouldn't leave. Could she and Scarlett go with him back to Australia?

She tried to flick the thought away. No. Canada was home. Nan needed her. And Jack already knew she couldn't return to the life she'd had in Australia—the fancy meals, the flash cars, the big house, the designer label clothes. That might suit Jack, but it wasn't for her.

But the thought hovered and refused to leave.

Something else twisted in her heart.

Jack said he'd changed and for the most part, she could see he had. At least she could see he was trying. But had *she* changed?

If she was honest, no. She was the same cold, hurting person who'd walked out on him eighteen months. He'd sought help. And she'd done nothing except continue to wallow in her hurts. Last night had gone a long way to resolving some of the hurt, but a little piece of her was still holding on, not believing him, not trusting him, and she needed to do something about that.

One of Nan's phrases sprang into her head so clearly it was almost as though Nan was in the room with her. 'Hurt people hurt people, Olivia.'

She had hurt Jack. The very thought was like a stab to her core.

She'd spent so long blaming him for the pain he'd caused her, she never once considered what she'd done to him. She'd focused all her unhappiness and disappointments on him, blaming him and his lifestyle for the breakdown of their marriage. As if he was the only reason everything had gone wrong. But that wasn't fair. There were two people in the marriage, and they both had to take some blame. He'd come to Canada and owned up to what he'd done wrong and she'd done nothing.

It had been the same for the entire relationship. Rather than speak up and make an honest effort to communicate, she'd stayed quiet. She could scarcely blame him if she'd never told him what made her happy. Instead, she'd always sat back and quietly shone her halo, making sure everyone knew about all the sacrifices she was making for her husband. All the moves, all the late nights, all the missed dinners.

Tears filled her eyes when she turned the lens onto herself and realised how many sacrifices Jack had made in order to make her happy. He *thought* he was doing the right thing because that's how he was raised. It wasn't his fault he hadn't met her needs, because she hadn't told him what her needs were. Or at least, not told him in a way he understood.

She thought back over the last few days again. They'd been so much better than she'd expected. Jack had done nothing except ask for a second chance and set about showing her how much he'd changed.

It was time for her to take a few steps towards him. It was also time to remember that perhaps living in Australia wasn't such a bad thing after all.

Movement at the door made her sit up straighter. Jack was being wheeled into the room. She'd expected him to be drowsy, but he was sitting up in bed smiling and cracking jokes with the orderly. His arm was in plaster above the elbow and strapped to his chest in a sling. He waved to her with his left hand and gave her a wide grin.

She stood and waited for the orderly to position the bed, plug it into the power point in the wall and leave.

'Hi,' she said, feeling shy all of a sudden. 'How are you feeling?'

'I'm fine.' He frowned. 'Better than you by the look of it.' He patted the bed. 'Come and sit here. You look like you've been crying. I told you it's just a broken arm.'

How could she tell him that wasn't the reason she was crying?

She let the side rails down and sat on the edge of the bed facing him. His eyes searched for hers.

'Liv. You're worrying me. What's wrong?'

Her tears fell in earnest and for the next few minutes she poured out her heart, telling him about her phone call with Maddie and how she'd realised how much she was to blame for their marriage breakdown.

'I'm so sorry, Jack,' she said finally, sniffing and searching for a tissue. 'If you want to go back to Australia, I'm willing to do that for you.'

He shook his head. 'No, Liv. I'm making the right decision. Maybe one day we'll live in Australia again, but for now, it's your turn. You've made sacrifices for me and it's my turn to let you go after your dreams.'

Julie, the nurse, came in to check Jack's obs. He was keen to get out of bed so Julie and Olivia helped him stand and put on the sweatpants and T-shirt Olivia had brought. Sensing they needed privacy, Julie ducked out of the room as quickly as she could, closing the door behind her and leaving them alone again. Olivia was grateful for hospital insurance that had allowed Jack a single room.

He walked over to where she'd stowed his bag in the cupboard, pulled it out and placed it on the bed. Unzipping an inside pocket, he retrieved a familiar little velvet covered box.

She gasped and her heart began to pound.

Awkwardly, he fell to one knee and held the box out to her. 'Do you know what this is?'

She nodded and tried to swallow the lump in her throat and blink back more tears at the same time.

'I brought you this as a special Christmas gift, but until now it wasn't the right time to give it to you. I know you don't want presents, but this is different.' He paused, searched her face. 'Will you accept this one?'

She nodded again, not trusting herself to say a word but love blossomed in her heart.

With some difficulty, because he could only use one hand and it was shaking, he flicked open the lid of the box. Lying inside were her engagement and wedding rings, the diamonds catching and sparkling in the light.

He closed his eyes, took a breath and opened his eyes again. 'This is not how I planned to do this, but Olivia Louise Donahue, will you give me a second chance?'

She knelt before him, as close as she could get and this time when the tears pricked, she didn't fight them. Jack was crying too.

She was done with hurting. Done with blaming Jack. Done with being angry. It was time to start over.

'Yes, Jack. I'll give you a second chance.'

Spreading her fingers wide, she held out her shaking left hand while he slid the rings back where they belonged.

Epilogue

Twelve Months Later

Olivia sat at the water's edge in a bikini, scooping sand into buckets. After lunch Scarlett had announced she wanted to build the world's biggest sandcastle.

Gentle waves lapped over Olivia's legs. Legs Jack couldn't stop looking at. She was so beautiful, and he refused to listen to her when she complained about being fat. He stood and watched her for a moment. Pregnancy suited her.

'Daddy, Daddy, come and help us,' Scarlett said, grabbing Jack's spare hand and dragging him towards the water.

Olivia looked up at him and smiled. His heart melted. Her skin was brown, her face freckled and she looked like a model. He didn't know what he'd done to deserve such an incredible woman.

He handed her a bottle of ice-cold water. 'Thought you might need this.'

'Thanks. I can't believe how hot it is.'

It was the third day in a row with temperatures reaching forty degrees. A vast difference from the previous Christmas.

'Is Nan doing alright?'

'She's fine. She and Paul have headed back to the house for a rest.'

It was the afternoon of Christmas Day and after a simple BBQ lunch they had headed to the beach to cool off.

'Thanks, Jack.'

'For what?'

'For this.' She indicated the white sandy beach, the blue skies, the bushland that extended up the hill. 'I'd forgotten how pretty it was.'

'Are you missing the snow?'

She shook her head. 'No.' Winter had arrived in October and when he'd suggested they fly to Australia for Christmas and take Joan and Paul with them, she'd gone online immediately and booked flights. He'd been concerned about her flying so late in her pregnancy, but the doctors had assured them she was perfectly safe.

He sank into the wet sand beside her and pressed a hand to her belly.

'Is he asleep?'

'He's never asleep,' Olivia said with a chuckle. 'I tell you, this kid is going to take after his daddy.'

'And that's a bad thing?' he asked.

'I'll reserve my judgment.'

'It's been a crazy year, hasn't it?' he asked, resting back on his elbows.

She nodded. 'This time last year we were tobogganing. It's almost hard to believe.'

'And then we went dog sledding.'

She flashed him a look. 'Don't remind me.'

Jack chuckled. 'When will you believe me when I say it was an accident?'

'I could have killed you.'

'And you didn't.'

They sat in comfortable silence, watching Scarlett. The beach was almost deserted although as the afternoon wore on, more people were coming out of their houses, full of Christmas lunch, for a swim or to just sit and relax in the water like they were doing.

'Does Scarlett need any more sunscreen?' she asked.

'No. Joan put some on her not long ago.'

They laughed at their daughter filling buckets of water and lugging them up the beach, tipping them into the moat Jack had built then bolting back to the water to do it all over again. She'd grown so tall in twelve months. He couldn't believe by the time the baby arrived she'd be starting school.

'I wonder what the community meal will feel like this year?' Olivia asked.

He knew she'd been worried about that. Because he'd had to close the restaurant for renovations, he'd expected a lot of disappointed people. Instead, another local restaurant had offered their venue so the dinner could still happen. Jack had already promised they could use *Home* next year.

'I'm sure it will be amazing. When I spoke to Beck she had everything sorted.'

Olivia looked out over the water. 'You're not going to want to leave this. Life is almost perfect here.'

She was partly right. But she was wrong too. He couldn't wait to get back to Canada. They had a busy year ahead of them.

He kept telling everyone he felt like he was having two babies. One was the little boy Olivia was carrying, the other was *Home*, the new restaurant he was opening on the long weekend in May.

After their trip to Huntsville, they'd returned to Niagara-on-the-Lake and he'd contacted Sally and Les and offered a generous figure for *Harbourside*. The sale had gone through without a hitch and he'd spent the next few months drawing up plans for the business. He was excited about linking with farmers to provide an Australian-style paddock-to-plate experience that showcased food and wine grown locally in the Niagara region.

Maddie had quit her job the moment he'd told her he wasn't

going ahead with *Globe* and he'd employed Olivia's friend Beck, who had a degree in marketing and years of experience with event management and hospitality to manage his business. She was a joy to work with and took so much pressure off him, rather than adding to it the way Maddie had for so many years. She was also a stickler in making sure he switched off from work on his days off and refused to email him or contact him after six o'clock at night unless it was urgent. Of course, once the new restaurant was up and running, it would be different, but he was already planning to structure things differently, so he was home a lot more during the day.

The production company had been excited about the prospect of extending his show into Canada so now he filmed for six weeks every year in Canada and six weeks in Australia.

Everything had worked out better than he'd dreamed. Especially his relationship with his wife.

He rolled over and straddled Olivia's legs, being careful of the bump between them. 'Did I ever tell you how much I love you?' he asked.

She giggled. 'The last time was about twenty minutes ago.'

'Oops, I'm falling behind my schedule.' He leaned in and kissed her tenderly on the lips. 'I love you, Olivia Carter.'

'And I love you, Jack Carter.'

He was about to kiss her again when Scarlett dumped a bucket of water over their heads. Olivia squealed and he jumped up and chased Scarlett along the beach, catching her easily and scooping her into his arms. He spun her round and round until all he heard was her giggles and Olivia's laughter.

Life was better than perfect.

ACKNOWLEDGMENTS

Firstly I'd like to thank my amazing family. My husband of nearly 28 years and our incredible "kids" Jeremy, Chloe, Zach and Toby. You guys are my world.

Thank you Tim for believing in me. When I lost my writing mojo, you told me to relax and see what happened. I took time off, I relaxed, and hey, look what happened! The muse returned and I wrote another book. Thank you for sacrificing coffee for a year too so we could have a trip of a lifetime in Canada—without it this story may not have come about.

I would like to thank an incredible group of women who have encouraged me to take the plunge into self-publishing. Firstly, Belinda Williams. If it wasn't for your "Nicki Edwards Self Publishing Crash Course" document, I never would have started, so thank you for everything you've done to help me.

Also, Lisa Ireland, Delwyn Jenkins, Ellie O'Neill and Alli Sinclair. You girls are amazing and I love our catch ups. I cannot put into words how grateful I am; especially to Delwyn for her amazing structural edits, to Ellie for critiquing those edits and for Marg Wigg for her proofreading.

Huge thanks also to Annie Seaton—one of the most generous authors I know. Thank you for working with me to produce this book. The cover is divine, your editing was excellent, and your help in getting it online was invaluable.

To my other special author friends, Andrea Grigg, Catherine Hudson and Narelle Atkins, thank you for always being on Messenger whenever I had a question. And I had lots! Thank you Andrea for opening your home and being with me in my darkest hour—when I lost every single word on my hard drive. Thank God (literally) you had copies saved on your computer.

There are always people I forget to thank and I'm sorry, I wish I could remember everyone. But most of all, I want to thank you, my readers. You've waited patiently for another book and when I announced I had a new one coming out, you were so supportive and encouraging. Without you, I wouldn't have gone searching for that muse. I'm so glad I did and I hope you are too.

ALSO BY NICKI EDWARDS

Escape to the Country series:
Book 1 – Intensive Care
Book 2 – Emergency Response
Book 3 – Life Support
Book 4 – Critical Condition

Escape to the Country novellas:
Operation White Christmas
Operation Mistletoe Magic

Other books:
The Peppercorn Project
One More Song
Country Hearts anthology

Coming January 2020:
Holding onto Hope

ABOUT THE AUTHOR

Nicki is a city girl with a country heart. Growing up on a small family acreage outside Geelong, she spent her formative years riding horses, hand rearing lambs and pretending the neighbour's farm was her own. After spending three years in a regional city in New South Wales in her 20's, Nicki's love of small country towns and rural life was further developed.

For years she dreamed of escaping to the country with her husband to live on land surrounded by horses, dogs, cows and sheep. Unfortunately, that's not likely to happen, so instead she continues to live vicariously through the lives of the characters in the books she loves to read and write. Nicki also dreams of living in Canada, but as that's also unlikely, she'll keep visiting there and setting some of my books in the country that stole her heart 30 years ago.

A voracious reader, Nicki always wanted to be an author. After returning to university as a mature aged student in her mid-30's to study nursing, she juggled full time study, part time work and raising four small children to achieve her dream of becoming a nurse in 2011.

Her other dream—the dream to write—never left. In January 2014 she wrote her first book and now divides her time between writing and working as a Critical Care Nurse in the Emergency Department, the Intensive Care Unit or in a busy local General Practice where many of her stories and characters are imagined.

Nicki and her husband Tim live in Geelong, Victoria and have four young adult children, two spoiled border collies and a Burmese cat. Life is always busy, always fun and definitely exhausting, but she wouldn't change it for anything.